MATT JENSEN, THE LAST MOUNTAIN MAN
SAVAGE
TERRITORY

MATT JENSEN, THE LAST
MOUNTAIN MAN
SAVAGE
TERRITORY

William W. Johnstone
with J. A. Johnstone

PINNACLE BOOKS
Kensington Publishing Corp.
www.kensingtonbooks.com

PINNACLE BOOKS are published by

Kensington Publishing Corp.
850 Third Avenue
New York, NY 10022

PUBLISHER'S NOTE
Following the death of William W. Johnstone, the Johnstone family is working with a carefully selected writer to organize and complete Mr. Johnstone's outlines and many unfinished manuscripts to create additional novels in all of his series like The Last Gunfighter, Mountain Man, and Eagles, among others. This novel was inspired by Mr. Johnstone's superb storytelling.

All Kensington titles, imprints, and distributed lines are available at special quantity discounts for bulk purchases for sales promotions, premiums, fund-raising, educational, or institutional use. Special book excerpts or customized printings can also be created to fit specific needs. For details, write or phone the office of the Kensington special sales manager: Kensington Publishing Corp., 850 Third Avenue, New York, NY 10022, attn: Special Sales Department; phone: 1-800-221-2647.

PINNACLE BOOKS and the Pinnacle logo are Reg. U.S. Pat. & TM Off.

ISBN-13: 978-0-7860-2000-3
ISBN-10: 0-7860-2000-8

First printing: February 2009

10 9 8 7 6 5 4 3 2

Printed in the United States of America

Chapter One

Fort Bowie, Arizona Territory

It was hot and dry at Fort Bowie, where elements of the Eighth Cavalry were conducting their daily exercises. New recruits, under the watchful eye of sergeants, were at drill, both mounted and dismounted. Older hands were conducting work details, from mucking out stables to rubbing down horses, to making needed repairs on the various buildings of the post.

One hapless soldier, wearing a sign that said I WAS INSUBORDINATE, was walking around the perimeter of the post in uniform, carrying a fully loaded pack and rifle. He would be performing this punishment detail from sunup to sundown, the entire day, taking only a short, five-minute break every two hours.

The U.S. Cavalry, operating under a set of tactics known as *Upton's Tactics,* was organized as ten regiments of three battalions each, with four companies to a battalion. Each company had one captain, one first lieutenant, one second lieutenant, and seventy-seven enlisted men.

The mounted trooper carried a light cavalry saber suspended from the waist belt. A pistol was carried on the right side, handle facing forward, in a large, flapped holster. He also carried a single-shot, breech-loading .45-caliber carbine, which hung from a carbine sling that was tucked into a leather socket affixed to the McClellan saddle just behind the trooper's thigh.

Newly minted officers and new recruits alike were made to learn, and recite, the paragraph in the manual that dealt with horses.

> Commanding officers must bear in mind that the efficiency of cavalry depends almost entirely upon the condition of the horse, which alone makes them able to get over long distances in short spaces of time. The horses must, therefore, be nursed with great care, in order that they may endure the utmost fatigue when emergencies demand it.

Elements of the Eighth Cavalry, under the overall command of General Crook, were stationed at Fort Bowie, and were engaged, and had been engaged for some time now, in pursuit of a militant band of Apache Indians led by Geronimo.

The bugle call for Officers' Call was sounded, and the officers of A Company, First Battalion of the Eighth, assembled in the headquarters building in response.

Matt Jensen was one of those who responded to the

bugle call. Although Matt was not an army officer, nor even in the army, he was currently employed as a scout for the army, and as such held the equivalent rank of a first lieutenant. He stood now at the window of the headquarters building, looking out over the quadrangle as he waited for the meeting to begin. Being a cavalry scout in pursuit of Apache Indians was not his permanent occupation. It was just an occupation that had temporarily caught his interest.

Matt was a wanderer, always looking for what was beyond the next line of hills or just over the horizon. When he was on the trail, he traveled light, with a bowie knife, a .44 double-action Colt, a Winchester .44-40 rifle, a rain slicker, an overcoat, two blankets, and a spare shirt, socks, trousers, and underwear.

Escaping from an orphanage when he was twelve, he was found more dead than alive by a man named Smoke Jensen. He learned everything he knew from Smoke, who took him in and raised him until Matt was old enough to go out on his own. It was then that Matt dropped the name Cavanaugh, which was the last name of his biological father, and took the name Jensen.

"Gentlemen, Colonel McKenzie," someone announced, and all the officers stood respectfully as the post commander came into the headquarters.

"As you were, gentlemen," McKenzie said. "Captain Trevathan has gone over his plans with me and I have given my approval. I leave you now to discuss your scout. Captain, the floor is yours."

"Thank you, sir," Trevathan said as Colonel McKenzie left. "Gentlemen, I call your attention to the Dragoon Mountains," Trevathan said, pointing out the mountain range on a map that was pinned to the wall. "If every man in this company will follow my plan to the exact detail, I am confident that we will rid this country of the savage Geronimo once and forever. Our Indian scouts tell us he has made his camp here."

Trevathan pointed to a spot on the map.

"Lieutenant Bristol, you will take your platoon out on scout to locate him. I will establish the rest of the company here. As soon as you locate him, send a heliograph signal informing us of the same. Once we receive your signal, we will launch the attack, smashing Geronimo once and for all."

"Excuse me, sir," Bristol said. "You are going to detach an entire platoon for a scout?"

"I am indeed."

"Wouldn't it be better if I just took a scout and a couple of signalmen with me?"

"I want the scout to be in strength, Lieutenant," Trevathan explained. "That way, if Geronimo attempts to escape, you can be in position to block him."

"Yes, sir," Bristol replied, though the tone of his voice indicated that he was not happy with his orders.

Trevathan sensed Bristol's unease. "I am going to be counting on you, Lieutenant. In order for this plan to work, I must be able to depend on you following my orders to the exact detail. You do understand the importance of that, do you not?"

"Yes, sir, I understand," Bristol said.

"Good. I'm glad that we understand each other. Now, gentlemen, I know that Geronimo has eluded the army for so many years that many of our troopers, I fear, have bought into the idea that he possesses mythical powers. But after this operation, that myth will be dispelled once and for all. If you follow my plan of operation to the exact detail, we will cut Geronimo to pieces, and the Eastern press will no longer make a hero of him."

"Captain," Lieutenant Bristol said. "With all due respect, sir, you have not encountered Geronimo before. You may find this operation more difficult than you realize."

"Yes, well, I realize this will be my first scout since arriving out West, but I have taught military tactics at West Point for the last four years, so it isn't exactly as if I am a novice in the art of warfare."

Lieutenant Bristol cleared his throat, but said nothing.

"Our civilian scout has not commented," Captain Trevathan said. He looked pointedly at Matt. "Mr. Jensen, what say you?"

"I'm not that impressed with your plan," Matt said flatly.

Some of the others who were attending the briefing gasped in surprise.

"Really," Trevathan said, obviously peeved by Matt's comment. "And pray tell, Mr. Jensen, if it isn't too much trouble, what is wrong with my plan?"

"I'll be happy to tell you what is wrong," Matt said, pointing to the map. "You have drawn this plan up as if you are engaging an organized army on a battlefield. You aren't attacking an army, Captain, you are attacking smoke. Do you have tactics you can use against smoke?"

"You description is quite colorful, Jensen, but you

are making my point. When you compare Geronimo to smoke, you are just perpetuating the myth. I will make allowances for your inability to understand the basic concept of this operation, Mr. Jensen, because you are just a civilian, and I cannot expect you to grasp the intricacies of military tactics. But this mission is one of classic cavalry deployment. And if we stick to our carefully prepared plan, as I fully expect us to do, the Indians will not escape."

"Captain, I've been out here for a couple of years now, and I know the way these Apache devils operate," Lieutenant Bristol said. "And I must confess that I believe there is something to what Mr. Jensen is saying."

Trevathan turned his attention away from Matt and looked directly at Bristol. "Lieutenant, if I may ask, how did you get your commission?"

"I got a direct commission from the ranks, sir," Bristol replied.

"A direct commission from the ranks?"

"Yes, sir."

"Lieutenant, I am not only a graduate of the Military Academy, but, as you well know, I taught military tactics there. Do you really intend to challenge me?"

"No, sir, I would never do that," Bristol replied.

"I would hope not," Trevathan said. "Now, gentlemen, by this time tomorrow we will have a victory to celebrate. Return to your men and prepare them for a midnight departure. I expect us to be in position, ready to strike, at dawn's first light."

* * *

By dawn the next day, in accordance with Trevathan's operational plan, the company, minus Bristol's platoon, had reached their debarkation point. Then, from a distant hill, there came a series of mirror flashes from the heliograph Bristol had carried with him.

"Lieutenant Manning," Trevathan called.

"Yes, sir?"

"You are a signal officer, Lieutenant. What does the message say?"

"Indians spotted, moving north along Bitter Water Creek," Manning read.

"By Godfrey, we've got him!" Trevathan said. "Men!" he shouted to the troopers. "Lieutenant Bristol has spotted the Indians! Get mounted. We are about to carry the fight to the enemy."

Sergeant Emerson mounted first, then started up the dry creek bed.

"Sergeant Emerson, where do you think you are going?" Trevathan called to him.

"I'm going to take the point, sir," Emerson replied.

"I want no one at point to give away our position."

"Beggin' your pardon, sir, but in terrain like this, you have to have someone riding point," Emerson said.

"Sergeant, you are forgetting your place," Trevathan said. "One more word from you and I will charge you with insubordination. Now, return to the company at once."

"Yes, sir," Emerson said and, as ordered, he returned to the main body as the others started toward their horses.

"Captain, if we are going to be riding up the

creek bed without a point, then we should at least have flanker riders on either side," Matt said.

"Thank you, Mr. Jensen, but you were hired as a scout, not as a tactician. Please refrain from any further suggestions along those lines. Flanker riders will slow us down."

"It's your command," Matt replied.

"Yes, Mr. Jensen, in that you are correct," Trevathan said. He stood in his stirrups, held his hand over his head, then brought it down.

"Forward, ho!" he ordered, and the company started forward at the trot.

Half an hour later, the dry creek bed narrowed precipitously, and Matt felt the hair on the back of his neck stand up.

"You thinkin' what I'm thinkin', Mr. Jensen?" Sergeant Emerson asked.

"If you mean do I think it looks like we're riding into a trap, yes," Matt said.

"Maybe the cap'n ain't noticed it," Emerson suggested. He called up to Trevathan, who was riding at the head of the column. "Captain Trevathan, have you noticed how them walls is closin' in on us?" Emerson asked. "This ain't good, Cap'n. This ain't good at all."

"Thank you for your concern, Sergeant Emerson," Trevathan replied. "We will continue according to the operational plan."

"Captain Trevathan, sir, I agree with Sergeant Emerson," Trooper Jones said.

"You, Trooper Jones? You agree with Sergeant Emerson? And so now I am to take advice from a private?"

"I haven't always been a private, sir."

"I'm well aware of the fact that you were an officer during the Civil War, Trooper Jones. But you are a private now, and I am in command."

"Yes, sir," Trooper Jones replied.

"Captain, you are aware of what happened to Custer, aren't you?" Matt asked.

"That will be enough from you, Mr. Jensen," Trevathan said. "As soon as we return from this scout, I intend to see Colonel McKenzie and have your service with the U.S. Army terminated."

"That won't be necessary," Matt replied. "As soon as we get back—assuming we do get back—I intend to resign from the scout service."

"Please do," Trevathan said. "I think that would be best for you and the army."

To Matt's relief, they were not attacked while they were in the narrow ravine, but they made contact with Bristol without ever encountering the Apache.

"Where are they?" Trevathan said, obviously angry that they had not encountered the Indians. "Your signal said you had spotted them and they were coming toward us up Bitter Water Creek."

"They were between us, sir. I don't know what happened to them," Bristol said.

"Are you sure you spotted them?"

"Yes, sir, we all saw them," Bristol replied.

"Well, they couldn't have just disappeared like—"

"Smoke, Captain?" Bristol said.

Trevathan glared at Bristol. "That's enough, Lieutenant. You are bordering on insubordination."

"Yes, sir," Bristol said.

"Lieutenant Manning," Trevathan called to his second lieutenant. "I want you to—"

"Injuns!" someone shouted, interrupting whatever order Bristol was about to give. A veritable cloud of arrows rained down on them, obviously a coordinated attack. The whishing sound of arrows was followed by cries from the horses, many of which had sustained multiple hits. There were also cries of fear and groans of pain from some of the men who had been struck.

"Dismount! Dismount! Form a skirmish line!" Trevathan ordered.

"Trevathan, no! We can't dismount here! We have to get to more open ground!" Matt shouted.

"Goddamnit, Jensen, I'm in command here!" Trevathan screamed. "I said dismount!" he ordered again.

"Cap'n, Mr. Jensen is right!" Emerson shouted. "We can't—*unh!*" Before he could finish his warning, a large-caliber bullet took off the back of his head, sending out a shower of blood, brains, and bone. Some of the detritus hit Trevathan in the face, and his eyes grew wide in shock as he wiped his face, then looked at his hand and realized what he was seeing.

"Remount," Trevathan yelled, his voice edged with panic. "We must retreat!"

"No, we need to attack!" Matt shouted.

Trevathan remounted, then swung his mount around. "Retreat!" he ordered, spurring his horse into a gallop even as he gave the order.

As the men watched in shock and alarm the panicked action of their commander, Trevathan was hit in the back by an arrow. He fell from his saddle, but his foot hung up in the stirrup and the panic-stricken horse galloped at full speed up the creek bed, dragging Trevathan behind it. Trevathan's head slammed against a big rock opening up a huge, gaping hole that left a trail of blood.

"Mount up!" Matt shouted to the soldiers, most of whom were staring at the scene of their commander being dragged through their midst.

"Bristol! Manning! Get your men in the saddle!" Matt said. "We need to attack now!"

"Mount up!" Lieutenants Bristol and Manning shouted, and the troopers, goaded into action, finally reacted.

"Column of twos, forward!" Matt shouted.

Mounted now, the cavalrymen felt a renewed sense of confidence in their leadership as they galloped out of the kill zone.

"Lieutenant Bristol!" Matt shouted.

"Yes, sir!" Bristol responded. Like the enlisted men, both Bristol and Manning had bowed to Matt's authority.

"The Indians are on both sides of us. You go left, I'll go right!"

"Yes, sir!" Bristol replied.

The galloping troopers split into two different directions. Very quickly, they came upon the Indians. The troopers had the advantage of superior numbers and mobility, and their surprise counterattack routed the Indians. Some were able to mount and ride away, but most of the others were on foot, and they ran from the attacking troopers, disappearing into the gullies and crevices that traversed the area.

"Company, halt!" Matt ordered, and the troopers, including the two lieutenants, responded to his command without question.

By now, nearly all the Indians had managed to escape. Then Matt saw one of them at some distance. The Indian was sitting on his horse, staring back at the cavalrymen without the slightest indication of fear.

"Trooper Jones, you know a lot of the Indians who left the reservation. Is that Geronimo?"

"No, sir," Jones said. "That particular Indian goes by the name of Delshay."

"Delshay?"

"Yes, sir. He isn't nearly as old as Geronimo, but he's damn near as smart."

For a long moment, Matt and Delshay continued to stare at each other. Finally, Delshay turned and rode away, his leisurely movement giving evidence of his disdain for the army troops who had been in pursuit.

"Lieutenant Bristol?" Matt said.

"Yes, sir?"

"It is your command, Lieutenant."

"Yes, sir. Thank you, sir."

Bristol, now being the senior officer present, took command and the company, with twelve killed, including Captain Trevathan and Sergeant Emerson, returned to Fort Bowie. Nine of the returning cavalrymen were wounded, a couple of the wounds severe enough that the soldiers had constructed travois to bring the men back. The bodies of the dead were brought back, draped over their horses. Six horses had been so badly wounded that they had to be destroyed, and that required doubling up some of the bodies on the remaining horses.

Colonel McKenzie met the dispirited company as they rode through the gate.

"Where is Captain Trevathan?" McKenzie asked Matt.

"Belly down on one of the horses," Matt replied.

"Lieutenant Bristol!" McKenzie called.

"Yes, sir?"

"I want you, Manning, Jensen, and the senior NCOs at headquarters as soon as you dismiss the men."

"Yes, sir."

Lieutenant Bristol gave the report, mercifully not condemning Trevathan for his mistakes.

"Mr. Jensen, you are the senior scout," McKenzie said. "It was your responsibility to keep Trevathan from riding into an ambush."

"I beg your pardon, sir," Bristol said. "But if it hadn't been for Mr. Jensen, our losses would have been much higher."

"Yes, sir," one of the NCOs said. "Mr. Jensen, he saved our lives, is what he done."

Matt Jensen tendered his resignation that very day. Two days later, he was on a train heading back up to Colorado, his experiment as an army scout concluded.

Chapter Two

Picket Wire Canyon, Colorado

To many, the metal bit jangling against the horse's teeth, the hooves clattering on the hard rock, and the creaking leather saddle might be little more than a cacophony of disparate sounds. But to Matt Jensen, it was music, a symphony that defined the life he had chosen to live. In the six months since Matt had resigned his position as scout for General Crook, he had earned his keep in a variety of ways, from riding shotgun for Wells Fargo, to transporting a prisoner for the sheriff of Fremont County, to delivering a string of horses from Higbee, Colorado, to Belle Meade, Kansas. He was just returning to Colorado from the horse-wrangling job now.

Matt wandered from occupation to occupation because he wanted to, not because he had to. In truth, Matt had a rather tidy sum of money earning interest in a bank in Denver, the result of a very successful operation in which he and his friend and mentor,

Smoke Jensen, had panned for gold. Smoke now owned a very productive ranch, and if Matt wanted to, he could probably own one as well. But Matt didn't want to. He enjoyed the idea of being as free as tumbleweed, feeling at home anywhere he happened to be, but putting roots down nowhere.

Dismounting, Matt unhooked his canteen and took a swallow, then poured some water into his hat. He held it in front of his horse and the horse drank thirstily, though Matt knew that the small amount of water would do little to slake the animal's thirst. Spirit drank all the water, then began nuzzling Matt for more.

"Sorry, boy," Matt said quietly. "That's the best I can do for now. But we'll reach Crocker's ranch before nightfall, and there will be water there for both of us."

Before Ian Crocker got married and settled down, he and Matt had wintered together in the mountains. But Crocker married a schoolteacher and started a ranch. It wasn't a large ranch, but it was successful enough that he was able to make a living at it. Now, Matt planned his trips so as to stop and call on his old friend from time to time.

Unbeknownst to Matt, even as he was approaching the ranch, there were four unwelcome visitors. The four were Burt Philbin, Deermont Cantrell, Abe Oliver, and Percy Morris. They had tried to hold up a bank in Bent Canyon, Colorado, only to run into a time-lock safe that prevented them from getting any money. Leaving the bank empty-handed, they barely escaped with their lives, and were forced to ride out of town under a hail of gunfire from the armed and angry population of the small town.

* * *

Matt reached Crocker's ranch at about the time the sun was a large orange orb sitting low in the western sky. The shadows of nearby aspen and cottonwood trees were long as he approached the house and barn. Dismounting, Matt saw four saddled horses tethered out front. He walked over to look at them. It was obvious they had been ridden hard recently and they had not been rubbed down, for streaks of salt stained their coats. There was something sticking out from under one of the saddles and as Matt examined it more closely, he saw that it was a sackcloth with two eyeholes.

It was a mask.

Matt walked away from the horses, then led Spirit over to a water trough where the horse began to drink.

The front door to the house opened, and Crocker stepped out onto the porch.

"What are you doing there, mister?" Crocker called.

Matt could see a look of concern in Crocker's face.

"I'm getting water for my horse."

"Water your animal and get. We don't like strangers around here."

"All right," Matt said. "I'm obliged for the water for my horse."

After Spirit drank his fill, Matt remounted, then rode away.

Philbin, Cantrell, Oliver, and Morris had been standing just inside the house when Matt approached. All four were holding drawn pistols, and Cantrell was peering through the crack between the dark green window shade and the window.

"Is he goin' away?" Philbin asked.

"Yeah, he's ridin' off," Cantrell replied.

The outlaw chuckled, then put his pistol away. He looked over at Crocker. "Well, now, you done that just real good, friend," he said. "Yes, sir, you done it real good. I don't think he suspects a thing."

Philbin turned toward Crocker's wife, who was busy in the kitchen. "How long till supper?"

"It's ready," she said.

"It's about time. I'm near 'bout starved to death here."

The five men walked into the kitchen where Katie was putting supper on the table.

"What the hell is this?" Philbin asked.

"Potatoes and eggs, cooked together in bacon drippings," Katie said.

"I ain't never seen 'em done like this before," Philbin said. He took a bite. "Oh, my, taters cooked like this is real good. Take my word for it, boys, this is just real tasty."

"Philbin, they ain't nothin' you ever et wasn't real tasty far as you're concerned," Cantrell said, and the others laughed.

Matt waited until after dark before he returned. Leaving his horse hobbled behind a stand of aspens, he slipped up to the side of the house.

From inside, a flickering light managed to escape. Also, it wasn't totally dark outside, because it was a cloudless night and the moon was full and bright so that the house and barn gleamed in a soft, silver light, like white blooms in a meadow.

The still night air was rent with the long, high-pitched trills and low violalike thrums of the frogs. For countermelodies there were crickets, the distant, mournful howl of coyotes, and from the stable, a braying mule and a whickering horse.

With his gun in hand, and staying in the shadows alongside the wall, Matt found a window and looked inside. There, he saw four men with Crocker and his wife. One of the men was pointing a gun at Crocker.

Because he had been on the trail, Matt was unaware of the fact that these four men had attempted a bank robbery earlier in the day. But he had known right away that they were the cause of Crocker's strange response when he had arrived earlier in the evening.

Katie Crocker was holding, clutched tightly to her chest, a silver candelabrum.

"Please," he heard Katie's pleading voice say. "We have given you water, food, and shelter. But you cannot take this. This candelabrum was made by my great-grandfather. He was apprenticed to Paul Revere."

"Who is Paul Revere?" one of the men asked.

The man holding the gun chuckled, but it was an evil chuckle.

"It don't matter who Paul Revere was. This here is silver, and I intend to have it."

"No," Katie said, clutching it even more tightly. "You can't have it."

"Woman, you better think about what you are doin' here. You are either goin' to give it to me, or I'm goin' to kill your man and you and take it. I'm goin' to have it either way, but if you don't give it to me, then you'll both be dead." He cocked his pistol.

Matt ran around to the back door and, finding it unlocked, pushed it open.

"Drop the gun!" he called.

"What the hell?" One of the men shouted. He was standing by the one flickering candle, and he snuffed it out. The inside of the house was immediately plunged into darkness as the man holding the pistol fired. Matt felt a hammer blow as a bullet slammed into his shoulder. He returned fire, using as his target the flame pattern from the discharge. He heard someone groan, then fall. A moment later, he heard the front door crash open, and he hurried through the house and out the back door to try and stop them, but they had already mounted and were galloping away.

By the time Matt got back inside, Crocker had relit the candle and he and Katie were looking down at the man Matt had shot.

"Damn," the wounded man said. "My belly hurts."

"Who are you?" Matt asked.

"Are you the one who shot me?"

"Yeah, I'm the one that shot you."

"I'm dyin', ain't I?"

"More than likely," Matt replied.

The man nodded. "Yeah, I thought so."

"Who are you?" Matt asked again.

"My name is Morris. Percy Morris."

"Who were the others?"

"Don't know their first names. I only hooked up with them a couple of days ago. We robbed a bank in Bent Canyon. So if you was lookin' for us, you found us."

"The only thing I was looking for was water," Matt said. "I didn't know you'd robbed a bank."

"The truth is, we didn't," Morris said. "I mean, don't get me wrong, we tried to rob it. It just didn't go all that well." Inexplicably, Morris tried to laugh, but it came out a hacking cough that spewed blood.

"Who were the men with you?" Matt asked, repeating the question.

Morris started coughing again, but this time the coughing spasm ended in a wheezing gasp, then silence.

"I wasn't sure you were going to come back," Crocker said. "After the way I acted when you were here first."

Matt laughed. "Ian, didn't you think I knew why you were acting like that?"

"I figured you would. I know that I sure hoped so."

"Oh, you are bleeding," Katie said, noticing the wound for the first time.

"Yes," Matt replied without elaboration.

"Where is your horse?" Crocker asked.

"He is outside, tethered behind the stand of cottonwood trees."

"I'll go bring him in while Katie cleans and bandages your wound. Then we'll fix you some supper and feed Spirit."

"Thank you," Matt said. He smiled. "Spirit thanks you as well."

Chapter Three

The Santa Rita Mountains of southern Arizona

Almost eight hundred miles south of Crocker's ranch, a band of Chiricahua Apache warriors—the same band Matt had scouted against—were still eluding General Crook's army. The leader of this particular band, Delshay, whose name meant Walking Bear, dismounted and held up his hand. This was a signal to the other warriors who were with him that they should stay down in the ravine. Getting down on all fours, Delshay crawled up the hill, then lay down and looked just over the crest.

Two weeks earlier, Delshay had led this same group of warriors in a bold attack on an army supply wagon. The attack had been successful, and without losing even one man in the raid, Delshay and his men had killed the six soldiers who were guarding the wagon. In addition to defeating the soldiers, Delshay's little band of Apache Indians had come away from the skirmish with a veritable treasure of powder and ball, as well as bacon, beans, and flour.

Delshay took his prize back to the main Apache camp, and that night the Indians had danced and sung songs in his honor. But some had complained that Delshay's raid had just increased the danger because, as a result of that operation, the army, under General Crook, had sent a fresh platoon after them. Delshay made a solemn promise that he would find and kill all the soldiers who came after them.

Now, from his position at the top of the hill, Delshay could see the thirty soldiers who had been tracking him for the last two days. Evidently, the soldiers were planning to make camp here, for already they had unsaddled their mounts, constructed a hasty enclosure for them, and stacked their carbines. The soldiers, who had no concept of light or sound discipline, had lit a couple of campfires, and they were blazing brightly as the soldiers busied themselves in the preparation of their supper.

"Hey, Sarge, is it really true that you can get two dollars for an Apache scalp at any saloon in Arizona or New Mexico?" one of the soldiers yelled.

"Not all the saloons will give you two dollars, but some of 'em will," the sergeant replied. "And some places, you can even get three dollars for a scalp. But purt' near any of 'em will at least give you a free drink."

"Well, then, I reckon by the time we finish this here little excursion, I'll have me a whole string of 'em to cash in," the soldier said.

The other soldiers, now in various stages of making camp, laughed.

"Dooley, you're full of shit," one of them said. "The truth is, you'd better look out that you don't wind up with your own scalp hangin' from some Apache's belt."

"His scalp, hell! More than likely some buck will cut off his pecker and hang it on his belt," another called, and again, the soldiers laughed.

Turning toward the warriors who were with him, Delshay signaled for them to come up the hill. One by one, and moving as quietly as if they were walking on air, the seven men of Delshay's small war party moved up the side of the hill, then got down on their stomachs and eased up to look over the crest.

Delshay took the first shot. He saw dust rise from the tunic of the man he shot, and he saw the man's eye's open wide in shock before he fell. This was the same soldier who had been bragging about carrying a string of Apache scalps, and Delshay took particular pleasure in killing him.

Delshay's opening shot was a signal to the others, and almost immediately, the warriors with him began shooting. The valley rang with the echoes of gunfire as the soldiers hurried to retrieve the weapons they had so carefully stacked a short while earlier. A few managed to get to their rifles and they began returning fire, though as Delshay and his men were both concealed and covered, the return fire was ineffective. As a result, the firefight was brutal, fast, and one-sided. In less than two minutes, all the soldiers of the little detail either were dead or had run away.

Shouting in victory, the Apache warriors swarmed down the hill, going to the bodies of all the soldiers to make sure they were dead. Then they went through the packs of the slain soldiers, taking whatever they found, including several bottles of whiskey.

One week later, Delshay was back in Goyathlay's mobile camp. Goyathlay was the head of the small band of warriors to which Delshay belonged. For over ten years, Goyathlay, better known as Geronimo, had raided Mexican and American settlements at will, easily avoiding the vast army that had been sent after him. And while Delshay had not been with him for all that time, he had quickly become one of Geronimo's most effective warriors and leaders.

The smoke of a half-dozen campfires lifted into the sky, perfuming the air with the aroma of cooking meat as Delshay walked out to the edge of the mesa. He stood there for a long moment, looking north. Goyathlay came up to stand beside him.

"You wish to go back to your woman," he said. It wasn't a question, it was a statement.

"Yes, Goyathlay," Delshay admitted.

"I think you should return."

"I cannot return."

"Why not?"

"Because to return would be to abandon you and my brothers. That I will not do."

"While you were with us, you fought well, *ciye*,"

Goyathlay said, calling him his "son." "You will not leave us, you can never leave us for no matter where you are, your warrior spirit will remain with us to fight with us against the whites."

"That is not enough. My warrior spirit cannot shoot a rifle," Delshay said. "My warrior spirit cannot shoot a bow. Only my body can kill our enemies."

"And only your body can look after your woman and your children. Go now. Be with them. It is the thing you must do."

"I have learned much from you, Goyathlay," Delshay said.

"Do not let the lessons you have learned here die with you," Geronimo said. "Our children, and our children's children, as well as the children of their children, must forever keep alive the spirit of the Chiricahua. I have had dreams, Delshay, and I have read the signs. I know that the time will come when there will be no Chiricahua. Then, the memories we pass on to our children will be all that is left of our people."

"This I will do," Delshay said. "You have my promise."

Geronimo reached out to put his hand on Delshay's shoulder. "My brother, the dreams and the signs I have seen are also about you. They tell me that there will be much sadness in the life that awaits you," he said. "But there will also be much honor, for you will become a leader whose name will be spoken with wonder for many seasons to come, even after you have died."

"*Ka dish day,* Goyathlay. Good-bye."

"*Egogahan,* Delshay. Until we meet again."

Chapter Four

New York City

Ken Hendel, a rather small, fastidious man, cleaned his wire-rim glasses, then carefully put them back on before stepping up to the window. He was in the third story of a brownstone mansion, and as he stood at the window, he looked down on Union Square and the statue of a mounted George Washington.

A street orator was giving a speech just outside the iron picket fence that surrounded the statue, and several were gathered around to listen. At the moment, the speaker was railing against the use of bicycles by women.

"The bicycle is a tool of Satan! To women of impure desires, this insidious device provides a ready means for facilitating the execution of depraved activity! Why, a young woman can be riding the wheel engrossed in the illicit pleasures of immoral behavior, all the while passing children who are totally innocent of the sin being perpetrated in their very midst!"

"Mr. Hendel?"

Turning away from the window, Hendel saw Dr. Petrie standing just outside the door to Mr. Montgomery's bedroom.

"Is he—is he still alive?" Hendel asked.

"Yes. For now," Dr. Petrie said. "He has asked for you."

Hendel nodded, then stepped into the room. Because the drapes were closed, the room was dark. And even though it was quite large, it seemed close. It was also redolent of the smell of scented candles, put into the room in an ineffective attempt to overcome the stench of putrefying flesh.

"Ken?" a weak voice called from the bed. "Ken, is that you?"

"Yes, Mr. Montgomery," Hendel answered.

"Come closer, Ken. Sit by me for a while."

Hendel moved a chair closer to the bed and looked at the man for whom he had worked for the last eight years after having assumed the same position his father had held for the previous thirty years.

Joel Montgomery, a shipping magnate, was a wealthy man. But now the seventy-six-year-old man was dying of cancer.

It was warm in the room, and there were beads of perspiration on the old man's forehead. Hendel took a washcloth from a basin on the bedside table and bathed Montgomery's forehead.

"You are a very good man, Ken," Montgomery said, his voice made thin by his weakened state.

"You have been very good to me, Mr. Montgomery," Hendel said. "And to my father before me."

"It is no wonder that you are a good man,"

Montgomery said. "For your father was as well. You come of good stock."

The two men sat in silence for a moment longer before Montgomery spoke again.

"I made a mistake, Ken," he finally said.

"I beg your pardon, sir?"

"I made a mistake," Montgomery said. "I should have never insisted that Cynthia marry Bixby. He is not the man I thought him to be."

Hendel did not respond to the comment. He had felt that way about Jay Peerless Bixby from the moment the old man pushed his beautiful young daughter into marrying him.

"You don't like Bixby, do you?"

"Not particularly," Hendel replied.

"You were against this marriage from the beginning, weren't you?"

"I wasn't sure it was the best thing for Miss Montgomery."

"For heaven's sake, man, why didn't you say something?" Montgomery asked. "Why didn't you speak out?"

"I am but an employee, sir," Hendel said. "It was not my place to speak out."

"Nonsense, my boy, you are much more than an employee," Montgomery said.

"I did not want to presume."

"Yes, well, it is all water under the bridge now," Montgomery said. He sighed. "I don't mind dying, Ken—death comes to us all. But it does gall me to think that I have compromised my daughter's future. I thought that, by having her marry Bixby, I was providing her with a husband who is a good businessman and who would look after her for the rest of her life. I fear now that all I have done is make it so that she will be beholden to him for the rest of her life."

"That is not necessarily the case, sir," Hendel said.

"What do you mean?"

"There is a way to insure your daughter's security. That is, if you are willing to take those steps."

"Yes!" Montgomery said, and with that one word, his voice was as strong as it had ever been.

There was a light knock on the door. "Papa?"

"Take care of that for me, Ken, will you?" Montgomery said. "Whatever you have to do, do it."

"I shall require your signature, sir."

"Then, by all means, do it quickly, while I still have the strength to hold a pen," Montgomery said.

"Papa?" the voice called again.

"Cynthia, yes, dear, come in, come in," Montgomery called back.

Cynthia opened the door, but seeing Hendel with her father, she hesitated.

"Oh, I'm sorry, I didn't mean to intrude. I'll return when your business is done."

"It's done, Ken was just leaving," Montgomery said.

"Miss Montgomery," Hendel said with a slight nod. Then quickly, he corrected himself. "I beg your pardon, I mean Mrs. Bixby."

Cynthia chuckled. "Mr. Hendel, you have known me as Cynthia Montgomery for my entire life. It isn't surprising that you would slip up."

"I suppose that's right," Hendel said. He looked back toward the figure lying in the shadows on the bed. "I'll get right on that, Mr. Montgomery."

"Good, good, I appreciate it," Montgomery replied.

"Papa, you are looking better this morning," Cynthia said, forcing the enthusiasm as she approached her father's bed.

"Nonsense, my dear, I am dying, and I am closer to death this morning than I was yesterday."

"Well, Papa, if you put it that way, we all are," Cynthia replied.

Cynthia's unexpected response tickled Montgomery's funny bone and he laughed out loud.

"I suppose we are at that," he said. "Thank you for coming by to see me, my dear. Have a seat and tell your papa all that you have been doing."

Hendel left before the conversation went any further, but he was happy to hear that the old man was still able to laugh.

When Hendel stepped into the parlor, he saw Jay Peerless Bixby sitting on the sofa, looking at photographs through a stereopticon.

"Mr. Bixby," Hendel said. "My business with Mr. Montgomery has concluded. If you wish to go in now, you may."

"Cynthia is here, she's his daughter," Bixby said without lowering the stereopticon.

"Oh, but I'm sure Mr. Montgomery would enjoy a visit from you as well."

"I'm not going in there," Bixby said. "It stinks in there. It smells like the old man has already died."

"I agree, it can get a little close in there," Hendel said.

"Where are you going when the old man dies?" Bixby asked.

"I beg your pardon?"

"When the old man dies, you'll be out of a job, won't you?"

"Yes, I suppose I will."

"So where are you going?"

"I don't know, I haven't actually given it that much thought."

"How would you like to come work for me?"

"You are offering me a job?"

"Yes."

"I'm surprised."

"Why are you surprised?"

"Because, to tell you the truth, Mr. Bixby, I've always had the belief that you didn't particularly like me."

"I don't like you," Bixby said. "You are just too damn meek for my tastes. I like a man who has a little gumption."

"And yet, you offer me a job."

Bixby laughed. "What does one have to do with the other?" he asked. "I'm wanting to hire you, not socialize with you. Besides, a little obsequiousness is not a bad thing for an employee. I don't want to be challenged."

"I see."

"And let's face it, I'll be taking over the old man's business," Bixby said. "Who knows his business better than you? I think it's a very good situation for both of us."

"What does Mrs. Bixby think?"

"It doesn't matter what she thinks. I'm the one hiring you, not her," Bixby replied. "But as a matter of fact, hiring you was her idea. Normally, I wouldn't listen to any suggestion she had to make, but in this case, I think it was a good one. So, what do you say, Hendel? Do you want to come to work for me?"

"Mr. Hendel! Mr. Hendel!" Cynthia called from the bedroom. "Please, come quickly! Papa is calling for you!"

Hendel hurried into the room and saw Montgomery sitting up in his bed. He was gasping for breath.

"Mr. Montgomery, you should lie back down, sir!" Hendel said, concerned over the old man's condition.

"The papers," Montgomery gasped. "The papers you want signed, give them to me now quickly."

"But they aren't made out yet," Hendel said.

Montgomery shook his head. "It doesn't matter," he said. "I'll sign at the bottom, you can fill them out later. Quickly, man."

"Yes, sir," Hendel said. Hurrying over to the old man's desk, Hendel rifled through it until he found three blank sheets of paper. He brought the papers and a fountain pen to Montgomery. Montgomery signed all three of them, then handed them to his daughter.

"Witness that you saw me sign these," he said.

"What are they, Papa?"

"Do you trust Mr. Hendel?"

"Yes, implicitly," Cynthia answered.

"Then sign them." Montgomery lay back on his pillow, as if exhausted.

Cynthia signed all three blank sheets of paper, then returned the pages to Hendel.

"I signed them, Papa, though I don't know what— *Papa!*" she screamed.

Montgomery was lying back on his pillow—his eyes open but already clouding over with the opaqueness of death.

"Papa!" she screamed again.

Hendel hurried over to the desk and picked up the telephone. "Number 271, please," he said. He looked over at the bed and saw that Cynthia was bent over at her waist, with her head on her father's chest. "Dr. Petrie," Hendel said when the doctor answered his telephone. "You had better return to the Montgomery home. I believe he has died."

Hanging up the phone, Hendel walked back into the parlor. Bixby was still there, but now he was reading the newspaper.

"Mrs. Bixby needs you, sir," he said.

"What for?"

"I'm afraid Mr. Montgomery has just died."

"So? What does she need me for? If the old man is dead, there is nothing I can do about it."

Bixby went back to reading the newspaper. "Says here there is a beef shortage," he said. "The price of cattle is going to go sky high."

Joel Montgomery left instructions that he was to be buried at sea. He wanted his funeral to be conducted at St. Paul's Episcopal Church, a small neighborhood church that had come into existence primarily because of Montgomery's generosity. He had paid for the building, and put enough money into the church coffers to hire a priest and organist. He had also been senior warden for the church, a position he held until the time of his death.

The church was filled to overflowing during the funeral, and it wasn't until then that everyone realized just how generous a man Montgomery had been in his life. He had donated money, not only to the church, but to several orphanages and needy families around town, and though during his lifetime he had kept his charitable contributions secret, his benevolence was well known to Ken Hendel, who, as his business manager, had set up many of the altruistic endeavors.

"My God, would you look at all this?" Bixby said as he read the pew sheet that told about Montgomery's beneficence. "With all the money he was giving away, it's a wonder he had any left at all. Well, I can tell you right now, that's all coming to an end. Hendel, the first thing I want you to do is contact all these people and tell them that the cow has dried up."

After the service in the church, Montgomery's body was taken by hearse down to the waterfront, where it was put on board the *Prometheus,* Montgomery's personal yacht, for transport to a spot far enough offshore for his body to be committed to the deep. Only his family and his closest friends were invited for that part of the rite, so Hendel stood by as the body was taken on board.

"Please, Mr. Hendel," Cynthia said. "You must come."

"There isn't room for me," Hendel said.

"Take my place," Bixby said.

"Oh, Mr. Bixby, I wouldn't want to put you out."

"You won't be putting me out. I'm not going, whether you go or not. I don't like boats."

"Please do come, Mr. Hendel," Cynthia pleaded.

"Very well, I would consider it an honor," Hendel said.

Hendel found a place at the bow of the yacht so as to be out of the way of the family. Then, when they reached the place where Montgomery was to be committed, he stood reverently while the priest intoned the interment prayer. As the body slid off the plank and into the water, he saw Cynthia making a strong effort to control her grief.

He knew at that moment that he could not totally abandon her to Jay Peerless Bixby. He would take the job Bixby offered.

Besides, in this job, he would be better positioned to make certain that the papers he had filed, after Montgomery's signature, were followed to the letter.

Chapter Five

The sound of flesh on flesh, followed by a woman's cry of pain, brought to a halt all conversation in the Hungry Miner Saloon in Fort Collins, Colorado. When the other patrons of the saloon turned toward the sound, they saw an angry Pogue Willis glaring at Juanita Simpson, one of the bar girls.

"When you bring me a drink, don't you be a-stickin' your finger down into the whiskey," Willis said angrily.

"Mr. Willis, I didn't have my finger down in your whiskey," Juanita said, her voice quivering in fright.

Willis slapped her again, harder this time than he did the first time, and her eye swelled shut almost instantly.

"Please, don't hit me again," she said.

"Then don't be a-lyin' to me," Willis said.

"Mr. Willis, I don't think you ought to be hittin' a woman like that, even if she did stick her finger down into your drink," one of the customers said. "It's such a pretty little finger anyway. Why, more than likely, all she done was sweetin' the drink a bit," he added, smiling to lighten his comment.

There was a nervous twitter of laughter from some of the others in the room.

Willis turned away from Juanita and looked toward the other end of the bar where the man who had spoken to him was standing, nursing his own drink.

"What's your name, mister?" Willis asked.

"It's Marcus. Lee Marcus," the man answered. "No need for you to introduce yourself, Mr. Willis. Why, I reckon ever'body in town knows you, if not ever'body in the whole state."

Marcus wasn't exaggerating. Pogue Willis had the reputation of being a gunman. It was a well-earned reputation, for Willis had put several men in their graves—at least fifteen and maybe as many as twenty-five, depending on who was doing the telling.

"What was it you was just sayin' to me?" Willis asked.

"Oh, nothin' much," Marcus replied. "I was just commentin' that there didn't seem to me to be no need for you to be knockin' around that young woman like you was doin'. Even if she did stick her finger down into your drink, you know it wasn't somethin' she done on purpose. And her bein' a woman and all, why, there's just no call for you to be beatin' up on her like that. I mean, when you think about, it don't seem all that gentlemanly a thing to do, does it?"

"I tell you what, Mr. Marcus. Maybe you'd like to take part in this fight," Willis said. "Because if you want to, I'll be more than willing to accommodate you."

"What? Fight? No, what are you talkin' about?" Marcus asked, wondering now if he had gone too far. "There ain't no fight here for me to take a part in. I was just commentin' as to how it don't seem right to me for a man to be hittin' a woman, that's all. I sure wasn't challengin' you to a fight or nothin' like that."

"Well, friend Marcus, it's too late," Willis said. "You done took a part in this fight. So what are you goin' to do next?"

"I ain't doin' nothin' next," Marcus said. "I aim to let this drop. Right here and right now."

Willis shook his head. "Huh-uh," he said. "It ain't a-goin' to drop. You started it, I am goin' to finish it."

"I didn't start nothin'! You're crazy, mister, and you're lettin' this thing get out of hand," Marcus said, the tone of his voice rising in fear. "I done told you, there ain't no fight goin' on here between you and me."

Pogue Willis was not a very big man. In fact, he was only about five feet six inches tall and he weighed no more than 145 pounds. His hair was a dirty blond, and the skin on his face had a blotch of red, whether from a birthmark or a burn scar, nobody knew. In a normal world, Pogue Willis would live his life as unobtrusively as possible.

But this was not a normal world. This was a world where a man like Pogue Willis, who should be little more than dust under a better man's boot, possessed two traits that lifted him from the obscure to the feared. He was fast and accurate with a pistol, but more significantly, he had no more compunction about killing a human being than the average person did about stepping on a cockroach.

Willis smiled, but instead of the smile ameliorating the situation, it exacerbated it, for the smile was not one of mirth or good cheer. It was an evil, sardonic smile that twisted the features of his face until it took on a demonic visage.

"You know what I think, Mr. Marcus," Willis said, his sibilant voice so low that even those who were the nearest to him had to strain to hear. "I think maybe me and you ought to get this here little difference of opinion settled between us," Willis said. "Otherwise, a thing like this, unresolved so to speak, is just goin' to start a-festerin' in my craw. And I don't like it when things gets to festerin' in my craw."

Lee Marcus owned a small producing silver mine. It had not made him rich, but it was providing him with a comfortable living, and just a few moments earlier, he had cashed out the results of his last six months of diggings for a little over two thousand dollars. He had come from the bank right to the saloon, and the cash was still in his pocket when he came into the Hungry Miner for a celebratory drink.

Now, in less than a minute, his entire world had changed. Marcus had gone from being very happy with his lot, to being irritated and concerned over the fact that a man was hitting a woman, to the sudden frightening realization that he was rapidly being pushed into a life-and-death situation. He was being drawn into a fight he didn't want.

Getting hold of himself, Marcus forced a smile,

making it as genuine as he could under these frightening circumstances. "Now, just hold on here, Mr. Willis, wait a minute, please," Marcus said. He spoke is as calm and friendly a voice as he could. "I think you would agree with me that it is pretty obvious that me and you have got ourselves off on the wrong foot here. I tell you what I'm goin' to do. I'm goin' to buy you a drink. Yes, sir, that's the best thing to do. I really didn't mean to say nothin' to put you to anger like I done, so why don't me and you just have us that drink I'm offerin' an' then we can start all over? Bartender, how 'bout you pour Mr. Willis another drink on me?"

"Sure thing, Mr. Marcus, I'd be glad to. Seems to me like that'd be about the best thing we could do, afore this here goes any further." the bartender replied, going along with Marcus's proposal. He poured another drink and set it in front of Willis. "There you go, Mr. Willis, compliments of Mr. Marcus."

Willis, with the demonic smile still on his lips, picked up the drink, held it up as if in toast, then, suddenly and without warning, tossed the contents of the glass into Marcus's face.

That sudden and unexpected action brought the rest of the saloon to total silence as every man and woman present looked toward the two men to see what would happen next.

Marcus had gasped in surprise, but checking his normal impulse to do or say anything that would make the situation any worse, he just reached down and pulled a towel from one of the towel rings on the bar, and wiped his face.

"Well, I guess I deserved that for buttin' in where
it was none of my concern," Marcus said. He forced
a chuckle as he continued to wipe his face. "Yes, sir, I
got to hand it to you, you got me good with that little
trick. So with all things bein' considered, I reckon
that makes me and you be just about even now."

"We ain't even," Willis said.

"Sure we are," Marcus replied.

"Are you callin' me a liar, Mr. Marcus?" Willis
challenged.

"What? No, I—why would I call you a liar?"

"Here's the thing, Mr. Marcus. Me and you ain't
goin' to be even till one of us is dead," Willis said.
His evil smile broadened. "And truth to tell, I got
me this feelin' that it ain't goin' to be me the one
that winds up dead."

"Wait a minute! Now, hold on here!" Marcus
called out, holding his hands out in front of him.
"This has gone far enough! Let's quit this foolishness now!"

"Foolishness? Are you callin' me a fool, Marcus?"

From somewhere, deep inside, Marcus felt a slow
calming begin to come over him. He knew there
was no way he was going to avoid this fight. He
could not explain why, but with that realization the
fear fell away to be replaced by a feeling of resignation and acceptance. There was going to be a gunfight, he was resigned to that fact. He knew also
that he was going to be killed, and he was resigned
to that fact as well. Finding a quiet courage that
he did not know he possessed, he quit cajoling.

"You are right, mister," Marcus said, his voice

calm and well modulated now. "One of us is going to die."

"That's right," Willis said. "And it ain't goin' to be me."

"You dried-up little son of a bitch, I'll be waitin' for you at the gates of Hell," Marcus said, his hand dipping toward his pistol even as he was talking.

Marcus broke leather before Willis even started his draw, and for a brief moment, he felt a sense of elation, a sense that he might actually win this fight.

But his hope was misplaced because in the wink of an eye, so fast that Marcus found himself wondering if somehow Willis hadn't had the pistol in his hand all along, he saw the muzzle-flash of Willis's .44. Before he could squeeze the trigger of his own gun, he felt a heavy blow in the middle of his chest. The impact of the bullet took his breath away and slammed him back against the bar. Even with the excruciating pain in his chest, he felt the blow of the bar against his back as he slid down to the floor, his gun hand by his side, his pistol lying, unfired, on the floor beside him.

Matt Jensen, fully recovered now from the gunshot wound he had received at the Crocker ranch two months earlier, was riding into town when he heard the sound of the gunshot. The single shot came from the other end of the street, and it put him on instant alert. Because Matt had lived an active and adventurous life, there were those who would like nothing better than to put a bullet in his head. He had managed to avoid that so far, not only by his own skill with pistols, rifles, and even knives, but also because of an acute power of awareness, the sixth sense that served men like Matt.

But he realized quickly that whatever the shot was, it wasn't meant for him. Relaxing from the momentary tenseness, he continued riding down the street at a leisurely pace.

Matt had come to Fort Collins in response to a letter he had received a few days ago from a friend:

Dear Matt Jensen—

I take pen in hand to write you to tell you of the success I have had in this here mine that you sold me. When you sold me this silver mine two years ago, you said it would pay out iffen someone was willin to work hard at it. They was them who told me I was a fool to trust anyone who was sellin a mine, but there was something about you that give me trust. I am happy to say that you was right. This here mine aint made me rich or nothin like that, but I have worked it regular since I bought it and it has paid out a lot more than I put into it so I thank you for it. On Wednesday the 15th instant I intend to be in Fort Collins cashin out my diggins from the winter previous. If you would care to meet me at the Hungry Miner saloon, I'd be that proud to buy you a drink then afterwards maybe you would let me buy you dinner at the finest café in town.

Your ob't servant
Lee Marcus

Matt had been in Trinidad, Colorado, when the letter caught up with him toward the end of last week, and because he had nothing else planned, he decided he would drop in to see Marcus. A colorful profusion of late-spring wildflowers, along with agreeable weather, had made the ride up from Trinidad quite pleasant.

When Matt dismounted in front of the Hungry Miner, he saw several people hurrying into the saloon. He surmised from the flurry of activity that the shot he had heard had come from the saloon. And for some reason that he could not explain, he suddenly had the feeling that somehow his friend might be involved.

Matt tied off his horse, Spirit, then joined the throngs moving in through the batwing doors.

You all seen it!" someone was shouting. Holding a pistol in his hand, he was waving it around as he shouted, causing the others to duck or move to get out of his way. "Is there anyone in here who didn't see him draw agin' me first?"

Looking over toward the bar, Matt saw Lee Marcus sitting on the floor, leaning back against the bar. The front of his shirt was covered with blood and though Marcus was still alive, Matt had watched enough men die to know that Marcus had but a moment or two of life left.

"Lee!" Matt called out. He hurried over to him, then knelt beside his friend.

"Hello, Matt," Marcus said. "Too bad you wasn't here a few minutes earlier. You missed all the excitement."

"What happened?"

"Me and this little feller here got into a bit of an argument," Marcus said.

Matt looked up at the small man.

"You do this?" he asked.

"Yeah, I did it. You plannin' on doin' somethin' about it?" the little man asked pugnaciously.

"Matt Jensen, this is Pogue Willis," the bartender said.

"You're—you're Matt Jensen?" Willis asked.

When he heard Matt's name, the little man's demeanor changed quickly. Instead of being arrogantly challenging, Pogue Willis suddenly became defensive. Quickly, he put his pistol back in its holster.

"It was a fair fight, Jensen, it was a fair fight," Willis said. "He drew first. You can ask anyone in here, your friend drew first."

"Is that true, Lee?" Matt asked.

"Yeah," Lee replied. He coughed, and blood came from his mouth. "I just got tired of listenin' to the feller go on so."

"See, I told you," Willis said. "Look there, he said it his ownself, he drew first."

"Shut up, Willis," Matt said.

"What? Now, see here, you can't talk to me like that," Willis said. "I don't care who you are, you—"

That was as far as Willis got, because Matt stood up and backhanded him across the face, hitting so hard that both his nose and lip began bleeding. Willis staggered back against the bar and his hand moved toward his pistol.

"Do it," Matt said calmly. "Please, pull your gun."

Without a saying another word, Willis stopped his hand just above his pistol, then moved instead to grab one of the bar towels.

"I wasn't goin' for my gun, I was reachin' for a

towel," Willis said. He began dabbing at the blood. At that moment, without a gun in his hand, there was nothing at all frightening about the little man.

"Matt," Marcus called. "Lean down here and listen to me. Don't pay no attention to that punk. I got somethin' else I want you to do for me if you will."

With another menacing, and warning, glance toward Willis, Matt knelt beside his friend.

"Matt, I got me a little over two thousand dollars in my pocket here," he said. "It's money from the diggin's. Take some of it and buy yourself a train ticket to St. Louis. When you get there, look up my brother, Andrew. You'll find him listed in the city directory. I want you to give him what money is left. Will you do that for me?"

"Yes," Matt answered, nodding. "I'll be glad to do that for you, Lee."

"I got me a pocket on the inside of this vest. Reach in there and get the money."

As Matt was reaching for the money, the sheriff arrived and, seeing Matt, he pulled his gun.

"Hold on there, mister," the sheriff called. "I ain't goin' to stand here and watch you steal from a dyin' man."

"No!" Marcus shouted, finding a last bit of strength. "He ain't stealin' it, Sheriff Allen. This here is my friend, Matt Jensen. I'm givin' it to him!"

"Matt Jensen?" Sheriff Allen said. He nodded. "Yes, sir, I know who you are. Go ahead."

Matt looked down at his friend again. "I'll get it to him, Lee, I promise. I'll get the money to your brother."

Marcus didn't answer, because Marcus was dead.

Matt continued to stare down at his friend for a long moment, then he turned his gaze toward Pogue Willis.

"What?" Willis said. He held both hands out in front of him. "Look here, Jensen, I got no quarrel with you," he said.

"Really?"

"No, I ain't got no—"

That was as far as Willis got, because Matt grabbed him by the scruff of the neck and the seat of his pants, picked him up, then with a mighty heave, sent him, belly-down, sliding for the entire length of the bar.

Those who were standing at the bar got out of the way as they watched in surprise while the gunman careened by in front of them, knocking over bottles and glasses. Willis fell off the far end of the bar, hitting the floor with a loud thump. When he got up, he had bits and pieces of expectorated tobacco quids sticking to him from those spittoon users who had been errant in their aim.

Everyone in the bar laughed loudly at Willis as he began picking the pieces off him.

"Sheriff, you seen it!" Willis said. "I wasn't doin' nothin' but mindin' my own business when he grabbed me and tossed me like that."

"Sheriff Allen, the reason Jensen done that is because Willis here is the one who killed his friend," the bartender said.

"That right, Willis? Did you kill Lee Marcus?" Allen asked.

"He drew on me first," Willis said. "Ever'body in

here will tell you that. That's why Jensen had no call to throw me down the bar like he done."

Allen pursed his lips and shook his head. "I agree with you, Willis. That seems like an awfully unfriendly thing for Matt Jensen to do."

"Yeah, yeah, that's right," Willis said, nodding.

"So if you want to throw down on him, why, I reckon I won't try to stop you."

"What?"

"Go ahead, draw if you want to," the sheriff said. "I'll stay out of it."

"No, wait, that ain't what I had in mind," Willis said. "That ain't what I had in mind at all."

"No, I didn't think it would be," Allen said. "I tell you what, Willis, why don't you just give your gun to me now and I'll take you into custody until after the trial."

"Trial? What trial?"

"Why, the murder trial, Mr. Willis. We're goin' to be tryin' you for the killin' of Mr. Marcus."

"But he drew first! Ever'one in here will tell you, he drew first!"

"Then the trial shouldn't be a problem."

Willis glared at the sheriff. It was obvious that he was considering this further, perhaps as far as drawing against the sheriff. But it was equally obvious that he was worried about the presence of Matt Jensen.

The glare changed to a forced smile and, slowly, using only his thumb and forefinger, he pulled his pistol from the holster.

"All right, Sheriff," he said. "Let's have the trial."

soiled dove who plies her avocation in the Hungry Miner Saloon.

Upon observing Willis striking Miss Simpson, Marcus reminded Pogue Willis of the responsibilities a gentleman has when dealing with women, suggesting that it was considered unseemly of Willis to strike Miss Simpson. There is no doubt that Marcus little dreamed that his innocent remark would hurl his soul into eternity before the sun had set.

Pogue Willis is a little man, standing but five feet six inches tall, but he more than compensates for what nature has denied him by making himself a man with a well-earned reputation for deadly skill in the employment of a pistol. It is well known that many men, all of whom were bigger, stronger, and better men than he in every respect, have fallen before his gun.

As it so happened yesterday, after a few remarks were passed back and forth between the two men, Willis, as is often the wont of small men with power beyond their physical attributes, began to show an ugly resentment toward Marcus and became very abusive.

The innocent exchange turned deadly when Marcus, goaded into it by Willis, made an attempt to draw his pistol. Now, whereas Marcus was a mining engineer and not a pistoleer, he was ill prepared to continue the fight, for Willis, upon seeing the clumsy attempt Marcus made, drew his own pistol and fired, his shot taking effect in Marcus's chest, the bullet piercing the lung.

Marcus fell to the floor of the saloon and soon expired. Sheriff Seth Allen arrived on the scene shortly thereafter, and promptly arrested Willis. Trial will be held in the morning before Circuit Judge Tony Heckemeyer.

Judge Heckemeyer arrived in Fort Collins in a black surrey with yellow wheels. The surrey was drawn by two black horses, each of which had a yellow tassel on its head. A rather large man, Heckemeyer had been summoned by telegraph, so he was not surprised to see that many in the town turned out to welcome him.

"Are you goin' to hang him, Judge?" someone shouted from the porch of the apothecary.

Believing a response, any response, would be beneath the dignity of the office, Heckemeyer didn't answer. Instead, he drove straight through town to the Hungry Miner Saloon. The irony was that Pogue Willis would be tried in the same saloon in which he had killed Lee Marcus.

"Hello, Judge, welcome to Fort Collins," Sheriff Allen said, greeting Heckemeyer just as he stepped into the saloon.

"Hello, Seth," Heckemeyer replied. Seeing two people standing at the bar, drinking beer, Heckemeyer pointed to the bartender. "Hodge, you know better than that," he said. "Shut this bar down."

"The bar is closed, Judge. They're just still drinkin'

what they bought before the bar was closed," Hodge replied.

"You two boys got three choices," Heckemeyer said to the two men who were drinking the beer. "Pour it out now, or leave the saloon with it and don't come back."

"You said three choices, Judge," one of the beer drinkers replied.

"Oh, yes. Your third choice is to be put in jail for thirty days for contempt of court."

Both drinkers immediately handed their beers over to Hodge, who, obligingly, poured out the rest.

"Let's get started, shall we?" Heckemeyer said.

Clearing his throat, Sheriff Allen turned and called out loudly: "Hear ye, hear ye, hear ye. This court is now in session, the Honorable Judge Anthony Heckemeyer presiding."

One table had been set up at the end of the saloon that was closest to the piano. Two other tables were set up, one for the defense and one for the prosecution. All the other tables had been moved to one side of the room and twelve chairs had been set up for the jury. The remaining chairs had been put in rows for the spectators.

There were only two lawyers in Fort Collins, and they took turns being the prosecutor. Today, the prosecution was being handled by George Dempster, and the defense by David Craig.

Dempster called witnesses who testified that Pogue Willis had goaded Marcus into finally drawing his gun.

Juanita Simpson was called to the stand. One of her eyes was black and nearly swollen shut. There was also a bruise on her cheek, both being visual evidence of the treatment she had received from Pogue Willis.

"Miss Simpson, Would you tell us, please, in your own words, what happened?" Dempster asked.

"Mr. Willis asked me to bring him a drink and when I did, he accused me of stickin' my finger into it."

"Did you stick your finger into the drink?"

"No, sir, I did not. And I told him I didn't, but that didn't make no never-mind. He hit me anyway. Then, Mr. Marcus said to Mr. Willis that he didn't have no call to hit me like that. One thing led to another and, the next thing you know, there was shootin' and poor Mr. Marcus was dead."

Juanita's testimony was most poignant, and she broke down on the stand while testifying.

"Take your time, Miss Simpson," Dempster said.

Juanita wiped her eyes and blew her nose before she continued. "The thing is, Mr. Marcus died because he was takin' up for me," she said.

"Miss Simpson," Craig said in his cross-examination. "You say you did not stick your finger in Mr. Willis's drink?"

"No, sir, I did not."

"Why do you think he accused you of doing that?"

"I don't know."

"Oh, surely you know, Miss Simpson. Why did he accuse you of sticking your finger in the drink? Do you think it might be because you refused to do business with him?"

"Do business with him?" Juanita said.

"Yes, do business. I'm sure you know what I'm talking about, Miss Simpson. What sort of business are you in?"

"I work at the Hungry Miner."

"Is it true, Miss Simpson, that you are a whore at the Hungry Miner? And is it not also true that you angered Pogue Willis, not by sticking your finger in his drink, but by refusing to go upstairs with him?"

"Objection," Dempster said quickly. "Irrelevant!"

"Withdraw the question," Craig said. "Miss Simpson, did you actually see the gunfight?"

. "Yes, I saw it."

"Who drew first?"

"You don't understand. Pogue Willis just kept on goading Mr. Marcus. He just wouldn't leave him alone. He was wantin' Mr. Marcus to draw his gun."

"Who drew first?" Craig repeated.

"Well, it was Mr. Marcus, but he—"

"Thank you, Miss Simpson. I have no further questions of this witness, Your Honor."

When all the witnesses had testified, Judge Heckemeyer invited the counselors to give their closing arguments. Counselor for the defense was first.

"Gentlemen of the jury, you have heard the witnesses to this shooting and, since it happened right here in the saloon during a busy time, more than a dozen were able to testify."

Craig paused for a moment.

"More than a dozen witnesses had a good enough view of the shooting to be able to give us a very detailed description of what happened. And, gentlemen of the jury—" Craig paused and held up his forefinger. "No one, not one witness, testified that Willis drew first. In fact, every eyewitness who testified before this august court and honorable judge testified that it was Marcus who drew first."

Craig pointed to Willis.

"You may not like Pogue Willis. Indeed, few do, for he is not a very likable man. But you cannot find him guilty of being unlikable. And if you are honest with yourself, you know that you cannot find him guilty of murder either."

Dempster stood up when Craig sat down. It was time for him to give his closing argument, but he stood silent for a long moment, then shook his head.

"An unlikable man?" Dempster said, speaking very quietly. "Unlikable?" he repeated, just a little louder. Then he pointed to Willis. "He is not merely unlikable—he is an evil spawn of Satan!"

Dempster shouted the last phrase.

"This *unlikable*"—he twisted his mouth as he said the word—"man has killed fifteen human beings! Do you fully understand that? Fifteen men, men who were someone's son, brother, husband, and father, fifteen men were killed by Pogue Willis.

"And now we are asked to find him innocent because the other man drew first? You have heard witness after witness testify that Pogue Willis goaded, cajoled, beleaguered, and intimidated Mr. Marcus until he felt that he had no choice but to draw. It has also been testified here that Pogue Willis had a smile on his face as he pulled the trigger.

"I ask that you find this man guilty, and that the judge sentence him to hang."

"Hear, hear!" someone in the gallery shouted.

Judge Heckemeyer quickly restored order by the judicious use of his gavel. Once order was restored, he charged the jury and they adjourned to the back room of the saloon to make their decision. After only a few minutes of deliberation, the jury returned.

"Mr. Foreman," he said. "Has the jury reached a verdict?"

"We have, Your Honor," the foreman answered. The foreman was Al Frakes, owner of Frakes Photography.

"Please hand the verdict to the bailiff."

Frakes gave a little piece of paper to the bailiff, who took it over to the judge. Heckemeyer read the verdict silently.

"Mr. Willis, approach the bench," he said sternly.

Although Matt Jensen had already bought a round-trip train ticket to St. Louis, he'd stayed in town long enough to attend the trial and now, as Pogue Willis approached the bench, Matt studied the expression on his face. Throughout the trial Willis had displayed arrogance and bravado. Now, however, being summoned to stand before the judge, he began to show a little bit of apprehension.

Matt could understand Willis's concern. For Willis, a prison sentence would be as deadly as a sentence to be hanged. Willis had made a lot of enemies during his short, but very brutal, career, and many of his enemies were now in prison. On the outside, where he could carry a pistol, Pogue Willis feared few men. But, if he had to go to prison, he would be unarmed. Without a gun, Pogue Willis would be dead within less than a week.

"Pogue Willis, it has been testified to in this court that when a Good Samaritan saw you hitting a woman, he asked you politely to quit. It has further been testified to that you took issue with that Good Samaritan and, for no good reason, began goading him, challenging him, and pushing him beyond reasonable limits until he was forced to draw against you.

"If it were my case to decide, I would find your sorry carcass guilty and sentence you to hang within the week. But it is the law of our land that you are to be tried by your peers, and your peers, following the letter if not the intent of the law, have ruled that, because Lee Marcus drew first, you are not guilty."

"Ha!" Willis shouted happily. "I know'd I was goin' to beat this one."

"I am going to acquiesce to the ruling of the jury, for I have no other choice," Judge Heckemeyer said. "However, sir, I am now issuing this court order. You are to vacate the town of Fort Collins and the state of Colorado. If you return to Colorado, I will have you arrested and thrown into prison for violation of this court order. I do not think, Mr. Willis, that you would fare very well in prison."

"Judge, you got no right to run me out of the state," Willis protested.

"You are free to appeal my decision, Mr. Willis," Heckemeyer said. "But in order to make that appeal, you will have to remain in the state. And if you remain in the state, I will put you in prison, where you will remain until that appeal is acted upon. So your choice is simple. Leave the state, or make an appeal from behind prison walls. Now, which shall it be?"

"I'll, uh, leave the state, Judge," Willis said.

"I thought you might see it my way. Sheriff, escort this man to the depot and put him on the next train," Heckemeyer said. He banged the gavel down on the table that was serving as his bench. "This court is dismissed."

"Gents! The bar is open!" the bartender shouted, and there was a rush to the bar as the patrons hurried to quench the thirsts that had been generated by the trial.

Chapter Seven

At the Fort Collins train depot, Matt Jensen stood with his arms folded across his chest as he watched the activity on the platform. Pogue Willis, unarmed, meek, and unchallenging, was here also, sitting on a bench under the watchful eyes of one of Sheriff Allen's deputies. As it happened, both Matt and Willis would be taking the same train south from Fort Collins, though when Matt reached Denver, he would transfer to a train heading east, while Willis and the deputy would continue on with the train heading south, toward New Mexico Territory. The deputy would stay with Willis until they reached the state line. At that point, Willis would be released and the deputy would come back.

Although Matt was disappointed by the outcome of the trial, he realized that technically the jury had come in with the correct verdict. No matter the provocation, Lee didn't have to draw his gun. That meant that in the final analysis, it was his own fault. Matt just wished that he could have arrived a few minutes earlier. He was sure that if he had been there, none of this would have happened.

"Mr. Jensen?"

Turning, Matt saw the bar girl Willis had been beating.

"Yes, uh, Miss Simpson, isn't it?" Matt replied.

The girl smiled and, even with the bruises, the smile softened her features. It was obvious that, before the dissipation of her profession had taken its toll, Juanita Simpson had been an attractive woman.

"Here, folks was callin' me miss all durin' the trial, and now you're callin' me miss, too. Don't hardly nobody ever call me miss no more," she said. "Not what with me bein' a bar girl an' all. Most folks call me much worse. You can call me Juanita if you want to."

"I'd be pleased to call you Juanita."

"You was a friend of Mr. Marcus, wasn't you?" Juanita said. "I seen that you and him talked some right there at the end, just before he died."

"Yes, we were friends," Matt said.

"You was friends, and now he is dead. And it was all my fault him gettin' killed all 'cause of the way he took up for me like he done."

"It wasn't your fault, Juanita. Not at all," Matt said. "Don't be blaming yourself for it. The person to blame is that little pipsqueak over there." Matt pointed to Pogue Willis."

"He don't look very scary now, does he?" Juanita said.

"No, not at all."

Juanita walked over to the bench where Willis was sitting.

"Mr. Willis, there's somethin' I owe you," she said.

"Yeah? What is that?" Willis asked.

Suddenly and totally without warning, Juanita swung her hand around, putting all her weight into it. With her doubled up fist, she hit Willis on the cheek just under his eye, hitting him with enough force to send him tumbling off the bench.

"Why, you bitch, I'm going to—"

"Do nothing, except sit back down on the bench and shut up," the deputy said.

The others at the depot, having seen what happened, laughed.

"Hey, Willis, you ain't much of a man without a gun, are you?" someone called.

Glaring, Willis sat still and stared down at the ground between his feet.

Juanita turned and walked away from him.

"Good for you, miss," someone said, and a few others joined in with their own positive comments.

Matt chuckled when Juanita returned.

"Feel better?" he asked.

Juanita smiled. "I feel a lot better," she said. "Oh! Do you think I was wrong?"

"No, Juanita, I think you were very right," Matt said. "To be honest, I've been standing here wishing I could do it myself. But it's even better coming from you."

Juanita laughed. "I hope Mr. Marcus is lookin' down from heaven and saw it."

"I'll just bet he is," Matt said.

"Oh, I almost forgot," Juanita said. She stepped back into the depot, then came back out a moment later, holding a package. "I made this for you while you are on the train," Juanita said as she handed the package to him. "I know I'm nothin' but a bar girl, but I'm also a pretty good cook. And I'm just particular good at bakin' cookies. This here is my mother's recipe. I made a batch of 'em for you."

"Well, that's very nice of you," Matt said. "I don't know what I did to cause you to want to make cookies for me, but I appreciate it."

"Like I said, you was Mr. Marcus's friend," Juanita said. "And you treated me real nice durin' the trial and all."

In the distance, they heard a train whistle.

"Eastbound!" the station manager shouted, coming out onto the platform. "This here train is for Eagle, Sherwood, Wolcott, Allentown, Minturn, Rock Creek, Wheeler, Pano, Denver, and all points east, north, and south."

"I reckon that's your train," Juanita said.

"Yes."

"If you wanted to stay here a couple days, maybe I could—uh—well if you wanted to stay here a couple of days, you could—what I mean is . . ." she said, not completing her thought.

"I appreciate the invitation, Juanita," Matt said. "But I made a promise to Lee that I intend to keep."

"Yes, sir, and you are the kind that keeps his promises," Juanita said. "Mr. Marcus was lucky to have a friend like you."

The train pulled into the station then, arriving with a rush of steam, a rattle of connectors, and the squeal of steel on steel as the brakes were applied.

The station manager walked out to the engine and held a sheaf of papers up to the engineer, who took them. The engineer filled his pipe as the engine sat at rest, venting steam from the pressure-relief valve.

Arriving baggage was taken from the baggage car while departing baggage was loaded. The conductor stood on the platform, self-assured in his importance, as the arriving passengers stepped down. He pulled out his pocket watch and examined it, then put it back.

"All aboard!" he shouted.

With last-minute good-byes, the outgoing passengers began loading onto the train. Matt watched as the deputy and Willis climbed onto the first car behind the baggage car. Matt boarded the next car behind the one that the deputy and Willis had taken, then took his seat for the start of what was going to be a very long trip.

Matt watched the other passengers settle in— a drummer with his wares, an older couple, two young cowboys, and a young woman with a baby. When the young woman tried to put her grip in the overhead rack, one of the cowboys came to her aid, saluted her with a touch to the brim of his hat, then took his seat beside his friend.

Matt heard the whistle of the train; then the train started, causing a series of jerks to be distributed down through the line of cars as the slack was taken from the couplers. As the train pulled out of the station, he looked through the window toward Juanita, who, like many of the others, was still standing on the platform. He waved at her and, with a quick and grateful smile, she waved back.

For a moment, Matt wondered what there was about Juanita that generated in him a feeling of warmth for her; then he realized that it was because she reminded him of Tamara.

The train began gathering speed and, as it did so, Matt leaned his head back on the seat, closed his eyes, and remembered Tamara. Both he and Tamara had been orphans at the Home for Wayward Boys and Girls. It was run by a man named Mumford, an exceptionally evil man who insisted that all call him Captain, though he had no military experience, and all the children of the home were victims of his cruelty. Unwilling to take any more of it, Matt ran away from the home when he was twelve years old. Tamara, who was fourteen, ran away from the home with him.

Matt wasn't sure exactly what time it was when he left.* He knew it was late at night because everyone was asleep and he could hear the snores and rhythmic breathing of the others. It was getting colder outside, and he had no overcoat, so he decided to take the blanket off his bed.

He walked down to the hall and stood just outside the girls' dormitory. When Tamara didn't show up, he was about to leave without her, but suddenly she was there.

"When I saw you with the blanket, I thought that might be a pretty good idea," she whispered. "So I went back to get mine."

"All right, let's go, but keep quiet," Matt said.

Once outside, they looked back toward the building that housed the Home for Wayward Boys and Girls. For a

___

*The passages in italics in the following pages are from *Matt Jensen: The Last Mountain Man*.

moment, he almost went back in. It wasn't much, but it was the only home he'd had for the last three years. For some of the residents, it was the only home they had ever known.

"Are you sure you want to go with me?" Matt asked. "I mean, when you think about it, the Home kept us warm in the winter, gave us a place to sleep, and provided meals."

"Such as they were," Tamara said.

"We are giving up a safe haven for the unknown," Matt said.

"Who are you trying to talk out of going? Me or you?" Tamara asked.

"I don't know," Matt answered honestly. "Both of us, I guess."

The moon was full and bright, and it lit the path for them. A cool night breeze caused Matt to shiver, though in truth he didn't know if his trembling was entirely from the cold, or from nervousness over his uncertain future. He pulled the blanket around himself, then began walking.

The Home for Wayward Boys and Girls was three blocks from Muddy Creek and while that had not been a conscious goal, Matt quickly found himself on the bank of the creek, looking down at the water. That's when he saw the boat.

"There," he said excitedly, pointing to the boat. "That's our way out of here!"

"We're going to steal a boat?" Tamara asked.

"Nah, we're not stealing it," Matt said. "We're just borrowing it. You keep a watch out while I untie it."

Scrambling down the creek bank, Matt started untying the boat. That was when he heard the dogs barking.

"Tamara!" he called up the embankment. "Tamara, what is it?"

"Someone's coming," Tamara called down.

"Come on, hurry!"

"No!" *Tamara said.* You go ahead. I'll lead them away from the water."

"Tamara, no, come on!" *Matt said.* "Hurry, we have to go now!"

"You go on!" *Tamara called.*

Matt saw Tamara turn and run away from the top of the bank.

"Help!" *Tamara called.* "Help me!"

"What are you doing out here, girl?" *a man's voice asked.*

"I don't know," *Tamara answered.* "I think I must have been walking in my sleep, I just woke up out here. I'm lost and frightened. Please, help me get back to the Home."

By distracting the man, Tamara had given Matt the opportunity to get away and Matt took advantage of it. Wandering around in the mountains, he very nearly died of starvation and hypothermia until he was found, nearly frozen, by Smoke Jensen. Not yet widely known, Smoke was well on his way to becoming one of the West's most enduring legends.

Smoke not only saved Matt's life, he took in a boy with potential and began schooling him in such things as horsemanship, marksmanship with a rifle or handgun, the quick draw, how to fight with knife or fist, hunting, tracking, and how to survive in the woods, mountains, or desert.

But most of all, Smoke instilled in the boy the knowledge of right and wrong, a sense of justice and fair play, and an awareness of when to use his skills as a gunman—and when not to. Having started as a boy, Matt had graduated as a man who, like

Smoke, was well on his way to becoming a legend in his own right.

It was six years after he and Tamara parted on the bank of that river before Matt saw her again.

"You don't recognize me, do you, Matt?"

Matt stared at her. It couldn't be. This woman looked ten to fifteen years older than he was, not a mere two years older.

"My God," he said with an expulsion of breath. "Tamara?"

"I wondered when you were going to recognize me," Tamara replied. "Have I changed that much? I recognized you right away."

"No, it's not that, it's just that—well, I never expected to see you—here."

"You mean you didn't expect to see me whorin'," Tamara replied.

Matt didn't answer.

Tamara got out of bed and padded, naked, over to a chair where she had put her clothes the night before.

"What did you expect would happen to the girls at the Home?" she asked as she began dressing. "Mumford had us on the line by the time we were fifteen." She looked up at him, and he saw tears sliding down her face. "I told you that. You do remember, don't you, Matt, that I told you that?"

Matt nodded. "Yes," he said. "I remember. I tried to take you with me."

Tamara's expression softened, and she nodded.

"I know you did, honey. But I guess it just wasn't in the cards."

"If it hadn't been for you, I don't think I would have

*gotten away that night," Matt said. "You led them away
from me and the boat."*

*"I know I did. And don't think that I didn't think
about it a lot of times. I thought sure you had died up in
the mountains, and I figured that if you had, it would
have been my fault."*

*"As you can see, I didn't die," he said. "And even if I
had, it would not have been your fault. Like I said, I
thank you for helping me out that night."*

*Suddenly, there was the tinkling sound of broken glass
as something whizzed through the window, followed by a
solid "thock," like the sound of a hammer hitting a nail.*

*Tamara pitched forward, even as a mist of blood was
spraying out from the back of her head.*

"No!" Matt shouted in a loud, grief-stricken voice.

Matt had avenged Tamara's death, but he had
never forgotten her, and even now, many years
later, he continued to think of her.

Had Matt loved Tamara? He had thought about
that many times over the years. He knew that he
had not been "in love with" Tamara, at least not in
the classic sense. But she was a part of his youth,
and he could not deny that he had loved her, any
more than he could deny his own heritage.

Chapter Eight

Grand Central Station, New York

The coach-and-four rolled onto the Park Avenue Bridge, crossing 42nd Street as it approached the great stone edifice that Cornelius Vanderbilt had constructed for his railroad. Inside the coach, on the backseat facing forward, sat financier Jay Peerless Bixby, a rather plump, balding man who wore chin whiskers and muttonchop sideburns. Bixby was dressed in a three-piece suit, as befitting a man of his economic station. He was in his late fifties, but because his wife, Cynthia, was an exceptionally beautiful woman in her mid-twenties, she was often taken for his daughter.

Riding in the coach with Bixby was Ken Hendel. Hendel, in his early thirties, was a small man who wore wire-rim glasses and, at the moment, was wearing a suit and tie.

"Are you sure you made all the arrangements so I can transfer the funds as needed?" Bixby asked.

"Jay, dear, you have asked Mr. Hendel that same question at least three times since we left the house," Cynthia said.

"Yes, well, one can never be too careful when dealing with employees," Bixby said, speaking of Hendel as if he weren't present. "For the most part, they tend to be unreliable."

"I have never known Mr. Hendel to be anything but reliable," Cynthia said in defense of the man who was their business manager.

"You can understand my apprehension, I'm sure," Bixby said. "After all, there is a great deal of money involved, and when I am done, I will be the largest landowner in the entire territory of Arizona. Why, I'll own a ranch that will be the envy of the West."

"For the life of me, I don't understand your obsession with owning a ranch," Cynthia said.

"I am buying a ranch to make money, my dear. The cost of beef is rising every day."

"But you've never even been west of the Hudson River," Cynthia pointed out.

"That's why I will do well," Bixby said. He laughed. "Can you imagine those Western cretins doing business with me? I will be their superior in every respect."

When the coach stopped in front of the station, a footman hurried around to open the door. Once outside the coach, they could see the many omnibuses and cabs standing below them. They were met by three porters who picked up the baggage that the footman off-loaded from the coach.

"Hendel, you go with the porters to make certain our luggage gets checked through," Bixby ordered.

"Very well, Mr. Bixby," Hendel replied.

"And before you come back, check to make certain the train is on time."

"He doesn't have to do that," Cynthia said. She pointed to a big blackboard. "You can see right there that the train is on time."

"It may have changed and they may not have changed the posting," Bixby replied to his wife.

Just beyond the north wall, under the great vaulting roof, trains were arriving and departing. As they did so, the rumble of heavy wheels rolling on the tracks caused the floor to shake and it filled the large cavernous room with echoes.

Through doors and portals that opened onto the tracks, they could hear the rush of steam, the clang of bells, and, occasionally, the blowing of a whistle.

"Oh, Jay," Cynthia said, her eyes shining brightly. "Have you ever seen anything as exciting as this place?"

"Sometimes, Cynthia, you are such a child," Bixby said gruffly.

Cynthia wrapped her arms about her shoulders as if hugging herself. "I don't care," she said. "I think this is so exhilarating!"

Bixby turned his attention away from his wife. "You," he called to a uniformed railroad employee who was passing by. "Are these miserable accommodations the best you have for your passengers of means?"

"I beg your pardon, sir?"

"Do you not understand what I am saying? I am

a very wealthy man," Bixby said. "A man of my class and means should not have to sit on hard benches in a noisy room with the common passengers. Where are your upper-class accommodations?"

"I'm sorry, sir, I'm not aware of any such facility," the employee replied. "If you'll excuse me, sir."

"You, come back here!" Bixby ordered. "Well, I never," he said in exasperation as the railroad employee hurried away without looking back. "I will certainly write Cornelius Vanderbilt a personal letter and complain about this insolence. And I shall inform him that this is no way to run a railroad."

"Oh, Jay, don't be so disagreeable," Cynthia said. "Look at all these people and think about the journey they are about to make. Imagine just how many stories are here to be told."

"Ha!" Bixby said with a mocking laugh. "I can think of nothing more dreary than to listen to some of the stories of these poor wretches. No doubt they are going to see Grandmother or some such thing in some awful place like Indiana or Arkansas."

"Why must you always be so hateful, Jay?"

"I'm not hateful, my dear, I am merely practical," Bixby answered. "Ah, good, Hendel is back. It is about time. Well?" he asked as the young man approached.

"The luggage is checked through, sir."

"The schedule, man, the schedule," Bixby said. "Will the train leave on time?"

"Oh, yes, sir," Hendel replied. "In fact, it is already here and I expect they'll be loading in just a few moments."

"The train is already here? Well, why didn't you say so, man?"

"Jay, he did say so. He just this moment returned," Cynthia said.

Almost as if on cue, someone stepped through one of the doors that led out into the train shed. Lifting a megaphone to his mouth, he began shouting an announcement.

"Now loading on track number nine, the Western Limited to Albany, Buffalo, Cleveland, Indianapolis, Springfield, and St. Louis. All passengers please proceed to track number nine!"

"I wonder how long it will take us to get there," Cynthia said.

"Two days to St. Louis," Hendel said. "From there, another three days to Denver, then three days from Denver to Phoenix."

"We shall be but one week and one day in transit," Bixby said. "We do live in a marvelous age. I'm told there was a time, in the early days of the Western migration, when it would take upwards of three months to cover the same distance we shall in a few days."

Antonito, Colorado

The car was dimly lit by no more than four low-burning, wall-mounted, gimbal lanterns. When the train came to a halt, Pogue Willis looked out the window toward the depot. The building, constructed of unpainted, wide planks, was totally dark. A white sign, with black letters, hung from the eave of the roof.

ANTONITO,
Colorado

The conductor came through the car then, moving quietly so as not to awaken any of the sleeping passengers. He leaned over the seat where Willis and Deputy Kinsley were sitting.

"Deputy, this is our last stop in Colorado," he said.

"Thank you," Kinsley said. "Uh, the next train back to Denver is at six in the morning. You got any idea where I can stay until then?"

The conductor pulled out his watch and looked at it. "That's only about three hours," he said. "There is a bench inside the depot. You can wait there."

"It's closed, ain't it?"

"Well, there is nobody there now, but the building remains unlocked," the conductor said. He chuckled. "They don't keep anything of value there."

"All right, thanks, I'll wait there," the deputy said. He looked over at Willis. "Come on, Mr. Willis, this is where we get off."

When Willis and the deputy stepped down from the train, they encountered a pretty stiff wind and the beginning of a rain. A streak of lightning flashed across the sky.

"Looks like it's starting to rain," Kinsley said. A crash of thunder followed his words.

"Yeah," Willis said.

"I expect you're going to get wet."

"What do you mean I'm goin' to get wet? You mean we, don't you?"

Kinsley shook his head. "No, like the conductor said, I'll be waitin' in the depot till the next train north."

"So what about me?"

"There is no what about you," Kinsley replied. "I was told to take you to the state line, then see that you got across, and that's what I'm about to do." He pointed to a marker alongside the track. "That marker is the state line," he said. "On this side is Colorado. On the other side is New Mexico."

Another lightning flash, and more thunder.

The train whistle blew a couple of times, then started forward, enveloping both Willis and Kinsley in a cloud of steam.

"Why did I have to get off the train here? If you're sendin' me to New Mexico, why didn't you get me a ticket all the way to Santa Fe, or some such place?"

"The judge said to get you out of the state, he didn't have no word as to where you was to be—just where you wasn't to be," Kinsley said. Again, he pointed to the marker. "You ain't to be in Colorado, and this is the last town inside of Colorado. That there marker gets you out of the state. Now, come along."

The rainfall intensified as they walked alongside the track toward the state-line marker.

"Look, couldn't I just wait there in the depot with you until morning? Or at least, until this rain stops?"

"The depot is in Colorado," Kinsley said pointedly.

"So?"

"My job is to get you out of the state," Kinsley repeated.

"So then are you just goin' to leave me here? What about my gun? Where's my gun?"

"More than likely, your gun is on the train we just left."

"What?"

"Sheriff Allen sent your gun on ahead by U.S. mail.

You can call for it at general delivery at the post office in Santa Fe."

"That ain't right," Willis said.

"Think about it, Willis. Do you really think I would turn you loose out here with a gun?"

All the time the two men were talking, they were walking. At one point, Willis tripped and fell against Kinsley, but he recovered quickly.

"Watch where you're walkin'," Kinsley said irritably.

After a few more steps, they reached the marker.

"Here we are," Kinsley said. "From this point, you are on your own."

There was another lightning bolt, this one so close that it was followed almost immediately by a huge clap of thunder.

"Ha," Kinsley said. "If I was you, I'd be findin' me a rock to crawl under or a hole to crawl into," he said. "Otherwise, you're purt' near goin' to drown out here."

Willis didn't reply.

"Well, so long, Willis. I'll be seein' you. Oh, no, I won't, will I? I mean, seein' as you can't come back into Colorado no more."

Turning, Kinsley laughed as he started back toward the small depot.

"Deputy?" Willis called.

Kinsley stopped.

"Ain't no sense in you callin' after me, Willis," he said. "You heard the judge's rulin' same as me. I done just what he said for me to do. Now, like I said, your best bet would be to find you a place to get out of the rain."

"Turn around, Deputy Kinsley," Willis said.

There was something in Willis's voice that caught Kinsley's attention and he turned back toward him. When he did, he gasped at seeing a gun in Willis's hand.

"What the hell?" Kinsley said. "Where did you get that?"

"It's your gun," Willis said. Another lightning flash showed that a wide, demonic smile had spread across Willis's face. "I got it when I fell against you a while ago."

"No," Kinsley said, holding his hands out in front of him and shaking his head. "Willis, no!"

Willis pulled the trigger, but the muzzle flame was obliterated by another lightning flash, and the sound of the shot was covered by the crash of thunder from the previous lightning flash.

Kinsley fell forward, the blood from his wound streaming out into the mud puddle.

Stepping over to him, Willis went through his pockets, relieving him of all his money.

"Three dollars?" he said with a snort of disgust. "All you got is three dollars? Damn, they don't pay you lawmen nothin', do they?"

A further search turned up a railway ticket to Denver, and another from Denver back to Fort Collins. Willis took the two tickets, then removed the deputy's star and stuck it into his pocket.

Willis pulled Kinsley's body up the berm, then laid it down lengthwise between the rails. After that, he walked back to the depot. Once there, he stepped into the building to get out of the rain. One hour later, a freight train passed through and Willis walked to the edge of the platform and looked down to where he had put Kinsley's body. The train had not slowed down, and Willis smiled as he knew that the body would now be impossible to identify.

It was two and a half hours before the stationmaster arrived. He lit a lantern, then walked around behind the ticket counter. That was when he saw Pogue Willis sitting on the bench. Seeing him there startled the stationmaster and he jumped.

Willis chuckled. "I didn't mean to startle you there, friend," he said.

"That's all right," the stationmaster replied. "I just didn't expect to see anyone here. Can I help you?"

"Yes, I have tickets for Denver and Fort Collins, but I've changed my mind, I'd rather go to Santa Fe. The only thing is, I don't have enough money to buy a ticket on to Santa Fe, so I was wondering if there was any way I could just change these tickets to Santa Fe."

"Why, of course you can, there's no problem there," the stationmaster said. "I can change those tickets around for you. You just give them to me, and I'll issue a new ticket down to Santa Fe."

"Well, mister, that's real nice of you," Willis said.

The stationmaster took the tickets from Willis, and handed the one from Denver to Fort Collins back. "I won't need this one," he said. "Your ticket back to Denver is all I need. This one is still good. Or, you can just cash it out if you want to."

"Yeah," Willis said. "Cash it out for me."

"Very well, sir, the Denver and Rio Grande will be happy to accommodate you."

The stationmaster gave Willis his new ticket,

plus two dollars in cash. As the transaction was completed, they heard the whistle of an approaching train.

"Well," the stationmaster said with a broad smile. "We got that business taken care of just in time. That will be your train."

Chapter Nine

St. Louis

Matt had read somewhere that St. Louis was a booming metropolis of over 300,000 people, and he could believe it by what he was seeing just outside the window. The city sprawl seemed to go on forever. It wasn't just the spread of houses and business establishments; it was the traffic on the streets. At every crossing, Matt could see wagons, coaches, surreys, and carriages drawn up in a long line, waiting for the train to pass.

"This your first time in St. Louis, young man?"

Matt, who had been looking through the window, turned to see the conductor standing in the aisle.

"Yes," Matt said.

"I thought it might be, because of the way you were looking through the window. Beer and shoes. And coffins," he added.

"I beg your pardon?"

"That's what St. Louis is known for," the conductor continued. "Beer, shoes, and coffins. Oh, and the traffic on the Mississippi. If you've never seen it, you must go down to the river and see all the boats that are drawn up there. Yes, sir, that is quite a sight to see."

"Thank you, maybe I will," Matt said.

"I hope your visit to our fair city is a pleasant one," the conductor said before moving on through the car.

The train continued on for several more minutes; then the scenery outside the window changed. Instead of streets and buildings, Matt saw a huge network of tracks. There in the marshaling yard, the train stopped, and began backing. As it did so, it backed under a high roof, and now his view was blocked because the tracks were very close and there was another train on either side. Finally, the train stopped altogether, and Matt and the others stood up and began filing toward the end of the car and the exit.

Stepping down from the train, Matt found himself in a shed that rumbled and echoed with arriving and departing engines. The walkways between the tracks were crowded with humanity. Steam drifted across the walkways, then rose, with the smoke from the smokestacks, to gather under the eaves of the great roof. Matt moved with the crowd toward the main hall, then, after claiming his luggage, stepped out onto Market Street. Outside the depot, he saw several cabs and carriages drawn up in front of the station, the drivers openly soliciting passengers.

"Cab, sir?" one of the drivers said to Matt.

"All right," Matt answered.

"Where to?" he asked.

"I don't have any specific place in mind. Can you recommend a hotel?"

"Oh, I can indeed, sir," the driver replied. "I recommend the Travelers' Rest on Washington Street." The driver took Matt's bag and put it into the cab, then pulled a portable step out from the carriage for Matt. Matt climbed up into the seat, then settled back for the ride.

The traffic Matt had sensed from the train was even heavier once he was actually out in it. The city was noisy, with the sound of the electric trolley cars rolling down the tracks without benefit of a horse, the clatter of hundreds of hoofbeats on cobblestone streets, the rumble of heavy freight wagons, and the incessant whistles of the traffic policemen who stood at every intersection, their movements as graceful as the ballet dancers Matt had once seen in Denver. The policemen wore blue uniforms with high-domed hats, and he watched as one held up a hand to stop the north and south traffic, thus allowing the east and west traffic to proceed, then gracefully turned and, with white gloves, signaled the east and west traffic to proceed.

The Travelers' Rest hotel occupied a large, six-story brick building that sat in the middle of the block. A marquee extending from the front of the hotel announced its name, and the cab driver pulled his rig off Washington Street and into the circle drive that passed under the porte cochere. When the cab stopped in front of the hotel, a uniformed doorman stepped out to the cab to take Matt's bag.

"Welcome, sir," he said. He blew his whistle and a bellboy came out to retrieve the bag. "My name is George. If there is anything I can do to make your stay here more comfortable, please let me know."

"Thanks," Matt said as he paid the driver, adding a quarter for a tip.

"Thank you, sir," the driver said.

"Tell me, George, where do I check in?" Matt asked.

"Just inside, sir, the desk is to your right," George said.

"George, you tell Mr. Dixon I brought him this customer," the driver said as he snapped the reins against the back of his team.

"I'll tell him, Tommy," George replied with a half salute toward the driver.

Matt followed the bellboy into the hotel lobby.

"Right over there, sir," the bellboy, who was a black man, said.

"Thank you," Matt replied. He walked over to the desk and began signing the register.

"Well, Mr. Jensen, is it?" the clerk said, looking at the register. "My, I see you are from Colorado."

"Yes."

"Welcome to St. Louis. I'll put you on the sixth floor. That way you will have an excellent view of the city."

"Thank you. Tell me, what would be the best way to find someone in this city?" Matt asked as he took the key.

"Most of the cabbies know the city pretty well,"

the clerk answered. "Just give them the address, they'll take you there."

"That's just it. I don't know the address," Matt said.

"Oh, my, well, that does make it a bit more difficult, doesn't it?" the clerk replied. "Do you know the person's name?"

"Yes."

"Well, if he has a telephone, you can call him. As a guest of the hotel, you are authorized to use the public phone in the lobby."

"Telephone?"

"Have you not used a telephone before, sir?"

"No, I haven't. I've read about them, though."

"It's really quite simple. You turn the crank to signal the operator. She will then ask you what number you wish to call, and once you give it to her, she will connect you."

The clerk showed Matt how to look up the number. Matt thanked him, looked through the directory, and found an Andrew Marcus. The number beside his name was 109J.

Matt turned the crank, then held the receiver to his ear.

"Number, please."

The voice was tinny, but quite audible.

"Ha! I'll be damned!" Matt said.

"I beg your pardon, sir?"

"Oh, I'm sorry," Matt said. "Excuse me, it just surprised me to hear how this thing works."

The woman chuckled. "You've never used the telephone before?"

"No, ma'am."

"Well, do you know the number you are calling?"

"Yes, ma'am, it's one zero nine J."

"One moment, please, and I will connect you," the operator said.

Matt heard a ringing sound in his ear and he jerked the receiver away. "What's that?"

"It's all right, sir," the operator explained. "What you are hearing is the telephone of the party you just called. The party answering the phone will say 'Hello.' Then you can talk."

Almost as if waiting for a cue, the phone was answered.

"Hello?" It was a woman's voice.

Matt didn't respond.

"Hello?" the woman said again.

"Go ahead, sir," the operator said.

"Uh—hello," Matt said. "I'm trying to find a man named Andrew Marcus."

"This is Mrs. Andrew Marcus," the woman said. "How can I help you?"

"Mrs. Marcus, I was a friend of Lee Marcus, Andrew's brother. I've come to—"

"You have the wrong number," the woman on the other end of the line said.

"The number I have is one zero nine J," Matt said.

"This is one zero nine J," the woman replied. "But my husband has no brothers. He has two sisters, but no brothers."

"Oh," Matt said. "I'm sorry. I apologize for disturbing you."

"That's all right," the woman said. "I hope you find your party."

That was the only Andrew Marcus with a telephone, though there were two other Andrew

Marcuses in the city directory. Writing down the
addresses, Matt went up to his room to leave his
suitcase, then went back down to hail a cab.

The first house he went to was on South Grand.
Asking the driver to wait for him, he walked up to
the house and knocked on the door. It was answered by a man who appeared to be in his late sev-
enties. His name was Andrew Marcus, but he had
no brother named Lee.

The next address was an apartment on Olive.

"You have the right address in that Andrew
Marcus used to live here," the man said. "But he
moved away last month."

"Do you know where he moved to?"

"No, sir, I'm afraid I can't tell you that. Oh, but I
can tell you that he works at the Anheuser Beer
brewing company."

"Thanks," Matt said.

Matt had seen small breweries before, but never
had he seen anything as large as the Anheuser
company. It was located in a huge building and
bustling with activity. Large wagons moved about,
some empty, but many loaded with big barrels of
beer. In addition to the wagons, there were also several railroad spurs on which stood freight cars
being loaded with beer.

When Matt checked in at the front office, he
learned that Andrew Marcus was no longer an employee of the brewery.

"Do you know where he is now?" Matt asked.

"I don't know," the personnel clerk replied, "but

I'll bet Cain knows. Cain worked with Marcus. You'll find him inside at the mash kettles. Cain and Marcus were both brewmasters."

"Is it all right for me to go find Mr. Cain?"

"Sure," the friendly clerk said. Getting up from his desk, he took Matt over to a large window, then pointed down onto the floor where there were several huge copper pots. "Do you see the tall fellow with the mustache there on the third kettle?"

"Yes."

"That is Gregory Cain," the clerk said. He pointed to a door. "Go through that door and down the steps."

"Thank you," Matt replied.

The door led to an open platform that was elevated above the level of the many mash kettles that occupied the floor. From there, one could see every mash kettle and every corner of the large room.

The room was filled with a very strong, but not unpleasant, aroma of barley, hops, and malt. It was also warm, as the mash was being cooked in the giant kettles.

Matt walked down the two levels of unpainted stairs, then up between the mash kettles until he found Cain. Cain was on a ladder, looking down into the kettle.

"Mr. Cain?"

"That's me," Cain answered.

"I wonder if I could—"

Cain held his hand up to stop Matt. Then, closing the top of the kettle, he climbed back down the ladder. Picking up a towel, he began drying his hands. Then he smiled at Matt.

"Yes, sir, what can I do for you?" he asked.

"My name is Matt Jensen, Mr. Cain. I'm looking for Andrew Marcus."

"Well, I'm afraid you are a little late," Cain said. As another man walked by, Cain called out to him. "Gary, we need a little more barley in number seven."

"Yes, sir, I'll get right on it, Mr. Cain," the other worker said.

Cain turned his attention back to Matt. "Why are you looking for Andy?"

"First, I need to know if this is the right Andrew Marcus," Matt said. "Does he have a brother named Lee?"

"Lee? Yeah, I think that's his name. Andy used to talk about him a lot. He lives out west somewhere, Colorado, Texas, some such place. I know that Andy said he was a fool for buying a gold mine from some scoundrel out there. Or maybe it was a silver mine, I don't rightly remember now." The man chuckled. "Anyhow, he used to talk about how dumb his brother was for doing such a thing."

"Then he is the one I'm looking for."

"Is it something about his brother?"

"His brother is dead," Matt said. "Before he died, he asked me to get in touch with his brother to let him know what happened."

"Oh," Cain said. "I'm sorry to hear that. Andy set a great store by his brother. Even though he went on about how dumb he thought Lee was to buy that gold mine, I think that secretly he admired and maybe even envied his brother for doing that." Cain chuckled. "In fact, I think that's why he took off for Phoenix."

"Phoenix?"

"Yep. Andy went out there last month. He's planning on starting a brewery out there." Cain laughed. "I told him his brother probably had a better chance with the gold mine than he would with a brewery, but, like I said, I think it was his brother doing what he done that inspired Andy, so to speak."

"Thank you, Mr. Cain. You've been very helpful."

"Glad I could be of help. Oh, and when you find him, tell him I asked about him and tell him that I'm sorry about his brother."

"I'll do that," Matt said.

"Mr. Cain, we've got a boil over here!" someone shouted.

"I'd better get on that," Cain said, hurrying away. "Good luck finding Andy!" he called back over his shoulder.

Chapter Ten

Santa Fe, New Mexico Territory

In New York's Hell's Kitchen, where Pogue Willis grew up, his size had been quite a disadvantage. Strength and the ability to uses one's fists were what established the hierarchy of Willis's neighborhood. Bullied by those who were larger than he was, Willis had his earlier years shadowed by intimidation and shame. Then one day, in desperation, Pogue Willis grabbed a shotgun and blew a hole in the guts of one of his tormentors. No one else in the neighborhood had ever seen an argument settled by any means other than sheer strength. When they saw the strongest of their number brought down by the weakest, they were visibly frightened and gave Willis a new, and unexpected, respect.

Willis discovered two things about himself that day. He found that had no compunctions about pulling the trigger, and he learned that he liked the feeling of power he experienced by seeing the others cowering before him. It was a feeling he didn't intend to surrender ever again.

However, one didn't just shoot someone in New York without answering to the law. Willis had to flee the city and when he did, he came West. It was the best thing to ever happen to him. There he learned a secret. It wasn't really how fast you were with a gun that counted. What counted was a person's willingness to kill. And that willingness—in fact eagerness—to kill gave Pogue Willis a tremendous advantage. Within less than two years after leaving New York, Pogue Willis had established a reputation as being one of the deadliest killers in the West. It was a reputation that he cherished.

Willis had been in Santa Fe for three days when he saw the report in the newspaper:

GRUESOME DISCOVERY

On Tuesday, a trackwalker who was making his normal sojourn along the tracks leading south from Antonito discovered the mutilated body of a man who had been run over by a train. As there was no identification found on the body, it is believed to be that of a transient who attempted to board a passing freight train only to slip and fall beneath the wheels.

Anyone with any information as to who this unknown party might be is asked to contact the city marshal at Antonito, Colorado.

Willis was in the Occidental Saloon when he read the article, and he smiled in satisfaction. So far, the body hadn't even been identified, and they were treating the death as an accident.

Willis had waited in Santa Fe only long enough for the body to be discovered. Now, seeing that he was under no suspicion, he decided it was time to move on. The only problem was, he needed money to do that, and he was flat broke.

Even as he was thinking about the problem, it was solved for him when he saw the tall, gray-haired man at the bar flash several bills.

"Damn, Johnny, what are you doin' carryin' so much money around?" the bartender asked.

"Don't worry, Pete, I don't intend to carry it with me for long. I'll be puttin' it in the bank first thing tomorrow," Johnny replied. "I just sold a string of horses to Wells Fargo and they give me two hundred dollars."

"Hey, Johnny, want to play a little poker?" one of the cardplayers called out. "We'd love to have your money."

The other cardplayers laughed.

"Now, if I played poker with you boys and lost this money, Martha would be down here to clean house. And trust me, you don't want to see my wife mad."

This time, not only the cardplayers, but the other customers, laughed as well.

"Speaking of Martha," Johnny said. He picked up his beer mug and tossed the rest of it down. "I reckon I'd better get on home now or I really will be in the doghouse."

"Good night, Johnny," several of the others called.

"Be seein' you," Johnny tossed back over his shoulder as he left.

Willis got up from the table then and went through the back door of the saloon, as if he were stepping out to the outhouse. Once outside, he ran up alongside the saloon to see which way Johnny was going. He was heading west, but he stopped to say a few words to someone on the street.

The delay gave Willis the opportunity he was looking for, and he hurried down to the west end of the street, then stepped behind a barn.

He didn't have to wait very long. No more than a couple of minutes later, Johnny came riding up the street. Willis waited until Johnny was even with him; then he stepped out behind him, aimed, and fired.

Johnny gasped, and fell from his horse. Willis ran up to him and quickly found the money.

The gunshot started some dogs to barking, and in the house nearest the barn, someone came outside carrying a lantern.

"Hello?" the man with the lantern called. "Anyone out here?"

The dogs continued to bark and a mule began to bray.

"What is it, Clyde?" a woman's voice called from inside the house.

"I don't know," the man with the lantern answered. "I thought I heard something, but it must have just been the dog."

The man with the lantern went back inside, and when he did so, Willis, with money in his pocket, mounted Johnny's horse and rode away.

St. Louis

Matt was in the Old Strong Tavern on Lafayette Street, reading the telegram he had just retrieved from Western Union.

> AS PER YOUR REQUEST YOUR HORSE
> WILL BE SENT TO SUNDOWN CORRAL IN
> PHOENIX STOP SPIRIT WILL BE THERE
> WHEN YOU ARRIVE STOP WILL SETTLE
> ACCOUNTS WHEN YOU RETURN STOP
>
> REDCLIFF STABLES

"Mr. Jensen? Are you Matt Jensen?"

Looking up from the telegram, Matt saw a man with long hair and a full gray beard. There was something familiar about the man, but Matt didn't recognize him right away.

"Yes, I'm Matt Jensen."

A broad smile spread across the man's face. "I'm J. C. Jones."

When Matt didn't respond, the man added, "You may remember me as Trooper Jones."

Now Matt smiled as well, and he stood up quickly and offered his hand. "Yes!" he said. "Yes, of course I remember you." Matt motioned toward the man's clothes. "But the last time I saw you, you were wearing an army uniform."

"Yes, but no more," Jones said. "When my hitch was up this time, I left. Oh, I might have stayed if Sergeant Emerson was still around. Me and Emerson was pards and had been since we was in the war together. But, as I am sure you remember, Sergeant

Emerson got hisself killed when that fool Trevathan led us into that ambush."

"Yes," Matt said. "I remember well."

"You was smart to leave when you did. Not long after you left, Lieutenant Manning—I reckon you remember him—took a platoon out lookin' for Delshay." Jones shook his head. "Manning didn't have enough sense to pour piss out of a boot, and he made camp down in a ravine, didn't post no lookouts or nothin'. Delshay attacked him and killed more than half his platoon, includin' the civilian scout that was with him."

"I'm sorry to hear that," Matt said. "I didn't scout very long, but I met several of the soldiers and liked them."

"Yes, one of them killed was Angus Pugh. I know you remember him."

"I remember him very well," Matt said.

"Ole Angus—he was a colonel in the Confederate Army," Jones said. "Not a lot of folks knew that."

"I know he was a good soldier," Matt said.

"So, Mr. Jensen, what are you doin' in St. Louis?"

"A friend of mine was killed and I came to St. Louis to give the news to his brother."

"Oh, that's got to be hard to do."

"I haven't done it yet. Turns out he's in Phoenix, so I have to go out there to find him. I'll be taking a train back tomorrow."

"Damn, that means you'll be goin' right back into Delshay country," Jones said.

"I guess I will," Matt said. "But I don't expect to run into him this time."

"Well, I hope not, for your sake," Jones said.

"I tell you the truth, ever'body knows about Geronimo—but for my thinkin', Delshay is a lot meaner and smarter than Geronimo."

"He's smart all right," Matt said. "He was the one who set up the ambush that Trevathan led us into."

"Only, if Trevathan had listened to you, there wouldn't have been no ambush," Jones said. He stuck his hand out. "I have to be going. I'm a deck-hand on a riverboat now and we'll be pulling out tonight. It was good seeing you again, Mr. Jensen. Good luck—and don't run into Delshay."

Chapter Eleven

San Carlos Indian Reservation

After taking his leave of Geronimo, Delshay returned to the reservation, where he was greeted warmly by his wife and children.

"Delshay," someone said and, looking toward the sound of the voice, Delshay saw two Indians wearing the uniform and accoutrements of the Indian police.

"Sentorio, have you become a running dog of the white man?" Delshay asked, recognizing a young man with whom he was raised.

"I am a policeman," Sentorio replied.

"Yes, like I said, a running dog of the white man. What do you want?"

"Agent Baker heard you were back. He has sent us to bring you to him."

"Am I your prisoner?"

"You are to come with us," Sentorio replied without being any more specific.

"And if I choose not to come?"

Sentorio and the other Indian policeman looked at each other, and it was obvious they were frightened at the prospect of having to force Delshay to come with them.

Delshay laughed. "Do not be frightened, friend of my youth," he said. "I will go with you to see the Indian agent."

Agent Eugene Baker was sitting on a stool under an umbrella, on the edge of a long, deep trench. There were dozens of Apache down in the ditch, digging with pickax and shovel. The ditch was the brainstorm of Agent Baker, ostensibly to be an irrigation ditch to bring water to the reservation from Salt River. As there were times during the year when the Salt River was dry, the irrigation ditch seemed a waste of time, but as Baker said to the representative from the Indian Agency who questioned him, "It keeps the bucks busy."

"Agent Baker, we have brought Delshay to you," Sentorio said.

There was a table beside Baker's chair and on the table was an apple. Baker picked up the apple and began paring it as he spoke.

"So, Delshay, you have come back to us, have you?" Baker said. "Did you find that riding with Geronimo was more difficult than you thought it would be?"

"I have been hunting," Delshay replied. It wasn't exactly a lie, it just wasn't the entire truth.

"Oh, yes, I have no doubt but that you have been

hunting. Tell me about the hunting you have been doing, Delshay. Was it with Geronimo?"

Delshay didn't answer.

"Uh-huh, that tells me all I need to know. Hunting for white scalps, more than likely. How many white men did you kill while you were with Geronimo?"

Delshay still did not answer.

"I have no doubt but that you have the blood of many white men, women, and children on your hands," Baker said. "Well, if you want my opinion, Delshay, I think you should have stayed with that renegade, because there is nothing for you here."

"My wife and children are here," Delshay said.

"Ah, yes, your wife and children," Baker said. Out of the corner of his eye, Baker saw one of the Indians climbing up from the ditch.

"Here!" Baker called to him. "I did not tell you that you could quit."

"I want water," the Indian said.

"You can get a drink when it is time. You don't want to leave the others to do your work, do you? Now get back down there and keep digging."

The Indian who had tried to climb up from the ditch glared at Baker for a moment, but he turned and went back down into the ditch.

"Now, where were we?" Baker asked. "Oh, yes, your wife and children. The truth is, Delshay, your wife and children are better off without you." The apple now pared, Baker quartered it. "Just make certain you do nothing that will put you on my bad side," he said as he popped a piece of apple into his mouth. Then, using his knife as a pointer, he continued his admonition. "I will tell you the truth,

Delshay. If I had it my way, I would hang you right now. At the very least, I would put you in prison. But the Great White Father in Washington has ordered that I treat humanely all the Apache who are willing to surrender to authority, so I have no choice but to accept you back onto the reservation."

After doing all in his power to humiliate Delshay, Baker dismissed him, once more warning him to do nothing that would incur his wrath.

Hachita, New Mexico Territory

Philbin, Oliver, and Cantrell reached the tiny town of Hachita just after midnight. Cantrell bought a bottle of tequilla at the cantina, then picked up a Mexican whore, taking her as much for her bed as for any of the "special" services she could provide for him.

Hachita was a scattering of flyblown, crumbling adobe buildings laid out around a dusty plaza. It was less than ten miles from the Mexican border, and what made it attractive to people like Philbin, Cantrell, and Oliver was its reputation as a "Robbers' Roost," or "Outlaw Haven."

The town had no constable or sheriff, and visitations by law officers from elsewhere in the territory were strongly discouraged. There was a place in the town cemetery prominently marked as "Lawman's Plot." There, two deputy sheriffs and one deputy U.S. marshal, all uninvited visitors to the town, lay buried.

Cantrell woke up the next morning with a ravenous hunger and a raging need to urinate. The *puta* was still asleep beside him, and she didn't wake up when Cantrell crawled over her to get out of bed and get dressed.

There was an outhouse twenty feet behind the little adobe crib, but Cantrell disdained its use, stepping out into the alley and going against the wall instead.

"Oliver," he called as he stood there, relieving himself. "Oliver, you still in there?"

Oliver had gone with the *puta* in the next crib over.

"Yeah, I'm in here."

"You goin' to sleep all mornin' or what?"

"I'm comin' out."

Cantrell heard a sound from within the shadows of the crib; then Oliver appeared in the doorway. He was wearing his boots, hat, and long underwear. He joined Cantrell at the wall.

"Philbin, where are you?"

Philbin didn't answer.

"You seen Philbin this morning?" Cantrell asked as they stood there relieving themselves. He shook himself, then put it away.

"Not this mornin', I just woke up. I seen him last night, though. He went in there," Oliver said, pointing to one of the other cribs.

Cantrell walked over to the crib and looked inside. The whore Philbin had been with was still asleep, but she was alone in the bed.

"He ain't here," Cantrell said.

"So where the hell did he go?" Oliver asked.

"Beats me. I ain't goin' to worry about it right now. I'm goin' over to have breakfast. You want to come along?"

"Yeah, I reckon so," Oliver replied.

* * *

In the Casa del Sol cantina, Cantrell rolled a tortilla in his fingers and, using it like a spoon, scooped up the last of his breakfast beans. He washed it down with a drink of coffee, then lit a cigar just as Philbin and Meechum came in.

"Well, I'll be damn," Cantrell said. "Look here, Oliver. Look who has just showed up."

"Meechum," Oliver said. "I didn't think we'd ever see you again."

"I sent word about the time lock on the safe in that bank back in Bent Canyon. It ain't my fault you didn't get it."

"If you'd done a little more lookin' into it than you done, you wouldn't have had to send word about nothin'," Cantrell said angrily.

"And if you hadn't left early, you would of got the word," Meechum said. "The truth is, you got greedy and was plannin' on keepin' all the money for yourself, wasn't you?"

"What money?" Oliver asked bitterly. "The only thing we got out of that was damn near killed. And Morris did get hisself killed."

"Do you want to sit around here and argue about that? Or do you want to do a job that will make us some money?"

"What's the job, and how much money?"

"I don't know," Meechum said.

Cantrell's laugh was gruff.

"You set us up with a bank robbery that got us no money and damn near got us killed, now you want to set us up with another job, but you don't know what it is and you don't know how much money,"

Cantrell said. "Meechum, you ain't makin' a hell of a lot of sense, you know that?"

"I'm not the one setting up the job," he said. "But I know who is and, knowin' him, I figure there's goin' to be a lot of money involved. Otherwise, someone like him wouldn't waste his time with it."

"Someone like who?" Oliver asked. "Who are you talkin' about?"

"He's talkin' about Pogue Willis," Philbin said, unable to keep quiet and let Meechum tell them.

"Pogue Willis?" Cantrell said, his demeanor changing. "Is this for real?"

Smiling, Meechum nodded. "Yeah, it's for real," he said. "I run into Willis back in Arizona and he asked me if I knew where I could get a few good men for a job he had in mind."

"He didn't tell you what the job was?" Oliver asked.

"No."

"And you didn't ask?"

"You don't ask a man like Pogue Willis," Meechum said. "If he says he has a job lined up, I believe him. And like I say, a man like Pogue Willis ain't goin' to be wastin' time with a job that don't pay a lot."

"Yeah, that's what I think," Philbin said.

"Philbin, you're willin' to go along with this?" Cantrell asked.

"Yeah."

Cantrell nodded. "All right," he said. "You was in Bent Canyon, same as me and Oliver. I reckon if this is good enough for you, it's good enough for me." He looked at Meechum. "Where is this job?"

"It's over in the Arizona Territory," Meechum said. "About five days ride."

Chapter Twelve

San Carlos Indian Reservation

For the first month after he returned, Delshay felt isolated from the rest of the people. Many, he knew, blamed the slow delivery of meat and other supplies to the reservation on Goyathlay, and, by extension, Delshay as well, since he had ridden with the raiders. And because Delshay was the only one of Geronimo's band present at the reservation, some took their anger out on him.

However, there were as many on the reservation who respected and looked up to Geronimo because he was carrying the fight to the white man. And because Delshay had ridden with him, they treated him with respect and honor.

From his cousin, Chandeisi, whose name meant Broken Nose, Delshay learned to make jewelry from the silver and turquoise that they were able to mine on the reservation. Sagozhuni, Delshay's wife, was particularly skilled in weaving baskets of various shapes and sizes, all incorporating beautiful and intricate designs.

It had been two months since returning to the reservation, and Delshay was sitting in front of his hogan when Chandeisi came to see him.

"I have spoken with Baker," Chandeisi said. "He has given permission for us to go to Picket Post to trade jewelry and baskets."

Delshay spat on the ground. "Are we children, that we must have permission?"

"Delshay, it is the way of life on the reservation," Chandeisi explained. "If we live here, we must follow the rules."

"Cousin, are you content to follow the rules of the white man?"

"I have no choice," Chandeisi said. "I have a family, as do you. Would you rather be with Goyathlay than with Sagozhuni and your children?"

Delshay looked over at his youngest child, who was sitting on a blanket.

"Soon, the child will be old enough to go and I will take my family and leave this place."

Chandeisi looked around quickly to make certain no one overheard.

"Delshay, you must not speak of such things," he said. "If the Indian police hear you, they will report you to Baker and Baker will put you in jail."

"Maybe," Delshay said. He smiled. "Or maybe I will kill the Indian police before I leave."

When Delshay saw the shocked look on Chandeisi's face, he laughed out loud. "I am making the joke, cousin," he said.

"I think one should not joke about such things."

"Very well. Tell me about the trading we will do."

"The white men like the jewelry and the baskets. Tomorrow, we will go to the white village called Picket Post and trade."

Before the sun rose then next morning, Delshay and Chandeisi, along with their families, left the reservation for the twenty-five-mile trek into Picket Post. When they were within two miles of the town, they halted.

"Wait here for us, Sagozhuni," Delshay said. "Chandeisi and I will go into town and see if they will trade."

"Very well, Delshay, my husband. I will feed the children while you are gone."

Delshay's wife found a place in the shade and spread a blanket for the three children. Because some of the merchants of the town resented the Indians coming in to trade, Delshay and Chandeisi thought it would be best to leave their inventory behind as they went into town to invite customers out to trade. The Indians would trade for tobacco, coffee, blankets, and other goods and trinkets that would make their life on the reservation somewhat easier.

Meechum, Philbin, Cantrell, and Oliver had been on the trail for three days, and were now giving their exhausted horses a much needed rest.

"I gotta take a piss," Meechum said. He walked a few feet away from the others, then stopped. "Well, now," he said, looking over the edge of a rock. "What do we have here?"

"What?" Cantrell asked.

Meechum put his finger across his lips. "Be quiet," he hissed.

"What is it, Meechum, what do you see?"

"Come here and take a look for yourself, but be quiet and don't show yourself."

The other three men came up to stand beside Meechum.

"What is it?" Oliver asked.

"Look down there," Meechum said, pointing to two Indian women and children.

"What?" Cantrell asked again. "All I see is a couple of squaws."

"Yeah, that's 'cause you don't know what you're lookin' at. Why do you think they're out here?" Meechum asked.

"I don't have no idea," Cantrell said.

"Me neither," Oliver said.

"Why do you think, Burt?" Meechum asked.

"I don't know for sure, but if I had to guess, I would say that it is more than likely they've come to trade," Philbin said.

Meechum smiled and nodded. "My cousin is smarter than any of you," he said. "That's right."

"You mean them squaws has just come out here in the middle of nowhere to trade?" Cantrell asked. "That don't make no sense."

"They ain't by themselves," Philbin said. "Not really. Whenever they come out to trade like that, they never actually go into town. If you was to ask me, I would say that the men that was with them have prob'ly rode on into town to get it all set up."

"Burt is right," Meechum said. "And you know what that means, don't you?"

"I don't know," Cantrell answered. "I reckon it means the men is in town."

"Yes, and that also means there ain't nobody watchin' over their trade goods but them two squaws and the young'ins," Meechum said.

"So, what does that have to do with us? What do they have that we would want to trade for anyway?" Cantrell asked.

"Could be they got some of that turquoise and silver jewelry. Them Indians is just real good makin' them things. And it's right down there just waitin' for us," Meechum said, pointing to the Indian women and children.

"What's that got to do with us? What do we want with a bunch of Injun jewelry anyway?"

"You don't never think, do you, Cantrell?" Meechum said. "We can sell it."

"We ain't got nothing to trade for it."

"We ain't goin' to trade. We're just goin' to go down there and get it," Meechum said.

"Go get it?" Cantrell replied. "Meechum, it ain't very damn likely they are goin' to just give it to us."

Meechum chuckled. "Hell, I didn't say we was goin' to go down there an' ask for it. I said we was goin' to take it. Their men are gone. How much trouble can a couple of squaws and a few snot-nosed kids be?"

"Yeah," Cantrell said. "Yeah, I reckon I see what you are talkin' about now. We can sell it, you say?"

"Yeah, we can sell it. We need to go someplace away from here like, say, Phoenix or some such place, but we're headed that way anyway. Once we get there, we can sell the jewelry for fifty, maybe as much as a hundred dollars. I'd kind of like to have a little money in my pocket when we talk to Willis, wouldn't you?"

"Yeah, I would," Cantrell agreed.

"Come on, boys," Meechum said, mounting his horse. "This is goin' to be the easiest money we ever made."

"Sagozhuni, white men are coming to trade," Chandeisi's wife, Natanh, said. "I do not understand why they would come before our husbands return."

Sagozhuni looked toward the four men who were riding in single file down the slope of the hill.

"Natanh, hide the jewelry," Sagozhuni said quickly. "I do not think they are traders."

Natanh laid a blanket over the turquoise and silver.

"Hello, ladies," the man who rode in front said. He touched the brim of his hat. "Have you got something to trade?"

"These baskets," Sagozhuni said, holding up one of the baskets that had the most intricate design.

"Baskets? Is that all? I was thinking more along the lines of turquoise and silver."

"We have baskets," Sagozhuni said. "They are very beautiful. Your wife will like them."

"My wife?" the rider said. He laughed. "Did you hear that, boys?" he said to the others. "Our wives will like the baskets."

The other riders laughed as well, but rather than easing her fears, their laughter frightened Sagozhuni even more.

The rider in front quit laughing and a snarl crossed his face. "Don't lie to me now, you redskin bitch. Give us all your jewelry and we'll just ride away and leave you alone. Otherwise, we'll have a little fun with you two women, then take the jewelry anyway."

"Aiyeee!" Natanh yelled, rushing toward one of the men, brandishing a knife.

"Natanh, no!" Sagozhuni shouted.

Sagozhuni's shouted warning was too late. Natanh slashed out with her knife and brought blood from the leg of one of the riders.

"You crazy bitch!" the wounded rider shouted. Jerking on the reins of his horse, he managed to pull away from her before she could make a second swipe at him.

Natanh's attack was answered with a flurry of gunshots, and Natanh went down. With a shout of anger, Sagozhuni grabbed Natanh's knife, but before she could get to any of the men, she was shot down by a second volley.

"Son of a bitch!" Meechum said angrily. "What the hell did they do that for?"

The children began crying.

"What about the damn brats?" Philbin asked.

Meechum shook his head. "We got no choice," he said. "Shoot the little bastards." He shot one of the children and the others, following his lead, began shooting as well. For several seconds, the valley echoed and reechoed with the sound of gunshots.

Finally, with the air stinking of spent gunpowder and the last echo dying away, the four men, who had not even dismounted, sat their saddles, looking on, shocked at their own actions.

"Son of a bitch, Meechum, did we have to do this?" Oliver asked.

"Didn't look to me like we had all that much choice," Meechum said as he dismounted. "Let's find the silver and turquoise and get the hell out of here."

"You sure there's any here?"

"Yeah, I'm sure," Meechum said. "Otherwise, they wouldn't of put up such a fight."

Meechum turned back one of the blankets, and was rewarded with the sight of a pile of silver and turquoise trinkets. He smiled and looked up at the others.

"Well, now, lookie here, boys, lookie here what I just found."

The other three riders dismounted and began gathering up the jewelry.

"Damn," Meechum said. "This is fine stuff, and there's a lot of it. I wouldn't be surprised if we didn't get two hundred dollars for it."

"Two hundred dollars?" Cantrell said. "That's fifty dollars apiece."

Meechum chuckled. "Ahh, you are all for it now, I see. Maybe you think ole Meechum is pretty smart after all."

"Well, this don't quite make up for sendin' us to rob a bank that didn't have no money," Cantrell said. "But it makes up for a little of it."

"It wasn't that the bank didn't have no money," Philbin said. "It had lots of money."

"Which we couldn't get to because of the time lock," Cantrell said. "So, as far as I'm concerned, that was the same as having no money."

"Let's quit the palaverin' and get out of here before the men come back," Meechum said. He ran his hand over the top of his head. "I've grown just real partial to my scalp."

Delshay was feeling good as he returned to the campsite. He and Chandeisi had found at least ten people who agreed to come out and trade with them. He thought of the smile he would get from his squaw when he traded for some bright red silk.

Even as he was riding back, Delshay began planning the display for them. He knew that if the silver was highly polished so that it shined brightly in the sun, the white men would be willing to give more than they would if the silver was tarnished. He didn't know why that was so. It was the same silver, whether tarnished or shining, and it was very easy to make the silver shine, yet the whites would sometimes pay twice as much for a shiny piece as they would for a piece that was tarnished.

As the two men continued the ride back toward the camp, however, Delshay began to feel a sense of apprehension. He didn't mention it to Chandeisi, because he had no reason to be perturbed and he had no wish to cause Chandeisi worry. But even before the camp came in sight, he began to feel anxious.

Why was he so uneasy?

"Delshay, there is no smoke," Chadeisi said. "We should see smoke."

"Perhaps our dinner has already been cooked," Delshay said.

"Yes, I think that is it," Chandeisi agreed.

Despite Delshay's reassurance, the restlessness continued. Then, the disquiet grew to a strong fear when he saw the large, circling black birds.

Delshay didn't have to speak to Chandeisi. He saw the circling turkey vultures as well. Delshay slapped his legs against the side of his horse, urging it into a gallop.

They were all dead, both women and every child. All had been shot, even Delshay's infant child. The silver and turquoise was gone; only the colorful and intricately woven baskets remained.

Chapter Thirteen

St. Louis

Matt didn't really want to go to Phoenix, but he had made a promise to Lee to find his brother and give him the money, so, checking out of the hotel, he returned to the depot and bought a ticket.

"You will be aboard the Western Flyer, sir," the ticket clerk said as he began stamping on the long folded train ticket. "The train will depart from track five at two o'clock this afternoon."

"There isn't one earlier?"

"I'm afraid not, sir."

"All right, thanks," Matt said, taking the ticket and putting it in his pocket. Looking up at the big clock on the wall, he saw that it was just after eleven, which meant that he had three hours to kill. He walked down to the newsstand and bought a copy of the *St. Louis Democrat,* then found a bench in a remote and quiet part of the waiting room.

With another glance at the clock, he sat down to read. He found an article that made him chuckle.

Hokum Balloon Ascension

A balloon ascension that took part on the riverfront yesterday was deemed an absolute failure. The proprietor of the magnificent airship, Professor de la Smith of Paris, promised to take up not only a bridal party, but every reporter in the city. He ascended alone two hours before the time allotted, and the few people who saw him declared that he was so frightened that his teeth chattered. After ascending no more than one hundred feet at the end of a tether, he began calling for help. The balloon had to be pulled down by the rope, as he was incapable of even so small a thing as pulling the valve. Afterward, he admitted that he had never been up before, and that he had stolen the balloon from a proprietor in Ohio, doing so with the idea of making money by giving rides to those who were willing to pay for ascensions.

Glancing up once more at the clock, Matt saw that it was slightly after twelve, so he went into the dining room to have lunch. He had just ordered when he heard a loud and angry voice.

"You ignorant swine! This soup is cold!"

The complaint came from an irritated diner who was sitting with two others, a woman and another man, at the next table.

"Very good, sir, I shall take it back to the kitchen and have it warmed," the waiter said.

"I don't want it warmed, you ignorant dolt. I will require another bowl! I swear, the farther west one goes in this country, the more savage the people and the more incompetent the help."

The man complaining was short, pudgy, and bald. He was sitting with a quiet, studious-looking man and a very pretty woman.

"Jay, please, can't you just eat your soup without making such a fuss? There are a lot of people in here and you can see how busy the waiter is," the young woman said. "I have tasted the soup. I find it quite warm enough."

"Yes, I am quite sure it is warm enough for you, Cynthia, but you must understand that is only because you are willing to accept inferior as adequate and mediocrity as standard," Jay replied. "I am not. I demand satisfactory service in all things and I say that being busy is no excuse for ineptitude. And just because you are content with less than acceptable conditions, that is no reason for me to be. You and Hendel are such mice that you would just let people run all over you."

Cynthia did not reply, and she and Hendel ate their soup without complaint. Jay squirmed in his seat, waiting for the server to return with his soup.

Finally, the main course was brought, but there was still no soup.

"Oh, this is just unconscionable," Jay said in anger. "Now the main course is here and I still have not had my soup."

"I'm sorry, sir, I forgot," the waiter said. "I will bring your soup now."

"Well, no, you bungling oaf, there is absolutely no need to bring it now, for heaven's sake. You have already served the main course, so what good would it do me now? However, I do want it clearly understood that I will expect an adjustment to my bill"—he held up a finger pointedly—"and you, my incompetent friend, may disabuse yourself of any expectation of a gratuity."

Ignorning the obnoxious diner's complaints as much as he could, though it was difficult as the man was at the very next table and found much to complain about, Matt ate his own meal. Afterward, Matt left the restaurant and walked around the depot, killing time until his train departed.

Matt saw a line of railroad cars sitting on a track at the far end of the car shed, and because he was just killing time until his train left, he walked over to look at them. The cars had been there for some time, as evidenced by the fact that there were cobwebs formed on the wheel trucks.

"No! Help! Help me, someone! Please help!"

The call for help came from the other side of the line of cars, and quickly, Matt stepped between the cars, then looked up and down the brick pathway. That was when he saw someone being set upon by two assailants.

"Give us all your money!" one of the two men said angrily.

"You two!" Matt called, starting toward them. "Get away from that man!"

Hearing Matt's challenge, one of the two assailants

turned away from the victim and started after Matt, holding a club over his head.

"Mister, you're goin' to learn better'n to butt into somethin' that ain't none of your business," the club-wielding thug said. "Fact is, we'll just take your money, too."

The would-be assailant made a vicious swing with the club, but Matt ducked easily under the attack, then rising up again, caught the man with a hard blow to the chin. The attacker went down.

"What the hell!" the other thug yelled and, abandoning his attack on the victim, he came toward Matt holding a knife in his hand, low and turned sideways in the manner of someone who knew how to use a blade.

"Friend, this here is an Arkansas toothpick and I aim use it to gut you like a fish."

Matt crouched down and managed to avoid the attacker's first swipe at him. When the assailant made a second attempt, Matt stepped to one side, then kicked his adversary in the kneecap.

The assailant let out a loud yelp of pain, but he kept his feet and came after Matt with still another vicious swing. This time Matt stepped gracefully to one side, grabbing the knife-wielder's arm as he did so. He twisted the arm violently, and heard the snap of a breaking bone, even over the sharp yell of pain.

By now, the first man had regained his feet, but seeing that they were now both disarmed, and that his partner had been injured, he gave up any idea of continuing the encounter. Turning away from Matt, he started running toward the front end of the long line of cars—away from the depot itself and out into the marshaling yard.

The second assailant, now holding his injured arm, glared at Matt for a moment longer. Then, realizing that he had been abandoned by the other assailant, he ran after his partner, limping badly on his injured knee.

Matt turned to the would-be victim.

"Are you injured?" he asked.

"No, I don't think so," the man replied. "No thanks to those ruffians." He began brushing his clothes. "The name is Bixby, sir. Jay Peerless Bixby."

It wasn't until that moment that Matt realized this was the same obnoxious diner who had been sitting next to him in the railroad restaurant.

"I'm Matt Jensen."

"Well, Mr. Jensen, you have my gratitude for coming to my rescue."

"It was just lucky that I happened to be here at the right time," Matt said. "I'm curious. What would bring you to this remote part of the car shed?"

"You called it, sir, I was curious," Bixby said. "I grew weary of waiting for my train to depart, so I set upon an exploration of the depot. I wonder, though, if I could prevail upon you to accompany me back to my wife and employee. I do not want to take a chance on encountering anyone else such as these two hooligans. I would be more than happy to compensate you for your trouble."

"Oh, I wouldn't feel right in accepting money merely for doing what is the right thing to do," Matt said. "I will be glad to walk back to the depot with you."

"I shall be eternally grateful, sir," Bixby said.

Returning to the waiting room, Bixby pointed out his wife.

"This is my wife, Cynthia," he said. "Have you ever seen anyone any more beautiful?"

"Jay, please, you are embarrassing me," the young woman said. "I do not consider myself beautiful, and I find it uncomfortable for you to carry on so."

"Nonsense, my dear," Bixby replied. "Of course you are beautiful. Why else would I have married someone like you, if not for your beauty? It certainly isn't for your intelligence," he added with a raucous laugh.

Matt saw a flicker of humiliation pass across Cynthia's face as she glanced down in mortification.

"And this is my employee, Ken Hendel," Bixby added. "I keep him on because of his business acumen and—also—because he is, at heart, too frightened to ever challenge me."

As Cynthia had before him, Matt saw Hendel react to Bixby's harsh words. The reaction, however, suggested that Hendel might not be quite as subservient as Bixby believed, and when Matt smiled knowingly at him, he was pleased to see Hendel return the smile. It was as if Hendel had just verified Matt's observation.

"Tell me, Mr. Jensen, where are you bound?" Bixby asked.

"Phoenix."

"Phoenix? Well, what a wonderful piece of luck. We, too, are bound for Phoenix," Bixby said. "That means we shall be able to keep each other company during the journey."

Phoenix, Arizona Territory

"I'll give you one hundred dollars for all of it," the jeweler said.

"One hundred dollars?" Meechum complained. "These here necklaces is worth a lot more than one hundred dollars. Why, there's twenty of 'em here and I've seen just one of 'em bring twenty dollars in Denver."

"You aren't in Denver," the jeweler said. "Of course, if you don't like my offer, you can always take 'em to Denver to sell."

"Take the money, Billy," Philbin said. "It's better'n nothin', and right now nothin' is what we have."

"All right, all right," Meechum said disgustedly. "We'll take the one hundred dollars, but that ain't right and you know it. It ain't no way right."

"If it isn't right from you, consider the Indian you bought these from," the jeweler said. "I don't know what you paid for them, but I'd be willin' to bet you didn't pay no one hundred dollars."

"Hah! You got that right!" Cantrell said.

Meechum glared at Cantrell for a moment, then said, "Give us our money so we can get on about our business."

The jeweler counted out five twenty-dollar gold pieces. Meechum kept two for himself, than gave one each to the other three men.

"How come you get to keep two?" Oliver asked.

Meechum held the piece up. "This here is for all of us," he said. "We'll go over to the saloon, get us somethin' to eat and somethin' to drink, have some left over for some whores—and we'll still have twenty dollars apiece in our pockets."

"Yeah," Philbin said with a big smile. "Yeah, that sounds good to me."

The three men tied off their horses, then went into the Last Chance Saloon. The barkeep was at the other end of the bar talking to a couple of his patrons. He laughed loudly at something one of them said, then with the smile still on his face, moved down the bar toward Meechum, Philbin, Oliver, and Cantrell.

"What can I get you gents?"

"Whiskey," Meechum said. "Leave the bottle."

"What kind?"

"I don't care what kind. We want to get drunk, not give a party."

The bartender took a bottle from beneath the counter. There was no label on the bottle and the color was dingy and cloudy. He put four glasses alongside the bottle, then pulled the cork for them.

"That'll be a buck-fifty," he said.

Meechum slid the double-eagle gold piece toward him, then waited for the change.

Philbin poured four glasses, then passed them around. He took a swallow, then almost gagged. He spat it out and frowned at his glass.

"What the hell is this?" he asked. "This tastes like horse piss."

Cantrell took a smaller swallow. He grimaced, but he got it down. Meechum and Oliver had no problem at all with the whiskey.

"It's all in the way you drink it," Meechum explained. "This here is sippin' whiskey and it can't be drunk down real fast. What you got to do is, you got to sort of sip it." He demonstrated.

Philbin took another swallow, following Meechum's advice to sip it, and this time he, too, managed to keep it down.

"Yeah," he said, coughing to clear his throat. "Yeah, I guess it ain't all that bad."

They were on their second glass each, and the bottle was more than half empty, when another patron stepped into the saloon. He stood just inside the swinging batwing doors for a moment, taking everything in with one comprehensive sweep of his eyes.

"Whoa, get a load of that little dandy over there who just come in to the saloon," Oliver said, chuckling. "Ain't he somethin' now? I bet that little feller wouldn't dress out more'n seventy-five to eighty pounds. Ninety pounds at the most."

"I'd be careful makin' them comments about that little feller iffen I was you," Meechum said.

"Why, what's he going to do? Come over here and beat me up?" Oliver asked, laughing again.

"No," Meechum said. "But he might put a hole between your eyes."

"What do you mean, he might put a hole between my eyes? What are you talkin' about?"

"We're over here," Meechum called out, and the little man at the door started toward them.

"What the hell you invitin' him over here for?" Oliver asked, obviously irritated by the invitation.

"Men, I want you to meet Pogue Willis," Meechum said when Willis joined them.

Oliver had just taken another swallow of his whiskey, and he spat it out in surprise.

"Willis?" he said. "This is Pogue Willis?"

The others laughed at Oliver.

"Damn, Abe, iffen you ain't man enough to drink that whiskey, maybe you ought not to even try," Cantrell said, and they all laughed again.

"What do you say we find us a table at the back so we can talk?" Willis said. "Get another glass and bring the bottle."

Meechum grabbed the bottle and another glass, and they all went to a table at the back of the room.

"I told the boys you had a job for us," Meechum said.

"Only he didn't tell us what it was," Oliver added.

"Does it matter?" Willis asked as he poured himself a glass of whiskey.

"It don't matter as long as it pays off," Oliver said. "I just don't want no more bank jobs like the last one."

"I told you I sent word callin' that job off," Meechum said. "It ain't my fault if you got greedy and went before you was supposed to."

"Yeah, well, that one is behind us," Cantell said, "and there's no use in palaverin' over it now. What is this new job, and what do you want us to do?"

"The bank of—" Willis started, but Philbin interrupted him before he could continue.

"Whatever bank this is, I hope you checked out the safe so's there's nothin' like happened before," Philbin said.

Willis glared at Philbin with such intensity that Philbin had to look away.

"You boys goin' to let me tell you what this job is about? Or are you goin' to sit there and prattle on like a bunch of women?" Willis asked, his voice showing his irritation.

"I'm sorry," Philbin said. "I was just makin' a comment, is all, given what happened to us the last time we tried to hold up a bank."

"I am not in the mood to listen to any comments any of you might be wanting to make," Willis said.

The others were quiet.

"Like I was about to say, the Bank of Phoenix gets a transfer of funds from a bank in Colorado every Friday," Willis said.

"What is a transfer of funds?" Oliver asked.

"It means the bank in Colorado is sendin' a lot of money down to the bank here in Phoenix," Meechum said. "By train," he added.

"Son of a bitch, you're talkin' about robbin' the train, aren't you?" Oliver asked.

"No," Willis said. "We're goin' to rob a stagecoach. That's a lot easier than holdin' up a train."

"But I thought you said the money was comin' by train from Colorado."

"Yeah, I did. The only thing is, the train don't run all the way to Phoenix. Closest it comes is Maricopa. Then they put it on a stagecoach."

"How much money are we talkin' about?" Cantrell asked.

"From what I hear, they don't never transfer less that ten thousand dollars. Is that enough money to get you interested?" Willis asked.

Cantrell smiled broadly, then nodded. "Yeah," he

said. "Yeah, I think ten thousand dollars is enough money to get me interested."

"How are we goin' to pull this off?" Oliver asked.

"Don't be worryin' none about that," Willis replied. "I've got it all figured out."

Chapter Fourteen

San Carlos Indian Reservation

"Delshay, I know the impulse will be very strong for you to get revenge," Baker said after the funerals of those killed in Delshay's and Chandeisi's families. "But don't. Leave it up to the law."

"White man's law?"

"The law is the law," Baker said. "Just because it was Indians they killed, it doesn't make them any less guilty of murder. The law will find them and the law will punish them."

"How will the law find them?" Delshay asked. "Nobody knows who did it."

"Just leave it in the hands of the law," Baker repeated. "That is all I am asking of you."

Delshay nodded, but said nothing else. Then, at midnight on that very night, in the flickering light of a held torch, he spoke to the nine men he had managed to recruit. One of the recruits was Chandeisi; the others were young men, without families, who would be coming along for the excitement and adventure.

"If you are brave of heart, and can leave home without so much as saying good-bye to your mother and father, then you have the fighting spirit that you will need in the days to come," Delshay said as he looked into the fire-lit faces of the young men who were eager to become warriors.

"Come, we will strike fear into the heart of every white man and all will hear the name Apache and cower."

"All will hear the name Delshay and cower!" Chandeisi shouted.

"Delshay!" the others shouted.

There was some stirring from those who were still sleeping in their hogans, and Delshay held up his hand to call for quiet.

"Go to your horses," he said. "We ride."

San Carlos was made up of several small encampments that were scattered about the reservation. The wickiups were of traditional construction, animal skins, bark, woven grass, and mud. But at the center of the reservation, where the headquarters was established, stood the Indian agent's house. The equal to any fine home in any city, the agent's residence was a large, two-story house with white-painted leaded windows, dormers, clapboard sides, and a green shake roof. There was a swing on the deep, front porch where Baker and his family often sat in the evenings, enjoying the cooling breeze.

The sun had not yet risen when Sentorio rode

up to the front of the house, dismounted, and hurried up the brick walk.

"Agent Baker!" he called. He banged loudly on the door. "Agent Baker!" He banged on the door again.

A moment later, Baker, carrying a candle and still in his nightshirt, opened the door.

"What is it, Sentorio?" he asked irritably. "What do you mean by banging on my door at this time of morning?"

"It's Delshay, Agent Baker. Delshay, Chandeisi, and eight others."

"Delshay, Chandeisi and eight others? What about them, Sentorio? Make sense for God's sake."

"They are gone, Agent Baker," Sentorio said. "All of them."

"Gone? By gone, do you mean they have left the reservation?"

"Yes, Delshay and Chandeisi gathered several warriors to follow them and they left the reservation."

"Damn," Baker said, shaking his head in anger. "It wasn't Chandeisi. He didn't have anything to do with it."

"You are wrong, Agent Baker. Chandeisi is with Delshay," Sentorio said.

"Oh, Chandeisi might be with him, all right," Baker said. "But you can bet your bottom dollar that Delshay is in charge. Chandeisi is but a puppy that will go along with anything Delshay says. How long have they been gone?"

"I don't know."

"You don't know?"

"I did not see them leave," Sentorio said.

"Never mind. Round up the rest of the Indian police and see if you can find them."

"If they are off the reservation, we will have no authority over them," Sentorio said.

"I know that. That means you had better catch them before they get off reservation property."

"I think it may be too late for that," Sentorio said.

"Yeah, well, whether it is too late or not, you are going after them," Baker said. "And when you find them, bring them back bound and gagged. I want the others to see their—hero—humiliated." He set the word "hero" apart from the rest of the sentence, twisting his mouth around the word.

"I will do so," Sentorio promised.

At the very moment Sentorio and Agent Baker were discussing their absence, Delshay, Chandeisi, and the others were already off the reservation. Eerily illuminated by the flickering torches many of them were carrying, they sat on their horses on the crest of a hill that overlooked the Doogan Ranch near the little white settlement of Picket Post. Delshay looked down on the little collection of neat buildings that made up the ranch.

"All are asleep," Chandeisi said.

"Yes," Delshay replied.

"Delshay, are we at war?" one of the younger riders said.

"Yes."

"Will we join Goyathlay?"

"No," Delshay said. "We will make our own war."

He made a motion with his arm, then pointed toward the barn.

Delshay's riders rode quickly down the hill to the Doogan Ranch. Without any further directions, a couple of the riders broke away from the rest of the pack and headed toward the barn. One of them tossed a torch inside the barn, where it landed on dry hay. The other threw his torch up onto the dry-shake shingles of the roof. Within moments, the barn was on fire.

Another of the riders started toward the main house, but Delshay called out to him.

"Wait," he said.

The rider stopped, though it was clear by the expression on his face that he did not understand why Delshay had stopped him.

They waited for nearly two minutes. Delshay and the nine other warriors sat silently as they stared at the house, which, though not on fire, cast back the reflected flames of the burning barn. The popping, snapping fire licked up the sides of the walls and spread over the entire roof, growing in heat and intensity. The horses and cows trapped inside the barn realized their danger and began screaming in terror. Delshay reached down to pat the neck of his own horse reassuringly. The animal was very nervous at being that close to the blaze and it began to prance about.

The ten Indians waited, their faces glowing orange red from the fire. The illusion created an apparition of ten of Satan's mounted demons.

From inside the house, they heard a young boy's voice call the alarm.

"Pa! Ma! Wake up! Wake up! The barn's on fire!"

* * *

Alerted, his mother and she poked her husband awake. When Doogan opened his eyes, he didn't have to ask what was wrong, for by now the light from the burning barn lit up the bedroom as bright as day.

"What in the world! How did that happen? Sue, get the buckets! Donnie, Morgan, you boys turn out double quick! Turn out, boys, we've got to save the animals!"

Doogan and his two sons dashed out through the front door in their nightshirts, not bothering to take time to get dressed. They tumbled off the front porch, then were brought to an immediate stop by the sight of the ten mounted Indians. Backlit by the burning barn, the Indians looked as if they were ghost riders from Hell. Doogan shielded his eyes against the glare of the fire, but even though he stared hard at the riders, he couldn't make out any of their features. As a matter of fact, from his position he couldn't even tell that they were Indians.

It was Sue who made the connection.

"Indians!" Sue shouted. "My God, Paul, they are Indians!"

Doogan ran back into his house, then returned a moment later with a pistol. He started firing at the Indians, and Delshay returned fire. Those shots were a signal to the other Indians, and for the next several seconds the valley rang with the sound of dozens of gunshots. When the shooting stopped, Doogan, his wife, and both sons were sprawled out in the yard in front of the house. All four were dead.

On board the Western Flyer, somewhere in Kansas

Jay Peerless Bixby's insufferable manners had continued throughout most of the trip. He grumbled constantly, complaining about everything from the frequency of the stops, to the weather, to the food that was being served in the dining car.

"Is this the extent of your carte du jour?" Bixby asked, thumping his fingers against the menu card that was on the table before him. "Beef, ham, or chicken?" Bixby said. "No lamb? No fish? Just how primitive is this railroad anyway?"

"I'm sorry, sir, these selections have proven to be most popular with our travelers," the waiter said.

"Well, of course they would be," Bixby replied. "No doubt in this part of the country, your passenger list is composed of nothing but country bumpkins. But I would think that you would also make provisions for those of us who have a more refined palate. You do get travelers of some sophistication from time to time, do you not?"

"I wouldn't know, sir. I am merely a waiter," the waiter replied.

"Yes. Well, I will have the braised sirloin tips in hopes that the chef can render it edible."

As the trip progressed, Matt saw that Bixby's boorish behavior wasn't limited to the crew. He treated his wife and business manager with equal disdain. Once, when Cynthia asked Matt a question about ranching, Bixby interrupted her.

"Cynthia, please don't try to discuss business," he said. "It only exposes your total lack of knowledge."

"I'm just trying to take an interest, Jay," she

replied. "If we are going to have a ranch out here, then I want to be of some value to you."

Bixby laughed scornfully. "Your value to me, and your only value, is in your looks," he said. "Having a beautiful wife is an asset to a successful businessman. Though I must tell you, my dear, that the moment you open your mouth to show your ignorance, that asset is nullified."

Matt watched Cynthia's reaction to the hateful words, amazed that Bixby either didn't see how his words hurt her, or didn't care. On the other hand, Hendel seemed acutely aware of the way Bixby treated Cynthia and though he didn't say anything, he did get up and walk to the back of the car, then out onto the rear vestibule.

Matt waited for a moment, then walked out to the rear platform as well. Hendel was leaning against the railing, watching the track unwind beneath and behind as the train moved at a twenty-mile-per-hour pace.

"Mind if I join you?" Matt asked.

"Not at all, sir, not at all," Hendel said.

Matt pulled out the makings and rolled a cigarette, then offered the makings to Hendel.

"Thank you, no," Hendel declined. "I've never acquired the habit." He chuckled. "I tried, but can't seem to get the hang of pulling the smoke down into my lungs."

"Nothing to be ashamed of," Matt said as he leaned into the car and, using it as a shield against the wind, snapped fire onto the end of a match with his fingernail. He lit the cigarette, tossed the spent match out onto the track, then took a puff.

"I don't want to step on any toes here," Matt said, "but your Mr. Bixby seems to be a difficult man to please."

"You've noticed that, have you?"

Matt chuckled. "I think everyone on the train has noticed it."

"Yes, well, Mr. Bixby can be difficult."

"You seem to handle it well."

"I have had years of practice," Hendel said. He turned back to look out at the passing countryside. "It's funny, Mr. Bixby has been complaining about the fact that the country out here is so desolate, but I find it awe-inspiring."

"Your first time out here?"

Hendel smiled. "Yes, it is. As a matter of fact, this is my first time out of the city of New York," he said. "You seem to be a man who is well in control of things, the manifestation of what one thinks of when one thinks of the Westerner. Do you live out here?"

"Yes."

"Where?"

"Oh, that's hard to say," Matt replied. "I've been just about everywhere out here, from the Canadian border all the way down to the Mexican border."

"What is your occupation, if I may ask? I mean, what sort of job would afford a man so much opportunity for travel?"

"I've done a bit of everything, I reckon," Matt replied. "I've been a deputy sheriff, a deputy city marshal, and a deputy U.S. marshal. I've scouted for the army, I've been a railroad detective, I've been a cowboy, I've trapped fur. I've even done some mining for gold and silver."

"My, what an exciting life you must lead," Hendel said. "You truly are the stuff of legend—the kind of man that books are written about."

Matt smiled but said nothing, for in fact, two dime novels had already been written about his exploits.

"I must say that I not only admire you for living such an exciting life, but also for living it in such a magnificent environment."

"If you think this is magnificent, you haven't seen anything yet," Matt said. "Wait until we reach the Rockies in Colorado."

"I am looking forward to that," Hendel said. "It almost makes it . . ." He paused without finishing his sentence.

"Almost makes it worth working for a man like Jay Peerless Bixby?" Matt asked.

Hendel smiled. "I didn't say that," he said.

"No, you didn't, because you are too good a man, Mr. Hendel, and it doesn't take a strong sense of observation to see that," Matt said. He looked back into the car. "But I don't work for Mr. Jay Peerless Bixby, and I have no such restraints. I don't know that I've ever seen a more insufferable man, or a more long-suffering woman. I don't know why she puts up with him."

"She puts up with it because she feels a sense of obligation," Hendel said.

"A sense of obligation to who?" Matt asked.

"No who, so much as what," Hendel replied. "She feels a sense of obligation to honor. You see, this marriage was arranged by her father. It was his last wish—or, one might say, his last command to her—before he died. I wasn't able to talk him out of it, so the least I can do is . . ." Again, he left the sentence uncompleted.

"I'll be damn," Matt said with a chuckle. "That's it, isn't it? The only reason you work for Bixby is so you can look out for Cynthia."

"I don't know that I would put it quite that way," Hendel said. "But I do look out for her as best I can."

The door to the car opened and Bixby stepped outside.

"What are you two doing out here?" he asked.

"We just stepped out for a breath of air," Hendel said.

"It stinks of smoke and ash out here. Anyway, they are about to call the first setting for dinner. I would like to eat early, then have the porter turn my bed down. I have discovered that the more I can sleep on this accursed trip, the better it is."

"Yes," Hendel said. "I have discovered that as well."

Matt hid his smile.

Chapter Fifteen

Denver

The Western Flyer arrived in Denver at ten o'clock in the morning. There, it was necessary for Matt to collect his luggage and leave the Union Pacific depot. Boarding an omnibus that was drawn up outside the depot, he rode across town to the depot of the Denver and Rio Grande. There, he learned that the train for El Paso would not leave until two that afternoon.

Resolving himself to a four-hour wait in the depot, Matt decided to use the opportunity to get a haircut and take a bath. Coming out of the bathhouse a while later, he looked like a different man. Gone was the suit he had been wearing, to be replaced by jeans, a gray denim shirt, and a Stetson hat. He also strapped on his pistol, feeling comfortable in reacquiring that which he had abandoned during his trip to St. Louis.

Much more refreshed now, Matt had his lunch, then bought a newspaper and settled down to read.

INDIAN UPRISING!

Yesterday morning, in the dark hours of predawn, neighbors who lived near the Doogan ranch near Phoenix, Arizona Territory, reported seeing a fire. They gathered quickly for what they thought would be an excursion to extinguish the flames, and made haste to reach the scene in order that they might provide assistance to their neighbor.

When they arrived at the Doogan ranch, however, they were greeted with a sight that is almost too gruesome to describe. Mr. Doogan, his wife, and two sons lay mortally wounded in the yard. Their bodies had been riddled with gunfire and with arrows. The barn had burned to the ground, killing three horses and two cows, but the house was undamaged.

This newspaper has learned that markings on the arrows found in the bodies are consistent with the markings of arrows used by Chiricahua Apache. As the Apache renegade Geronimo is Chiricahua, it was believed at first that Geronimo, long an adversary to the army, might be responsible for the foul deed. But those who are knowledgeable in the ways of the wily Apache chief say that it is very rare for him to range this far north for his nefarious deeds.

A recent telegram was dispatched from Indian Agent Baker at the San

Carlos reservation to the Department of the Missouri Army headquarters in Chicago, telling of the unauthorized departure from the reservation of the Indian Delshay. Word then went out to General George Crook to widen his campaign against Geronimo to include Delshay.

Delshay is described as a man in his late twenties with the appeal of a medicine man to the other Apache. He is known to have ridden with Geronimo and, no doubt, has acquired much of the Apache chief's skills as well as his savagery.

Matt had just finished the paper when he heard the by now familiar, and unpleasant, voice of Jay Peerless Bixby. Looking up, he saw Bixby standing at the ticket counter, arguing with the clerk.

"El Paso? But isn't that in Texas?"

"Yes, sir, it is."

"But why must we go through Texas? I may not live out here, but I do know my geography, and I know that it is not necessary to go through Texas to get to Arizona Territory."

"It is, sir, if you are going by railroad," the ticket clerk said. "You will take the Denver and Rio Grande to El Paso, where you must change trains again, this time boarding the Southern Pacific cars."

"And how many more times must I change trains?" Bixby asked, his voice getting louder and more irritating.

"That will be your last train."

"Well, thank heavens for small favors," he said. "So, this train will take us directly to Phoenix?"

"No, you'll have board a coach from the Sun Valley Stage Coach Line at Maricopa for the last twenty miles into Phoenix."

"Oh, for heavens sake, when will the West catch up with the rest of the country?"

Earlier in the day, when Matt had stepped off the Union Pacific train in Denver, he considered waiting to take a later train down to El Paso, just so he would not have to put up with Bixby any longer. But he found that he actually liked Hendel, and he believed that somehow his being present helped Hendel bear the burden of being Bixby's employee. Although he had not known Hendel all that long, he felt that leaving now would be the same as deserting a friend, so he decided to continue his trip as planned.

"Mr. Jensen," Bixby said when he and the others came over to join him in the waiting room. "I didn't see you at the cab stand so I thought perhaps you might be on a different train. I'm glad to see that we shall be continuing our journey together. You have adopted a different mode of dress, I see."

"No," Matt said. "This is my normal mode of dress. I adopted a different mode of dress when I went to St. Louis."

"Well, I think it becomes you," Cynthia said with a pleasant smile.

"Thank you, ma'am," Matt responded, touching the brim of his hat.

"Oh, my, I see that you are wearing a pistol," Bixby said. "Is the West really so unsettled that one must wear a pistol?"

"It's sort of a habit I've gotten into," Matt replied. "You might be more comfortable, by the way, if you would take off your jacket and vest. For the rest of the journey, it is only going to get hotter."

"Thank you, but I've no intention of taking fashion suggestions from someone whose idea of proper dress includes wearing a pistol on his hip," Bixby said.

Matt smiled. "Like you said, Mr. Bixby, it was just a suggestion."

"Have you eaten, Mr. Jensen? We are about to take our lunch. Would you care to eat with us?" Cynthia invited.

"Thank you, I have had my lunch," Matt said.

"Very well. Come, Hendel, let's find the dining room," Bixby said.

"I've eaten as well," Hendel said.

"You have? And when did that happen?" Bixby asked, surprised by Hendel's response.

"While I was seeing to our luggage."

"Very well, you can wait here. Come, Cynthia."

Bixby and Cynthia left. Then Hendel indicated the bench next to Matt. "May I join you?"

"Yes, of course," Matt said.

"To be honest, Mr. Jensen, I wasn't sure you would be on this train."

Matt smiled. "I considered waiting for the next one," he admitted.

"Why didn't you?"

"I need to get there and get my business done," Matt replied. He decided not to add that he thought his presence might lend support to Hendel.

Hendel sighed. "Well, for whatever reason, I'm glad you are still with us. I confess that I have enjoyed our conversations during the journey, and it has helped pass the time in an enjoyable way. I just wish it could help Cynthia as well."

"I think your being here helps her," Matt said.

Hendel smiled self-consciously. "I hope it does," he said.

Later that afternoon, shortly after they boarded the train and left Denver, Matt saw Hendel lean across the space between the seats to speak to Cynthia.

"Mrs. Bixby," he said. "While we were in Denver, I bought something that might make the rest of the trip somewhat easier for you."

"Oh, Mr. Hendel, you didn't have to do anything like that," she said.

"Oh, but I wanted to," Hendel said. "You and Mr. Bixby have been so good to me that I wanted to do something." He reached down into a bag and withdrew a book. "This is *Sonnets of the Portuguese,* a book of poetry by Elizabeth Barrett Browning. I hope you enjoy it."

"Oh, yes, I know the book," Cynthia said enthusiastically. "I've read some of the poems and I love them. I'm sure I will enjoy the book, and I don't know how to thank you."

"Take pleasure in the book," Hendel said. "That is all the thanks I will need."

Rancho Grande

The sun was a great orange ball, poised on the eastern horizon, and Delshay and the others waited just over the crest of a ridge that overlooked the house. Despite its overstated name, Rancho Grande was barely a ranch, with no more than fifteen head of cattle.

Delshay could smell the aroma of cooking bacon and baking biscuits and he felt his stomach rumble in hunger. The back door of the little house opened and a man came outside, wearing a pair of trousers with suspenders. As he walked toward the outhouse, he loosened his suspenders and let them drape down to either side.

Using a bow, Delshay stood up, drew the string back, then let the arrow fly. He and the others watched it flash quickly through the air. It hit the man in the back, right between the shoulder blades. The arrow did not drop him, though, and he spun around with a surprised and pained expression on his face, reaching around, trying to grab the arrow, trying to pull it out. Looking up, he saw Delshay and the other Apaches standing no more than fifty yards away.

"Martha! Injuns!" He shouted. He started back toward the house but, with the need for silence gone, Delshay and the others opened up on him with rifles. He went down before he made it to the back porch.

From inside the house, they heard a scream.

Jumping up, Delshay ran toward the house with the others close behind.

"Mama, what—" The young boy's call was cut off by the sound of a gunshot.

Delshay leaped over the body of the rancher, then ran up the steps and burst through the kitchen door. He stopped in surprise at what he saw. There, lying on the floor, was a boy who looked to be about six or seven. His eyes were open, but unseeing. There was a hole in his forehead, from which a small trickle of blood oozed.

A woman was sitting on the floor next to the boy. Her eyes were wide in fright and she was holding a pistol to her temple.

"Woman, why did you kill the boy?" Delshay asked.

The woman didn't answer. Instead, she pulled the trigger and blood, bone, and brain sprayed out from the entry wound. Her arm dropped to her side, the pistol clattered to the floor, and she fell over against the body of her son.

"She killed herself," Chandeisi said, stating the obvious. "She killed herself and her child."

"Yes," Delshay replied.

"But I don't understand. Why did she do that?"

"It is what white women are told to do," Delshay said. Stepping over the body, he grabbed a handful of bacon and a biscuit and shoved it in his mouth.

Along the Maricopa-to-Phoenix road

Pogue Willis was sitting on a rock eating cold beans from a can. Burt Philbin had climbed up onto the ledge a little earlier and was looking toward the south. Deermont Cantrell and Billy Meechum were playing a game of mumblety-peg, and Abe Oliver had walked over into a little patch of woods to relieve himself.

"Hey, Pogue, I can see the dust," Philbin called down. "The stage is a-comin'."

Willis took the last mouthful of beans, wiped the

spoon clean on his shirt, then stuck it in his pocket. He tossed the can over his shoulder and it landed with a soft clanking sound. He stood up and brushed his hands together.

"Come on down, Philbin," Willis called. "Meechum, Cantrell, Oliver, you three get over here."

Meechum, Cantrell, and Oliver came over to join Willis as Philbin came down from the ridge.

"Now, do all of you have it straight as to what each one of you is goin' to do?" Willis asked.

"Yeah," Philbin said. "We pull a log across the road to stop the stage. When it stops, you and Meechum will be up here on the rock keepin' an eye open while I brace the driver and shotgun guard and Oliver and Cantrell pull all the folks out of the coach. We'll take whatever money they got, plus the money pouch."

"Right," Willis said. "Any questions?"

"Yeah, I got a question," Oliver said. "You ain't never said how much money you think this here coach will be carryin'?"

"Who knows how much it's carryin'?" Willis answered. "That ain't nothin' you can ever tell till you open the money pouch and look."

"Yeah, but how much do you think?"

"How much money you got now?" Willis asked.

"About half a dollar," Oliver answered.

"More than likely the coach is carryin' more than half a dollar," Willis said, and the others laughed.

"Look here, Oliver, you don't want to do this, you just ride on out of there now and I'll take your share," Philbin teased.

"I didn't say I wasn't goin' to do this."

"Yeah, I thought you might come around."

"All right, enough talkin'. Get the log across the road," Willis said. "Ever'one get ready."

Aboard the Sun Valley stagecoach

The team was pulling the coach down a slight downgrade so that the coach was moving at a fairly brisk pace. The driver, Moses Turner, was handling the ribbons with a very delicate touch.

Hal "Pinkie" Floyd, the shotgun guard, saw it first.

"Moses!" he said. "Look up! There's somethin' a-layin' across the road up there."

"Damn. It's a log," Moses said as he started hauling back on the reins. "It wasn't there this morning. How did it get there? There ain't no trees nearby to fall across the road like that."

"I don't know," Pinkie said. "But I sure don't like the looks of it." Pinkie picked up the shotgun, broke it down to make certain it was loaded, then snapped it back and held it, barrels up, with the butt on the seat right beside him.

"Whoa!" Moses called to the team. He put his foot on the brake as the coach slowed to a stop.

"Son of a bitch! It's a holdup!" Pinkie said as three masked riders appeared on the road. He raised his shotgun to his shoulder.

Chapter Sixteen

There were six passengers in the coach: Bixby, Cynthia, Hendel, Matt, a whiskey drummer, and a young man who was returning to school at Tempe Normal. Matt was napping when he heard a loud shout, then the unmistakable discharge of a double-barrel shotgun as well as several pistol shots.

Matt awoke with a start.

"Oh, what is it?" Cynthia asked, her voice edged with fear.

Though Matt hadn't seen anything, when he heard gunshots and loud guttural voices outside, he surmised at once what was going on. He loosened the pistol in his holster.

A masked man's head suddenly appeared in the window. He stuck a gun inside.

"Ever'one out of the coach!" he shouted.

"See here! What is this?" Bixby shouted indignantly as he stepped down from the coach. "Do you know who I am?"

"You are the man I'm robbin'," the gunman

replied. He brought his pistol down sharply over Bixby's head. Bixby groaned and fell back against the coach, though he didn't fall down.

"Jay!" Cynthia cried out in alarm.

"Anybody else?" the gunman challenged. "Maybe you folks didn't hear me when I said everyone get out of the coach."

Another gunman came around to join the first. He was also wearing a mask.

"Philbin's dead," the second gunman said. "The shotgun guard killed him."

"We get the money pouch?"

"We'll clean these folks out first," the second gunman said. He took off his hat. "Folks, what I want you to do is pretend you are in church and the plate is being passed. I want you to put all your money and valuables in this here hat. If you try and hold out on me, I'll shoot you. We'll start with you, mister," he said to Bixby, who, though streaks of blood were sliding down from the wound on top of his head, had managed to stay on his feet.

Bixby took out his wallet and put it in the hat.

"Your pocket watch, too."

Grumbling, Bixby disconnected his watch from his vest and dropped that in the hat as well.

"Hurry up down there!" someone called from the top of a large rock. Glancing up, Matt saw two masked men standing up there, looking down at the proceedings.

"We're hurryin', we're hurryin'," the gunman with the hat said.

"That bauble you're wearin' around your neck looks real pretty there," the robber said to Cynthia.

"But it's goin' to look even prettier in my hat." He giggled at his own joke.

When he got to Hendel, Hendel dropped in his own wallet and watch without complaint.

"You folks are doin' just real fine," the robber said. He stopped in front of Matt, but Matt had nothing in his hand.

"How come you are standin' here empty-handed?" the robber said. "What have you got to give me?"

"Just a bullet in the stomach if you don't give these folks their money back and ride away from here," Matt said.

"Ha! Hey, Oliver, did you hear what this fella just said?"

"Just shoot him and be done with it," Oliver said.

"Yeah, I reckon that's best," Cantrell said. He cocked his pistol.

What happened next happened so fast that it surprised everyone, robbers and passengers both. Even though both robbers were holding pistols pointed in the general direction of the coach passengers, Matt drew and fired so quickly that both were dead before either realized they were in danger.

Looking up to where the other two men were standing, Matt raised his pistol, but both dropped down out of sight on the other side of the rock. Matt climbed the rock and looked for them, but by the time he reached the top of the rock, they were already too far away for a good shot.

Putting his gun away, Matt climbed back down to the stage. Bixby, Cynthia, Hendel, and the other two passengers were gathered around the bodies of the two men he had shot. The body of the robber the guard had shot was lying on the road in front of the coach.

The guard was also dead, slumped over the edge of the seat with his arm hanging down. His shotgun was lying on the ground alongside the left front wheel, the stock of the gun red with his blood.

The driver was also slumped forward.

"How bad are you hit?" Matt called up to the driver.

"I don't rightly know," the driver answered, his voice racked with pain. "All I know is it hurts like hell."

Matt climbed up on the wheel to take a look. The driver was holding his hand over his side. Matt moved the driver's hand to one side, then breathed a sigh of relief.

"It looks like it cut a pretty good crease, but it didn't poke a hole in you," Matt said. He looked at the seat just behind the driver and saw a bullet buried in the front of the coach. Taking out a pocket knife, he pried out the bullet. "And it didn't stay in you," he said, holding the bullet out for the driver's inspection.

"Damn," the driver said. "That's as close as I ever want to come to getting' shot dead." The driver looked over at the shotgun guard. "Poor Pinkie. He wasn't as lucky."

"The robbers are gone. Do you feel up to driving?"

"Yeah, I reckon so," the driver said.

"We need to get you patched up first," Matt said.

"You know somethin' about doctorin', do you?" the driver asked.

"I've patched a few bullet holes in my day," Matt replied. "A couple of them on myself. I wonder if you are carrying anything we can use as a bandage."

Cynthia, who was tending to the wound on Bixby's head, looked up toward Matt when she heard him say he needed something for a bandage. "I can give you something to use as a bandage," she called up to him.

"What have you got that you could possibly give him?" Bixby asked.

"Just watch," Cynthia replied.

Reaching up under the hem of her skirt, she began to wriggle around a bit.

"Cynthia, stop that!" Bixby ordered. "You are disgracing yourself!"

After a few more moments of wriggling, she pulled a large piece of silk from under her skirt.

"How about this?" she asked Matt. "A silk petticoat."

"Cynthia!" Bixby gasped. "Have you lost your mind?"

"Oh, don't be silly, Jay," Cynthia replied as she handed the slip up to Matt. "I have two more on."

Up on the driver's seat, Matt unbuttoned Moses's shirt, then pulled it away from him. Some of the coagulating blood had caused the shirt to stick to the wound, and Moses winced in pain when the shirt was pulled away.

"I know that probably stung a bit," Matt said. "But the truth is, sticking to your wound like that is probably what saved your life. It acted like a bandage and it stopped the bleeding. If it hadn't, you might have bled to death."

As Matt worked to apply a bandage to the stagecoach driver, the drummer and the young student pulled the masks off the dead robbers.

"Look at them," the student said. "They are meanlooking, aren't they?"

The whiskey drummer chuckled. "They're

mean-enough-lookin' all right, but I'd say these boys picked the wrong coach to try and rob."

"They did that, all right," the student said.

"Wait a minute," Matt said, looking down at the three bodies. "I know these men."

"You know them?" Hendel asked, surprised by the announcement.

"Sort of. I don't actually know them by name," Matt said. "But I've seen them before."

These were the same men Matt had encountered at Ian Crocker's ranch almost two months earlier.

"I would imagine they were up to no good then as well," the drummer said.

"You are right about that," Matt replied.

"What are we going to do with them now?" the student asked.

"Well, if you two men will give me a hand, we'll lift them up onto the roof of the coach. I hate to lay the shotgun guard out there with the others, but we don't have much of a choice."

"You can put the shotgun guard inside the coach with us," Hendel suggested.

"What? How dare you make such a suggestion?" Bixby shouted, angrily. "Anyway, there is no room for him inside."

"There will be," Matt said. "I intend to finish the trip by riding up here with the driver."

"You will not put that dead man in the coach with us! I will not allow it!" Bixby said.

"You won't allow it?" the driver called down. "Mister, I'll have you know that as the driver of this coach, I am in charge. Me. Not you. Now, either Pinkie rides in there with you, or you can ride up on top of the coach with the dead outlaws, or you can walk. It's up to you."

"Your employer will hear from me, my good man! You can count on that," Bixby said.

"Oh, Jay, for heaven's sake. Be quiet, will you?" Cynthia said. She was cleaning his wound and she pressed down hard on the bump.

"Ouch!" Bixby called out. "What are you trying to do, kill me?"

"Don't give her any ideas, mister," the whiskey drummer said, and the student laughed out loud at his joke.

"Well, I'll be!" Bixby said, his face turning red in anger and embarrassment over being the butt of a joke.

Both Cynthia and Hendel managed to hide their smiles.

With the bandage applied to the driver's side, Matt climbed up onto the top of the coach, then called down to the drummer.

"You two start passing them up to me, I'll lay them out up here."

"I'll help," Hendel offered and, over the next few minutes, the three dead outlaws were lifted up to the top of the coach, then laid out side by side. After that, the student climbed up and helped Matt pass the dead guard down to Hendel and the whiskey drummer.

"Now we have to get the log moved," Matt said.

Once the log was moved, Moses picked up the reins, gave the team a whistle, and they resumed their run into Phoenix.

Chapter Seventeen

"Can you believe that?" Bixby asked after they got under way once more. "Mr. Jensen has just killed two men. Two men, mind you, yet to look at him and to hear him talk, you would think nothing had happened."

Bixby had a large, discolored bump on his head, clearly visible because of his baldness.

"To think that we had befriended him," Bixby continued.

"Surely, you aren't condemning him, are you, Mr. Bixby?" Hendel asked.

"I am indeed."

"But why? He saved our money, if not our lives."

"He is as savage as the others," Bixby said.

"I think he was courageous, even heroic," Cynthia said.

"Of course you would think such a thing, my dear," Bixby said. "As empty as your head is, you probably see him as a knight in shining armor. But I'm telling you now that someone who can kill as easily as he can is not someone with whom we need to associate. And I forbid you to speak to him again."

"But Jay," Cynthia said.

"Not another word. When we get to Phoenix, we shall go our way and, no doubt, he shall go his."

"It isn't as if I want to invite him over for tea," Cynthia said. "But I do think that you are wrong in your judgment of him, and I agree with Mr. Hendel. I think we are obligated to him for our very safety."

After leaving the aborted stagecoach robbery, Pogue Willis and Billy Meechum rode hard, dismounting occasionally to give the horses a blow. Even then they didn't stop, but continued to walk, always putting distance behind them. They did pause briefly late in the afternoon in order to eat a few bites of jerky and to take a few swallows of water.

Meechum chewed on the leathery jerky, then took a drink of tepid water from his canteen. He spat the water out in disgust, and wiped his mouth with the back of his hand.

"Here we are, drinking water that tastes like horse piss and chewing on jerky that tastes like saddle leather. You said we was all goin' to get rich. Well, the only thing that we got was my cousin kilt, two of my pards dead. And for all that we got nothin'."

"Quit your bitchin'," Willis said. "You got out alive, didn't you?"

"Yeah, I'm alive, as long as I don't starve to death or die of thirst," Meechum said. "There's got to be a town near here. Listen, Pogue, don't you think there's a town around here somewhere?"

"What if there is?"

"Well, if there is, I was thinkin' we could go in an' get somethin' fit to eat an' decent to drink," Meechum said.

"You was thinkin', was you? What makes you believe you have enough brains to think?" Willis asked.

"You got no right to talk to me like that."

"Anytime you want to call me on it, why, feel free to try," Willis said.

"No, you ain't goin' to goad me into pullin' a gun against you, no matter how hard you try. Maybe I ain't the smartest man around, but I got more sense than to do anything like that."

"Then try to have enough sense to keep your mouth shut for a while," Willis said. "I'm gettin' just real tired of listenin' to you."

Meechum seethed with frustrated anger, but he said nothing.

"Now, that's more like it," Willis said. "We're goin' to Phoenix. I figure if we didn't get the money while it was on the coach, then we'll take it from the bank."

"If we couldn't get it from the coach, what makes you think we can get it from a bank?" Meechum asked.

"Stagecoaches are moving, banks are still," Willis replied, as if that answered everything. "Get mounted, we have a long way to go yet."

Phoenix

It was late afternoon by the time the coach reached Phoenix. As they were coming into town, the driver shouted down toward the passengers. "Phoenix! This is Phoenix, folks!" he called.

Matt put his hand on Moses's forehead. He was relieved to discover that the driver had no fever.

"What?" the driver asked.

"I was just checking to see if you had any fever," Matt said.

"Do I?"

"I don't think so."

"Good."

"How do you feel?"

"My side is hurtin' like hell," Moses said. He smiled, then looked down at the bandage wrapped around his waist. "And I'm going to have one heck of a time explainin' to my wife why I'm wearin' a woman's petticoat."

Matt laughed. "If you've still got a sense of humor after all this, Moses, I think you are going to be all right."

After he climbed down from the coach, Matt walked over and stood against the wall of the stage depot, watching as some men pulled the three outlaws off the top of the coach and laid them out on the wooden platform. The moment the bodies were laid out, several people went over to look down at them. The crowd grew quickly as more and more people, not only employees of the stage depot, but citizens from the city, began congregating to look at the morbid show.

Fortunately, the shotgun guard was spared that indignity, as they decided to keep his body inside the coach until the undertaker could call for him.

The sheriff, having been notified of the attempted stagecoach robbery, hurried down to the depot. He looked down at the three bodies, then after speaking to the driver for a few minutes, walked over to talk to Matt.

"The name is Williams. Robert Williams," he said as he extended his hand. "I'm the sheriff here. I understand from the driver that you are the one who killed these three men."

"I killed two of them," Matt answered. "The guard got the other one."

"And who might you be, if you don't mind my askin'?"

"My name is Jensen. Matt Jensen."

The sheriff blinked in surprise. "Matt Jensen? Are you *the* Matt Jensen?"

Matt laughed. "I don't know if I'm *the* Matt Jensen, but I'm the only one I know."

"Of course you are *the* Matt Jensen," Sheriff Williams said. "Nobody else could have done this."

A wagon backed up to the coach and the guard's body was taken off. Because the wagon was closed, and was backed so close to the coach, few actually saw the body as it was removed. The driver of the wagon, a very thin, sallow-faced, hawk-nosed, pinched-cheek man wearing striped pants, a black coat, and a high hat, clucked at his horse and drove away. Only a few paid any attention to him, as most continued to gawk at the three dead outlaws.

"If you'll excuse me, now that they've taken the shotgun guard's body out of the coach, I think I'll just go on over there and get my bag," Matt said.

"I'll walk over there with you, if you don't mind, Mr. Jensen," the sheriff said.

Matt claimed his bag, then stepped out of the way so the other passengers could claim their luggage.

"Do you know who you killed here, Mr. Jensen?" Sheriff Williams asked, pointing toward the three bodies that lay out on the depot platform.

Matt nodded. "Yeah, I know who they are. I can't call them by name, but I know who they are," he said. "I ran into them a few months back, but it was up in Colorado."

"That sounds about right. I heard that they were up in Colorado for a while. I don't think they've been back down here for more than a couple of weeks."

"Do you know who they are?" Matt asked.

"Oh, yeah, I know them all right," the sheriff replied. He pointed to the three bodies. "The one on the left went by the name of Burt Philbin, the big one is Deermont Cantrell, and the other one is Abe Oliver. How did you happen to run into them in Colorado, if you don't mind my askin'?"

Matt told the sheriff about his encounter with them at Ian Crocker's ranch. "I didn't know it at the time, but it turns out they had tried to hold up a bank up in Bent Canyon. There was another man running with them then, by the name of Percy Morris. The only reason I know his name is because I killed him in the shoot-out."

"Hmm, don't know anything about a fella named Morris. They must'a run into him when they was up in Colorado," Sheriff Williams said.

"Hey, Sheriff," someone shouted from the crowd. "Is it all right if I tie these three boys up against some boards, then stand 'em up so's I can take a picture of them?"

"Sure, Gilbert, go ahead," the sheriff called back."

"Get 'em strapped to those boards there, boys,"

the photographer ordered, pointing to the bodies, and several men began tying the slain outlaws to the three two-by-six boards the photographer had brought to the depot just for this occasion.

"You say there was another fella with these three?" the sheriff asked as he watched the men work.

"Actually, there were two more with them," Matt said. "But they were both wearing masks, and I didn't get that good a look at them."

"Well, these boys also ran with an hombre by the name of Billy Meechum. Fact is, he was sort of the head of the little group, and I'll bet a dollar to a doughnut that he was one of the two that got away. Of course, without someone actually seeing Meechum there, I don't reckon I can rightly accuse him just yet." The sheriff shook his head. "As to who the other one was, though, I don't have the slightest idea."

"Okay, boys, get 'em propped up against the wall here," the photographer said.

At the photographer's orders, the three outlaws were picked up, then carried over and stood up against the adobe wall of the depot—their grotesque bodies making a grisly display.

"Hey, you, young feller," the photographer shouted over to Matt. "Bein' as you're the one who kilt these outlaws, how 'bout you come over here and stand alongside of 'em, holdin' up the gun that you done the killin' with?"

"I'd rather not," Matt replied.

"Why not? Come on, young feller, this will make you famous. Why, I'll send your picture back East and it won't be no time till ever'one in America will know who you are."

"No, thank you," Matt repeated.

"I'm just—"

"Gilbert, the man said no," Sheriff Williams snapped back, interrupting the man in mid-sentence. "Now just get your pictures took and leave us the hell alone."

"Whatever you say, Sheriff," the photographer replied. "I was just tryin' to do right by him, is all."

"I'm sorry about that, Mr. Jensen," the sheriff said.

"That's all right."

"People, people," the photographer called out to the crowd. "If any of you want your picture took with these here desperados, why, step up here now, give me a quarter, and I'll take your picture with them. You can pass them onto your grandkids someday, tell 'em you're the one that kilt 'em. By then nobody will ever know the difference."

Matt was surprised to hear such a blatant lie proposed, but scores of people crowded forward to take Gilbert up on his dishonest offer.

"Mr. Jensen, you are aware, are you not, that there is a bounty on these three men?" Sheriff Williams asked.

Matt shook his head. "A bounty? Well, I can't say that I am surprised, but no, I didn't know anything about a bounty. I'm not a bounty hunter, Sheriff, so I don't keep up with such things."

The sheriff chuckled. "Uh-huh. Well, we're talking fifteen hundred dollars here—five hundred on each of them. I don't reckon you'll be turnin' that money down, will you?"

Matt chuckled as well. "No, Sheriff, I won't be turning the money down. I understand from the driver that the guard was married."

"Pinkie was married, that's true."

"Give a thousand dollars of the reward to his widow."

"I can see her getting five hundred dollars," Sheriff Williams said. "I mean, seein' as how Pinkie got one of them. But you don't need to give her a thousand dollars."

"I know I don't need to. I want to," Matt said.

Sheriff Williams stroked his chin and nodded. "All right," he said. "I reckon you are as good a man as they say you are, Matt Jensen. By the way, I'm pretty sure these men you killed this mornin' are the same sons of bitches that got all our Indian problems started in the first place," the sheriff said.

"By Indian problems, you are talking about Delshay, not Geronimo, right?"

"That's right," Sheriff Williams said. "You know Delshay? I didn't think anyone outside Arizona Territory had ever even heard of the son of a bitch."

"The reason I know about him is because I scouted for General Crook for a while," Matt said. "I've never exactly met Delshay, but I have seen him."

Matt recalled his run-in with Delshay—remembering how the Indian had sat calmly on his horse, as if defying the army.

"I know Delshay rode with Geronimo. I didn't know he had gone out on his own, though, until

I read in the newspaper about one of his raids," Matt said.

"You're right, he did ride with Geronimo for a while. But then, for some reason, he decided to come back to the reservation. I think if it hadn't been for Meechum and these galoots here"—he pointed toward the three dead outlaws, alongside whom the citizens of the town were coming up, one by one, to brandish a pistol and pose for photographs— "Delshay would still be living just real peaceable-like out there."

"What makes you think these men had anything to do with Delshay leaving the reservation?" Matt asked.

"It's something Gene Baker told me, and I just put it together," Matt said. "Baker is the Indian agent out at San Carlos. It seems that Delshay and his cousin, Chandeisi, were going into the town of Picket Post to do some honest trading. They left their squaws and their children waiting for them on blankets just outside of town. The squaws were watchin' over the trading trinkets—you know, silver and turquoise necklaces and the like. But when Delshay and Chandeisi came back, their squaws and their children was dead and their trading goods was gone. Baker says he thinks that's what sent Delshay and Chandeisi and the others they was able to recruit out on the war trail.

"Anyway, a few weeks ago, right after that happened, Meechum and these three galoots showed up in Phoenix looking to trade silver and turquoise Indian jewelry. It ain't that far a stretch to figure that these is the same ones that killed the Indian squaws."

"If there was a bounty on them, why didn't you arrest them as soon as they came to town?" Matt asked.

"I wasn't in town when they came in," Sheriff Williams said. "I was down in Maricopa. And by the time I come back up to Phoenix, all four of them boys was long gone."

"Excuse me, Sheriff Williams?"

The man who spoke to the sheriff was the same one who had come for the guard's body a few minutes earlier. He was back, but this time he was driving an open wagon.

"Yes?" Williams replied.

"I wonder, Sheriff, if you would kindly call a halt to the circus Mr. Gilbert is conducting around the deceased so that I may get on with my business."

"Mr. Jensen, this here is Abner Prufrock. Mr. Prufrock, as you can tell by his attire, is the undertaker. Mr. Prufrock, your business with the county is compliments of Matt Jensen. He's the one who killed them." Sheriff Williams laughed. "Maybe you ought to give him a cut of your fee," he teased.

Prufrock cleared his throat. "Yes, Sheriff, well, I'm sure you are having fun with all this. But the truth is, regardless of whether these men were outlaws are not, common decency requires that they be given a proper burial."

"All right, I'll get your bodies for you," Williams said. "Gilbert, that's enough picture takin'," the sheriff called. "It's time to let Mr. Prufrock here get on with his business."

"If you say so, Sheriff," Gilbert answered.

"Kindly take them off those planks," Prufrock said as he walked over toward the bodies.

"I tell you what, Mr. Jensen, you do have my thanks and the thanks of the town," Sheriff Williams said, continuing his conversation with Matt. "You stopped a stagecoach robbery and, from what some are saying, you may have even saved a few of the passengers' lives as well."

"Too bad I wasn't able to do anything for the shotgun guard," Matt said.

"Yes, Pinkie was a good man," Sheriff Williams said. "I'm sorry for his widow, but at least I know that Moses and his wife and kids are grateful that you come along when you did and that you treated him."

"The driver's wound isn't all that serious. He should come through it just fine," Matt replied.

"I tell you what I hope," Williams said. "I hope that, once word gets back to Delshay that the sons of bitches who killed his family have been killed, that he'll come back to the reservation."

Matt and Sheriff Williams watched as the bodies of the outlaws were untied from the boards, then loaded on to the back of the undertaker's wagon.

"But that's never going to happen," Williams continued. "Delshay is going to hold every white man responsible for what happened to his family, same as white folks are going to hold all the Apaches responsible for what Geronimo, and now Delshay, have done."

Matt picked up his bag. "Can you recommend a hotel, Sheriff?"

"Well you might try the Phoenix House, though we do have a couple of pretty good ones and I wouldn't want to be accused of trying to steer you to one certain place."

"Phoenix House sounds good to me. Where is it?"

"It is right down at the end of this same street. You can't miss it."

"Thanks," Matt said.

"Oh, if you don't mind my askin', Mr. Jensen, I'm just curious. What brings a man like you to Phoenix?"

"I'm searching for someone."

"Searching for someone? I thought you said you weren't a bounty hunter."

"It's not that kind of a search," Matt replied with a chuckle. "This is personal. The man I'm looking for is the brother of a friend. I understand he came here recently."

"What's this fella's name?" the sheriff asked. "The one you're looking for?"

"His name is Marcus. Andrew Marcus."

The sheriff smiled. "You don't say? Well, I'll be damn. Andy Marcus, yes, I know him."

"Let me make sure this is the right one," Matt said. "The Andy Marcus I'm looking for is a brewer."

"Oh, yes, sir, that's the one all right," Sheriff Williams said. "Mr. Marcus hasn't been in town for very long, but the fact is, just about everybody in Phoenix knows him," Sheriff Williams said. "That's 'cause he's buildin' a brewery, and there isn't anyone here who wouldn't like to see us get a brewery. Only problem is, I don't know if Andy is going to be able to pull it off or not."

"Why not? I was given to believe that he is a master brewer. Those men know their stuff," Matt said.

"Oh, it's neither his skills nor his work habits I'm

concerned about," the sheriff said. "Why, Andy Marcus is as dedicated a worker as anyone you'd ever want to meet. But I ain't all that sure he's goin' to be able to raise the money."

"How much does he need?"

"I don't know exactly how much he needs. But it is more than he has, I know that. That don't seem to stop him, though. He ain't one to give up."

"Do you have any idea where I can find him?"

"Sure, you don't have far to go at all," the sheriff replied. He pointed to a building right across the street from the stage depot. "He plans to set up his brewery in that building right over there. Unless I miss my guess, you'll find him there now, and the fact that he didn't come over here to see the bodies of the outlaws when the whole rest of the town did ought to give you an idea of how dedicated he is to his work."

"Yes, it does," Matt answered. "And thanks for the information."

"Glad to be able to provide it," the sheriff answered. "And if you'll come down to my office tomorrow morning, by then I'll have the authorization to pay you your bounty money."

"Thanks, I'll be there," Matt said.

Matt decided to check into the hotel before he went to see Andrew Marcus, and as he walked down the street toward the Phoenix House, Prufrock drove by him with the three bodies lying in the back of his wagon. The one the sheriff had identified as Oliver was lying in such a position that, with his open eyes, it gave the illusion that he was staring accusingly at the man who killed him.

Matt stared back.

Chapter Eighteen

When Ken Hendel came down into the lobby of the Phoenix House, he saw Cynthia sitting in a chair in the streaming light of the window. She was reading *Sonnets of the Portuguese*, the book he had bought for her.

"Ah, Mrs. Bixby, reading the book, I see," he said, walking over to her. "I hope you are enjoying it."

"Enjoying it? Oh, Mr. Hendel, I simply love it," Cynthia replied enthusiastically. "How wonderful of you to buy it for me."

"I saw it, and I thought you might like it."

"But you must let me pay you for it," Cynthia said.

"No, no, I could never do that," Hendel said. "I bought this for you because I consider you my friend, and I hope you feel the same way about me."

"Oh, indeed I do," Cynthia said. "I consider you a very, very dear friend."

"I'm glad."

"May I read one of the sonnets to you?" she asked.

"Of course."

Smiling, Cynthia raised the book, cleared her throat, then began to read:

> *If thou must love me, let it be for nought*
> *Except for love's sake only. Do not say*
> *"I love her for her smile—her look—her way*
> *Of speaking gently,—for a trick of thought*
> *That falls in well with mine, and certes brought*
> *A sense of pleasant ease on such a day"—*
> *For these things in themselves, Beloved, may*
> *Be changed, or change for thee,—and love, so*
>   *wrought,*
> *May be unwrought so. Neither love me for*
> *Thine own dear pity's wiping my cheeks dry,—*
> *A creature might forget to weep, who bore*
> *Thy comfort long, and lose thy love thereby!*
> *But love me for love's sake, that evermore*
> *Thou may'st love on, through love's eternity.*

Cynthia drew the book to her chest, then looked up at Hendel. "Isn't that just the most beautiful thing you have ever heard?" she asked.

Hendel felt a flush come over him, and he cleared his throat to try and force it away.

"Yes," he said. "I must confess that Elizabeth Barrett Browning does have a way with words."

"I think reading a poem aloud gives it much more life than merely looking at words lying dormant on the page. But Jay would never let me read anything aloud to him—he says he doesn't have time for such nonsense. Thank you for allowing me to do that, Mr. Hendel, my dear friend."

Again, Hendel cleared his throat. Then, looking around, he saw Matt Jensen coming into the hotel.

"Oh, look, there is Mr. Jensen," he said, thankful to be able to extricate himself from a situation that was growing increasingly more uncomfortable for him.

"Mr. Jensen!" Cynthia called. "Hello!"

Matt set his bag down, then came over to greet Cynthia and Hendel.

"Hello," he said. "So, you have chosen this hotel as well, have you? That tells me the sheriff's suggestion was a good one."

"Oh, yes, I think you will be very pleased with it," Cynthia replied. "I know that we are."

"Really? Even Mr. Bixby is pleased with it?" Matt asked with a barely suppressed grin.

Cynthia laughed, a rich, deep-throated laugh. "Ah," she said. "How well you know my husband."

"Have you found the brother of your friend yet?" Hendel asked. In one of their more private talks, Matt had shared with Hendel his reason for coming to Phoenix.

"I think so," Matt said. "I haven't seen him yet, but the sheriff told me where to find him—and it has to be the same man."

"Will you be leaving as soon as you complete your business?" Cynthia asked. "If so, please stop by and tell us good-bye before you go."

"I'm not planning to leave right away. In fact, I've had my horse sent here," Matt said.

"Oh, how nice," Cynthia said. "Then we will be seeing each other again."

"Sir, are you checking in?" the desk clerk called.

"Yes," Matt said. Touching the brim of his hat, he smiled at Cynthia and Hendel, then walked over to the desk and signed the register.

After Matt checked into the hotel, he went over to the Sundown Corral to check on his horse.

"Yes, Mr. Jensen, your horse arrived four days ago," the stable keeper said. "I must say, he is as fine an animal as has ever boarded with us."

"Yes, thank you, Spirit has been a very good horse," Matt said.

Matt went back into the stall area. When Spirit saw him, he began nodding his head and pawing at the ground.

"Hello, old boy," Matt said, walking up to the stall. Spirit put his head down and let Matt pet him and pull on his ears. This was Matt's second horse named Spirit, and this one was so much like his first mount of the same name that he could almost believe that the "spirit" of Spirit One had somehow become a part of Spirit Two.

"Sorry I've been gone so long," Matt said. "But as soon as I get my business taken care of here, we'll do some riding together."

Walking back up front, Matt approached the liveryman. "Do I owe you anything?"

"Not yet, you don't," the liveryman replied. "The fella who arranged this for you has it all paid up for another week."

"Good, I expect we'll be here for at least another week, and perhaps longer. Thanks for looking out for him for me."

"My pleasure, Mr. Jensen. My pleasure."

* * *

When Matt reached the building the sheriff had pointed out as the one Marcus was using to build his brewery, he saw that the front door was open. Matt stopped at the door, but didn't go inside.

"Hello?" he called.

Not getting an answer, he stepped on into the building and called again.

"Hello?"

The inside was in shadows, poorly illuminated by the open door, a few open windows, and the bars of sunlight that streamed in through the cracks between the boards. Matt saw someone working on a large vat, and there was enough similarity in appearance to Lee that Matt knew immediately that he had found the right man.

"Are you Andrew Marcus?"

"Hand me that spanner, would you, mister?" the man replied, pointing to a wrench.

Matt picked up the wrench and handed it to him.

"Now, when I turn this, what I want you to do is look underneath this vat and see if it closes off the drain."

"All right," Matt said.

The man began turning the nut and Matt looked underneath the vat. He saw the drain close.

"Did that close it down?"

"Yes."

"Good, good, I've been working on that all morning. Thanks for your help."

Matt chuckled. "I didn't do a whole lot," he said.

"Sure you did. I needed another pair of eyes and

you came along at the right time." Marcus picked up a towel and began wiping his hands. "You got my name right, I'm Marcus. Who are you, and what can I do for you?" he asked.

"My name is Matt Jensen, Mr. Marcus, and I'm afraid I have some bad news for you."

"Bad news? Wait a minute, are you tellin' me there's some kind of law says I can't open a brewery here? Because if there is, it must be a new law. I read the law and all the statutes pertaining to brewing, and I didn't see anything that says I can't do it."

"No, it's not about that, it has nothing to do with the brewery. It's about Lee, your brother."

"Damn," Marcus said. "I knew it. He's in trouble with that mine he bought, isn't he? I told him he was a fool for getting mixed up in something like that."

"No, sir, I wish that was the worst of it," Matt said. He took a deep breath. "The truth is, Mr. Marcus, your brother is dead."

Marcus took a quick, surprised breath of air. "What?" he asked, his voice considerably softer now. He took a step back and put his hand on the side of the vat. "Did you—did you say Lee is dead?"

"Yes, sir. I'm sorry."

"How did he die?"

"He was killed in a gunfight."

"Lee? Killed in a gunfight? Mister, are you sure we are talking about the same man? Lee might get himself into a fistfight, maybe even a brawl, but he would never get into a gunfight."

"I'm sorry, Mr. Marcus. I am talking about your brother," Matt said. "Though I would give anything in the world if it wasn't true."

Andy walked over to sit down on the bottom step of a stairway that led to a platform that stretched out over the three vats.

"When did it happen?"

"Almost a month ago now," Matt said.

"Damn. That means he's already been buried. Here I've been so busy trying to get this brewery started that I didn't even know about it. And I didn't know about it because I was too damn self-ish. Hell, I wasn't even there for his funeral."

"I went to St. Louis to find you," Matt said. "Lee thought that's where you were."

"I'm sorry about that. I mean about you goin' to all that trouble and me not even bein' there," Marcus said. "But the truth is, Mr. Jensen, Lee didn't know where I was, because I didn't write to tell him I had left St. Louis. You see, I had sort of hoped I would have this brewery going before I had to tell him any-thing about it. Then I was going to ask him to give up that worthless mine of his and come join me. I wasn't even goin' to charge him anything, just take him on as a full partner." Andy sighed. "But it is too late for all that now."

"Lee left something for you," Matt said. Opening his bag, he took out an envelope and handed it to Marcus.

"What is it?" Marcus said. Opening the envelope, Marcus looked inside, gasped, then looked up at Matt. "What the hell? This is money!" he said.

"Yes. Exactly two thousand dollars, in fact."

Although Lee had told Matt to use some of the money to offset his traveling expenses, Matt had not used any of it, preferring to keep the entire two thousand dollars together.

"My God! You're tellin' me that there is two thousand dollars here and it came from Lee?"

"Yes," Matt said. "That is exactly what I am telling you."

"How in the world did Lee ever come up with that much money?"

"It turns out you were wrong about the mine, Mr. Marcus," Matt said. "The mine paid well for him."

"I'll be damn. And all this time I've been mad at whoever sold it to him. I wish I could meet that fella now, so I could apologize."

Matt smiled. "Well, Mr. Marcus, you just met him," he said.

"Wait a minute. You? You are the one who sold my brother the mine?"

"I am," Matt said. "Oh, and by the way, the silver mine belongs to you now." Again, Matt reached into the bag and pulled out a sheet of paper. "I've had all the paperwork drawn up transferring ownership to you."

"Mister, I'd like to shake your hand," Marcus said. "You may well be the most honest man I've ever met. You could have kept the money, and the mine, and I would have never known anything about it. So the mine paid off, huh?"

"Yes. Lee had to work it, and I won't tease you, it was hard work. But in the end, the mine did pay off for your brother."

Marcus ran his hand across his chin. "Oh, my. Well, now, that does present me with something of a quandary. I need to ask myself, should I pull up stakes here and go up to Colorado to work the mine? After all, it has proven itself. Or, should I stay here and build the brewery?" He held up the envelope containing the two thousand dollars. "This is all the money I need to finish."

"I intend to stay here for a few more days," Matt said. "Let me know what you decide. If you decide to sell out here and go up to Denver, we can go up together."

"You know the mine, do you think I should do that? Leave here and go up there, I mean."

Matt shook his head. "No, sir, Mr. Marcus, it's not my place to tell you. This is a decision you are going to have to make on your own."

"Yeah," Marcus said. "Yeah, I guess you are right about that. All right, I'll give it some thought over the next couple of days."

Chapter Nineteen

Even as Matt was visiting with Andrew Marcus, Pogue Willis and Billy Meechum were riding into town. Their attention was drawn to a group of people standing in front of a store identified by the red-painted sign on the false front as SIKES' HARDWARE STORE. The people appeared to be looking at something that was in the front window.

"Look at all them people standin' in front of that store over there," Meechum said. "What is it do you reckon they are lookin' at?"

"I don't know," Willis answered. "Why don't we just ride over that way and take a look?"

Willis and Meechum steered their horses across the street, then stopped just behind the people who were gathered in front of the store.

What they saw was three coffins, the bottom halves of which were closed, the upper halves open. The coffins, thus arrayed, displayed the bodies of Burt Philbin, Deermont Cantrell, and Abe Oliver. All three men were wearing jackets and ties, though

Meechum knew for a fact that none of them owned a jacket or a tie—and he was almost certain that none of them had ever even worn a jacket or tie.

Instead of the pallor of death, the three men showed color in their faces. In fact, it was far too much color, very obviously artificially applied by the undertaker.

"Damn," Meechum said. "It's Burt, Deermont, and Abe."

"I can see that," Willis said. "And if I couldn't, that damn sign there would tell me."

The sign Willis spoke of was painted on a square board that was standing on a tripod alongside the three coffins.

Burt Philbin
Deermont Oliver
Andy Cantrell

Robbers Beware!

These three outlaws were killed by
Matt Jensen
when they tried to hold up
the Sun Valley stage.

"Damn, look at that. They got the names all wrong," Meechm said. "They got Cantrell and Oliver's names all mixed up. And it's Abe, not Andy. We ought to do something."

"Do something? What do you mean, do something?"

Meechum pointed to the sign in the window. "That," he said. "We ought to at least tell 'em they got the names wrong."

"Right," Willis said. "And while you are at it, you can tell them that we was in on the same robbery."

"What? Well, no, I wouldn't do anything like that," Meechum said. He thought for a moment. "Oh," he said. "Yeah, I guess I see what you mean. But it don't seem right that they got the names all wrong."

"What difference does it make whether they got the names wrong or not?" Willis asked. "They're dead and if you get the names right, they ain't goin' to be any less dead, are they?"

Meechum thought for a moment, then he chuckled. "No," he said. I don't reckon they will be any less dead."

"Then why don't you quit worryin' about it and let's go get us a beer," Willis said.

A long board of wooden pegs nailed along one wall of the Dry Gulch Saloon stood about six feet above the floor and provided a rack for hats and coats. A card game was in progress near the back. At one of the front tables, there was some earnest conversation. Three men stood at the bar, each complete within himself, concentrating only on his drink and private thoughts. A soiled dove, near the end of her professional effectiveness, overweight, with bad teeth and wild, unkempt hair, stood at the far end. She smiled at Willis and Meechum when they came in, but getting no encouragement, stayed put.

"What'll it be, gents?" the bartender asked, making a swipe across the bar with a sour-smelling cloth.

"Beer," Willis said.

"The same," Meechum added.

The bartender drew two mugs of beer, then sat them in front of Willis and Meechum. "I think you'll like this beer, it's made local."

"What do you mean, made local?"

"Why, we got us a beer man right here in this town," the bartender said. "A master brewer come here from St. Louis. You won't get no better beer anywhere in the country than this."

"Beer is beer," Willis said, taking a swallow.

"You boys just ridin' through?" he asked.

Willis stared back at him, but didn't answer.

"The reason I asked is, you might not know 'bout some of the excitement goin' on."

"What excitement?" Meechum asked.

"Stagecoach robbery excitement," the bartender replied. He chuckled, "That is, some fellers tried to rob the stagecoach, only all they got for it was killed."

"Yes, we saw the bodies in the front of the hardware store," Meechum said. "Do the folks in this town put ever' dead body you got on display like that?"

"No, nothin' like that," the bartender answered. "But you can't blame Mr. Prufrock none. You see, he has his undertakin' business in the back of the Sikes hardware store—Mr. Sikes, he rents the space out. And these three galoots, bein' outlaws and all, don't have nobody payin' to bury 'em except the town, so Prufrock puts 'em on display like that to advertise his business."

"Tell me, what was them fellas lookin' to get by

robbin' the stagecoach?" Willis asked. "Was the coach really carryin' money?"

"I reckon the passengers was carryin' money," the bartender said. "Don't know if the coach was."

"It was carryin' some money, but it wasn't carryin' near as much as it'll be carryin' next week," one of the men down at the end of the bar said.

Willis took a swallow of his beer, then looked toward the man who had just spoken.

"Why do you say that?" he asked.

"'Cause, there's a fella in town now by the name of Bixby. Jay Peerless Bixby. You ever heard of him?"

"Can't say as I have."

"Well, he's one rich son of a bitch from what I hear."

"Bartender, I see my friend here's mug is empty. Give him another beer," Willis said, pointing to the talkative man at the end of the bar.

"Be glad to," the bartender said. He retrieved the mug, filled it, then replaced it. "There you go, Mr. Deckert."

Deckert held the full mug up toward Willis and Meechum, as if toasting them.

"I thank you, Mister—"

"Tell me more about this man Jay Peerless Bixby," Willis said, without supplying his own name.

"Oh, he's a rich one all right," Deckert said. "He's come out here to buy ranch land and they say he wants to own the biggest ranch in the entire territory. Anyway, to do that he's going to have to have a lot of money transferred."

"How much money is a lot of money?"

Willis asked the question over the brim of his mug as he took another swallow.

"A lot," Deckert answered. "In fact, some folks say it'll be as much as forty, maybe fifty thousand dollars, and it'll be comin' into town by stagecoach."

"When?"

"Next week sometime, from what I hear. You seem uncommon interested in all this," Deckert said.

Willis laughed. "Maybe I'm plannin' to hold up the stagecoach."

"Yeah? Well if you do, I hope you have better luck than them three boys that just tried it."

"They was just particular unlucky is all," the bartender said. "They happened to try and rob the particular coach Matt Jensen was ridin' on."

"You got that right," Deckert said. "I know there was only one of him and three of the robbers—"

"Five if you count the two that got away," the bartender said, interrupting Deckert in mid-sentence.

"Five then," Deckert corrected. "But here's the point I was gettin' at. They was five stagecoach robbers and only one of Matt Jensen, which means the robbers was outnumbered." He laughed.

For a second or two, neither the bartender nor anyone else at the bar reacted.

"Don't you get it?" Deckert said. "They's only one of Matt Jensen and they's three—maybe more of the robbers, but I said they was outnumbered."

There was still no reaction.

"Because he's so good," Deckert explained in an exasperated tone of voice.

"Oh, I get it now," the bartender said, and he laughed out loud.

"So you see, friend, if you really are plannin' on holdin' up the coach, you might want to think about it again, lessen you run into this here Jensen fella."

"There you go, friend, you just talked me right out of it," Willis said, laughing and holding up his beer.

The others in the saloon laughed as well.

When the Dry Gulch closed its doors for the night, Willis and Meechum, not having enough money to waste on a hotel room, rode just outside of town where they bedded down in an arroyo beneath the huge dark slab of the McDowell Mountains.

"We goin' to try and rob that stagecoach, are we, Willis?" Meechum asked.

Willis shook his head. "No, I don't think so," he said.

"Good, 'cause to tell you the truth, I wasn't lookin' forward to something like that again. I think waitin' till the money gets here, then robbin' the bank that it's put into, will be a lot better."

"We ain't goin' to do that either."

"What do you mean we ain't goin' to do that? Ain't that what we come here for?"

"We come here to get money the best way we can," Willis said. He smiled. "We'll just wait around until this here Bixby fella takes the money out of the bank. It'll be a lot easier takin' the money from him than it would be robbin' a bank."

A big smile spread across Meechum's face.

"Yeah!" he said. "Yeah, I see what you mean."

"So, all we got to do is spend a week or so here without gettin' into any kind of trouble."

After Meechum spread out his blanket, he stepped a few feet away to relieve himself. As he stood there, urinating, he happened to look up just in time to see a falling star. Long ago, his pa had once told him that every time you see a falling star, it meant someone was about to die, and he wondered if it was an omen for his own fate.

He shivered.

Chapter Twenty

Picket Post Road

The next morning, the sun was a quarter of the way up in the east as the wagon lumbered along the road. Its transit was accompanied by a symphony of sound, from the footfalls of the mules to the jangle of the harness, the rattle of the connecting pins, and the squeak of one of the wheels.

The driver, a grizzled old man, spat a plug of tobacco, wiped the back of his hand across his mouth, then turned to the boy sitting next to him.

"Dewey, did you grease that right rear wheel like I told you?"

"Yes, sir, Mr. Malcolm, I done greased it just like you said," the twelve-year-old replied.

"Do you hear that?"

They quit talking for a moment, the silence interrupted by the incessant squeak and chirp of the right rear wheel.

"Yes, sir, I hear it," Dewey Calhoun admitted.

"It sure as hell don't sound like you greased it now,

does it?" Malcolm asked. "If that axle is worn flat when we get back, I'm goin' to be takin' it out of your pay to buy a new one."

"Well, I done it, just like you told me," Dewey said.

They drove on for a few more minutes, then Malcolm tensed. "Get out of the wagon, boy," he said.

"What?"

Malcolm reached for the shotgun that lay in the floor beneath his feet. "Get out of the wagon and run find yourself a place to hide," he said. "I just seen some Injuns and I don't think they're friendly."

"Mr. Malcolm, I can't leave you to—"

"Damn it to hell, boy, I said get out of the wagon!" Malcolm said harshly. "I don't intend to be worryin' none about no snot-nosed boy!"

"All right," Dewey said.

"Jump out here, then go down the side of the hill and head north. When you reach the Salt River, turn left, it'll take you to Phoenix. It's about eight miles, but you can make it. Take the canteen."

"But there's only one canteen," Dewey said.

"You'll be needin' it more'n me," Malcolm said, holding the canteen out. "Now, do what I told you."

"Yes, sir," Dewey said. Taking the canteen Malcolm handed him, Dewey jumped over the edge of the wagon, then started down the hill digging his heels into the dirt to stay upright, and sending rocks rolling down before him.

Malcolm looked back just long enough to see Dewey get out of sight. Then he picked up the double-barrel shotgun and held it across his lap. When he came around the curve, he saw four Indians in the road in front of him.

"White man, what do you have in the wagon?" one of them asked.

"What I have in this here wagon ain't none of your business," Malcolm replied. "Now, get out of my way if you don't want to get gut-shot."

"I think if you give us some of what you have in the wagon, we will let you pass," the Indian said.

"To hell with that!" Malcolm shouted. He brought the shotgun up and fired. The heavy blast opened up one Indian's chest and he fell from his horse. The other Indians returned fire and Malcolm was hit with three bullets.

A quarter of a mile away, as Dewey was still hurrying down the side of the mountain, he heard the gunshots, echoing and reechoing through the mountains. He breathed a quick prayer for the soul of his employer, because he knew, without having to see, that Mr. Malcolm had just been killed.

Phoenix

At the very moment young Dewey Calhoun was running for his life, Ken Hendel was sitting in the lobby of the Phoenix House Hotel reading the *Arizona Gazette*.

INDIANS RAID RANCH !

Three Killed.

A Gruesome Scene.

On Wednesday last, George Gunter gathered his newborn calves for branding in the expectation that Joe

Clark, a helpful and friendly neighbor, would come over to lend him a hand in this necessary task.

When no small amount of time had passed after the appointed hour and Mr. Clark had not arrived as they had arranged, Mr. Gunter rode over to Rancho Grande for the purpose of ascertaining the reason for his neighbor's tardiness. That was when he was greeted with a scene that is almost too horrible for the sensitivities of the readers of this newspaper.

Joe Clark was found on the ground outside his house, foully murdered. It was not difficult to determine the cause of death, as there was an arrow protruding from his back, as well as several bullet wounds. It was obvious by Mr. Clark's position that he was making a brave attempt to protect his wife and child. That courageous effort, despite Clark's intrepidity, was to no avail, however, as further exploration resulted in the discovery of Mrs. Clark and their young son, both dead, on the kitchen floor.

While this might appear to be the work of Geronimo, Agent Eugene Baker of the San Carlos Indian Reservation has advanced his opinion that the Indian most likely responsible for the atrocities at Rancho Grande is the Apache Delshay. If that is true, there is a reason why Delshay's malevolent deed resembles those perpetrated by Geronimo. According to Agent Baker,

Delshay was, but recently, a member of Geronimo's nefarious band, leaving the war trail to return only because of the impending birth of his son.

Agent Baker says that he has no idea why Delshay abandoned his peaceful residence at the reservation to, once again, take up the warpath.

"We treat our Indians with kindness, providing them with food and shelter. It defies all logic and understanding as to why some of them would leave a situation where all the necessities of life are furnished, in order to take up the warpath against the very whites who feed, clothe, shelter, and protect them."

"Ah, there you are, Hendel," Bixby said, coming down the stairs into the lobby. "Have you located a conveyance?"

"Yes, Mr. Bixby," Hendel said. "The Sundown Corral will provide a buckboard and team for a dollar-fifty."

"A dollar-fifty?" Bixby replied. "Did you tell them I will only be using it for half a day?"

"Yes, sir, I did. Otherwise, it would have been three dollars."

"Why, that is an outrage! An absolute outrage. Could you find nothing less expensive?"

"I shopped around," Hendel said. "That was the best offer I could find."

"Very well, if that is the absolute best offer, then it will have to do. I do resent, however, that they are taking advantage of me because I am a visitor to this desolate place."

. "I believe that is the price they charge everyone," Hendel replied.

"Of course you would believe that. You are very good with numbers, Hendel, but you are very naive when it comes to business."

"If you say so, Mr. Bixby."

Bixby didn't reply because he didn't quite know how to react to Hendel's response.

"Yes, well, Cynthia and I will be taking our lunch now. We'll leave first thing this afternoon. If Dan Conway shows up at the hotel looking for me, tell him I will meet with him tomorrow morning."

"I thought Mr. Conway was going with you."

"I decided I would rather look at the land myself first. I don't want Conway trying to influence me."

"Oh, Mr. Bixby, I don't know if that is such a good idea," Hendel said.

"What do you mean?"

"I mean it may not be wise for you and Mrs. Bixby to go out on your own. I'm not sure it's all that safe."

"Don't be ridiculous," Bixby said. "Safe from what?"

"Indians."

Bixby laughed. "Indians? Where did you get such an idea?"

Hendel showed Bixby the newspaper he had been reading. Bixby looked at it for a moment, then handed it back.

"Stuff and nonsense," he said. "That's just a story to sell newspapers. Obviously, it's some fool Indian who has gone off on his own. It isn't as if there is an Indian war going on."

"Still, I would feel better if you had someone

local with you. Someone who knows the geography and can keep you out of trouble."

"You don't worry about me," Bixby said. "I will be just fine. What I want you to do is to make certain that the transfer of funds between my bank and the local bank is going through all right."

"Yes, sir," Hendel said. Looking toward the stairs, Hendel saw Cynthia coming down into the lobby, and he stood quickly. "Good morning, Mrs. Bixby. My, what a pretty green dress you are wearing."

"Why, thank you very much for noticing, Mr. Hendel," Cynthia said, smiling prettily. "Isn't it a lovely day today?"

"Yes, it is indeed," Hendel replied.

"Jay and I are going to take our breakfast now," Cynthia said. "Won't you join us?"

"Hendel doesn't have time to join us," Bixby said, speaking before Hendel could answer. "I have given him a task to perform and it must be taken care of promptly."

"I'm afraid Mr. Bixby is correct," Hendel said. "I do have a task to perform that may keep me busy for the rest of the day."

"Oh, such a shame," Cynthia said. She smiled again. "Perhaps you can take you lunch with us when we return."

"I shall endeavor to do so," Hendel said.

"For crying out loud, Cynthia, you aren't arranging a social," Jay said. "We are out here on business, and Hendel is an employee, not a personal friend."

"On the contrary, Jay," Cynthia replied. "Mr. Hendel has been a close personal friend for more years than I have even known you."

"Nevertheless, he is a mere employee, and I do wish you would remember to keep things at that level. Now, come, we can't tarry here all day."

Maison Doree Restaurant

Five hundred dollars richer, due to his share of the bounty paid for the three would-be stagecoach robbers, Matt Jensen was enjoying his breakfast in the Maison Doree, advertised in the paper as: *"The finest restaurant in Phoenix—meals served with European flavor—a new French Chef in residence."*

He had just started on his omelet when he saw Bixby and his wife come in. Cynthia saw him and smiled broadly.

"Mr. Jensen, how nice to see you," she said. "I hope you are having a pleasant meal."

Matt stood. "Thank you, Mrs. Bixby, I am enjoying my meal," he said.

"Cynthia," Bixby said gruffly. "I told you not to speak to that man. Come." He led her to a table in the back of the room and Matt, smiling and shaking his head, sat back down to finish his breakfast.

"Jay, there was no need for you to be rude to Mr. Jensen," Cynthia said as the two of them sat at their table in the rear of the restaurant.

"I told you I didn't want you to have anything to do with him," Bixby said. "The man is a cold-blooded killer."

"Oh, don't be ridiculous," Cynthia said. "He had every right to shoot those robbers. In fact, I think he may have saved our lives."

"Regardless of what you think of his heroics, you

are to have nothing more to do with him. Do you understand me?"

"I understand," Cynthia said.

"Good. Now, eat quickly. I want to go out and get a good look at the land I'm going to buy, and I expect that will take the rest of the morning."

At the other end of town, Sheriff Williams sat at the desk in his office processing the papers that had authorized payment of the bounty for the three would-be stagecoach robbers.

"One thousand, five hundred dollars," he said aloud.

"What?" The response came from Norman Keith, who was serving three days for public drunkenness.

It wasn't the sheriff's policy to arrest everyone who got drunk, but Keith had a habit of getting drunk and urinating in public, thus becoming a regular in the Phoenix jail.

"I said one thousand, five hundred dollars," Sheriff Williams repeated. "That's how much bounty we just paid to Pinkie's widow and that Jensen fella for killin' the three stagecoach robbers. That's a lot of money."

"I agree, fifteen hundred dollars is a lot of money. But consider this, Sheriff. When one engages armed robbers to earn it, one should certainly be allowed to keep the fruits of such a hazardous enterprise," Keith said.

"I don't know. I have to do that—that hazardous enterprise you were talking about—all the time because it's my job," Sheriff Williams said. "And I only get thirty dollars a month for doin' it." He pulled his pistol, looked at it for a moment, then spun the cylinder. "I suppose I could always quit being a sheriff and become a bounty hunter," he said.

Keith laughed.

"What are you laughing at?"

"I'm laughing at the notion of you being a bounty hunter," he said. "Come on, Bob, could you see your wife letting you do that? You aren't a bounty hunter, you're a sheriff. And I'll admit that you are a pretty good sheriff, but that's all you will ever be."

Williams laughed as well. "Oh, my, and comin' from the town drunk, I reckon I should be all worried about that," he said.

"I guess you got me there," Kieth said. "Only, just remember, I haven't always been a drunk."

Norman Keith was right, he hadn't always been a drunk. At one time he was an English professor at Tempe Normal, but a fire in his campus home had taken the life of his wife and two small children. Unable to cope with the grief, Keith had abandoned academia and begun drinking.

At the Sundown Corral and Equipage Company, Ken Hendel stood waiting beside the rig he had rented for Jay Peerless Bixby. When he saw them coming up the street from the restaurant, he stepped out to meet them.

"I have the buckboard here for you, Mr. Bixby."

"Were you able to talk them down any more?" Bixby asked.

"No, sir. It cost us a dollar-fifty."

"Very well, if we have to pay it we have to pay it," Bixby said. Without regard to Cynthia, Bixby climbed into the buckboard. Hendel offered his hand to help Cynthia into her seat.

"Thank you, Mr. Hendel," Cynthia said.

"Have you made the arrangement with the bank yet?" Bixby asked.

"I was there this morning. They are expecting the transfer of money on today's stagecoach."

"Well, stay on it," Bixby said, snapping the reins against the team.

"Yes, sir," Hendel said, stepping back quickly to avoid having his toes run over by the carriage.

Chapter Twenty-one

It was nearly noon when a bedraggled and exhausted Dewey Calhoun pushed open the door of the sheriff's office.

"Sheriff Williams! Sheriff Williams!" he called.

"I'm Sheriff Williams, what can I do for you?"

"It's Injuns, Sheriff," Dewey said. "I think they killed Mr. Malcolm."

"Are you talking about Pete Malcolm, the man that runs a freight service out of Picket Post?" Keith asked.

"Yes, sir, that's the one I'm talkin' about."

"Do you know him, Keith?"

"Yes," Keith said. "You know him, too, Bob. He's the one hauled in most of the material that was used to build the college."

"Oh, yes, I remember him."

"He's a good man," Keith said.

"Yes, sir, he was a good man. But more'n likely, he got hisself kilt savin' me," Dewey said.

"You say it was Injuns that killed him?" Williams asked. "Where did this happen?"

"It was on the Picket Post Road," Dewey answered. "Me 'n' Mr. Malcolm, we was bringin' a load a salt-peter to the Maricopa Chemical Company when the Apaches attacked us."

"Saltpeter?" Keith asked.

"Yes, sir."

"Damn, that isn't good," Keith said. "You put salt-peter with sulphur and charcoal and you can make gunpowder."

"I doubt the Injuns have enough sense to know how to use it," Williams said.

"Don't be selling the Indians short, Bob. I've known some that were very intelligent," Keith said. "What's your name, boy?"

"Dewey Calhoun."

"How'd you get away, Dewey?"

"Mr. Malcolm, he seen the Apaches before they attacked and he give me the canteen and told me to run. That's what I done, and that's how come I'm here."

"How do you know Pete is dead?" Keith asked from behind the bars. "Did you see the Indians kill him?"

"No sir, I didn't actual see it, but I heered it."

"What do you mean you heard it?" Williams asked.

"I heered Mr. Malcolm's shotgun go off—then I heered a lot more shots after that."

Sheriff Williams stroked his chin and nodded. "Yeah," he said. "Yeah, I'd say that's a pretty good sign he was killed all right." Williams walked over to take his hat off a hook. He also took down the ring of keys, then came back to open the door to Keith's cell.

"You aren't supposed to be let out till after lunch," the sheriff said. "But I may not be back by then, so

I'm lettin' you out now. And next time you have to take a pee, for heaven's sake, Keith, go out into the alley or some such place."

"I always do—when I'm sober," Keith said. "And I thank you for your kindness in letting me out half an hour early."

"Yeah, well, it also saves the county the money for buyin' your lunch," Sheriff Williams said. "Dewey, come with me, we'll go find Marshal Gilmore. This is more his jurisdiction than it is mine."

"Could I get me a drink of water first?" Dewey asked. "I drunk up all the canteen while I was walkin' here."

"Sure you can, boy," Sheriff Williams said. "There's a bucket and dipper back there against the wall."

Dewey hurried back to the water bucket and scooped out a dipper full. Turning it up to his lips, he drank deeply, letting the water run down both sides of his lips as he did so.

"Easy, boy, easy," Keith said as he stepped out of the jail cell. "You drink that too fast, you'll make yourself sick."

"Yes, sir, I know," Dewey said. "But I'm powerful thirsty."

Sheriff Williams found U.S. Marshal Gilmore having his lunch in Miller's Café.

"Marshal, this here is Dewey Calhoun. He came into the office a while ago tellin' a story about being attacked by Injuns. And seeing as dealing with Indians is more a federal thing than county, I figured we should, more than likely, bring you in on it."

"Where did this happen?" Marshal Gilmore asked.

"Out on the Picket Post Road," Dewey said.

"He was on a wagon, Marshal, and get this. The wagon was carryin' saltpeter. You know what that's used for, don't you?"

"Yes, I know."

"It's used for makin' gunpowder," Williams said, not to be denied showing his knowledge.

"Have you had your lunch, boy?" Marshal Gilmore asked.

"No, sir, it got left back on the wagon," Dewey said.

"Faye," the marshal called. "Bring the boy your blue plate lunch special."

"Sure thing, Marshal," a middle-aged woman answered.

"Now, boy, tell me all about it," Marshal Gilmore said.

On the trail with Bixby and Cynthia

The rig Bixby rented had been on the trail for the better part of the morning. The day had started out warm, and was now hot. As the steel-rimmed wheels rolled across the hard-packed earth, they picked up dirt, causing a rooster tail of dust to stream out behind them. The wood of the buckboard was bleached white, and under the sun it gave off a rather pungent smell. As Bixby drove the team, Cynthia sat in the sun on the dried seat of the wagon, looking at the map Bixby had given her.

"Do you see anything familiar?" Bixby asked.

"That obelisk over there has to be Weaver's

Needle," Cynthia said, pointing to the tall rock column. "And if it is, then we are right here."

"Why this—this is nothing more than desert," Bixby said. "I was led to believe I would be buying land that could easily be made into a ranch. How can one make a ranch of desert land? Are you certain of where we are?"

"You can look at the map," Cynthia said, handing it to him. "Perhaps you will read it differently."

Bixby studied the map for a moment, then sighed. "No," he said. "You are right. This is the property I was to buy. But no more. I will not be bamboozled. As soon as we return to Phoenix, I will stop the sale and we will return to New York."

Suddenly there was a creaking, snapping sound, and the buckboard lurched so badly that Cynthia was very nearly tossed out. She looked up from the map.

"Oh!" she gasped in a startled tone of voice. "What was that?"

"Whoa, horses," Bixby called, pulling back on the reins. The team stopped and the buckboard sat there, listing sharply to the right.

"Jay, what is it?" Cynthia asked. "What is wrong?"

"Oh, this is just too much," Bixby said. "I believe we have broken an axle."

"Can you fix it?" Cynthia asked.

"Now how can I fix it?" Bixby replied. "What do you take me for? A common tradesman? Oh, to provide customers with a conveyance that breaks down on you the first time you take it out is unconscionable."

Cynthia climbed down from the listing buckboard.

"Don't tell me you think you can fix it," Bixby said.

"No, I can't fix it. But we can't just stay here."

"What do you propose that we do?"

"I think we should start walking back."

"Walking? Walking where? All the way back to Phoenix?"

"If necessary, yes, all the way to Phoenix," Cynthia said. "But I believe Mr. Hendel will notice the lateness of our return, and will arrange for someone to come and collect us."

"You have more confidence in him than I do," Bixby said. "I doubt seriously that he will have the presence of mind to notice that we are late."

"You underestimate Mr. Hendel," Cynthia said. "I find him to be a very clever person. He is also very loyal and dependable."

"No doubt you should have married him, rather than me," Bixby said.

Cynthia did not respond, but Bixby was too self-centered to notice.

Superstition Mountain

Approximately five miles from where Cynthia and Bixby abandoned the buckboard, six men were prospecting at the foot of Superstition Mountain. They were used to working alone, but with the recent outbreak of Indian trouble, they decided it would be safer to prospect together. The little valley where they were working rang with the sound of their hammers as they chipped away at the hard rock, looking for "color."

"Listen," one of them said. He held up his hand. "Stop the hammerin' for a minute, will you?"

"What is it, Mickey?" one of the others asked. "I don't hear nothin'."

"Listen," Mickey said again.

All six were quiet for a moment, with the only sound the ever-present mournful wail of the wind through the rocks and peaks. Then, they all heard what Mickey had heard, the distant thunder of pounding hooves.

"Better get to your guns, boys," Mickey said. "We've got company comin', and I don't think it's anyone we want."

The battle was short and violent. Delshay moved in and out of gulleys, shouting with joy as he led the fight. The prospectors were all armed and they fired at him, but he was much too nimble to present an easy target for them, and not one bullet found its mark.

Within a short time after the initial attack, all six miners had fallen mortally wounded, and Delshay stuck both arms in the air, leaned his head back, and gave a loud shout of victory. The warriors who were with him, not one of whom had been wounded, shouted as well.

Delshay and the others went through the prospectors' camp, taking everything that was of any value— guns, knives, cooking utensils. One of them took a compass, and though none of the Indians had ever seen anything like it before, they were intrigued by the way the arrow always seemed to point toward the McDowell Mountains. They discussed the possibility of the compass being some sort of omen, and decided to smash it on the rocks.

On the road with Bixby and Cynthia

"What was that?" Cynthia asked.

The two were walking west on the same road over which they had come, and Bixby was now breathing hard with the effort.

"What was what?" he asked, panting.

"That sound," Cynthia said. "Didn't you hear it?"

"I haven't heard anything except the eternal and infernal howl of wind. What do you think you heard?"

"I don't know," Cynthia confessed. "It sounded like several pops." She laughed. "Rather like the sound popcorn makes when it is popping."

"Your imagination is working overtime," Bixby said. "Perhaps you are hearing the Mountain God. What did Hendel say the Indians call him?"

"Usen," Cynthia said.

"Usen, yes. Perhaps Usen is popping corn."

Cynthia laughed. "Why, Jay, you do have a sense of humor," she said. "I am surprised."

"I meant it as sarcasm, my dear, not as humor," Bixby said. "Oh, why did I ever think I might want to live out here?"

"But all you have to do is look around to answer that question," Cynthia said. "Why, I think it is beautiful out here. See the way the sun plays upon the mountains? And look at all the different colors it displays. It is magnificent."

"Only a fool could see beauty in this wild, trackless land," Bixby said bitterly.

Suddenly, over a ridge just before them, ten Indians appeared. The Indians drew back quickly, as surprised to see Bixby and Cynthia as *they* were to see the Indians.

"Oh, my God! Indians!" Bixby shouted in sudden panic.

Delshay held up his hand to stop the others and, for a long moment, the ten Indians just sat their mounts, looking at the strange sight of a white man and a white woman walking along the road all alone. Neither Delshay nor any of his men made a sound.

"Please, please, don't kill me! Don't kill me!" Bixby pleaded. Putting his hands on Cynthia's shoulders, he shoved her forward.

"Take her!" he said. "Do you see how beautiful she is? I know that Indians like white women. Take her, I give her to you!"

"Jay! What are you doing?" Cynthia asked, shocked by her husband's action.

"Kill him," Delshay said, pointing to the white man.

One of Delshay's men raised his club and started toward Bixby. He stopped when he saw the front of Bixby's pants suddenly grow wet. Realizing what had just happened, he laughed and pointed, then spoke in Apache.

"Look! The white man is so afraid that he has wet his pants!"

The others laughed and Bixby, realizing that the laughter was at his expense, began shaking and weeping.

"Wait," Delshay said. "Do not kill him."

The warrior who had started forward stopped.

"White man," Delshay said in English. "Would you give your woman to us to spare your life?"

"Yes! Yes!" Bixby said, nodding fiercely. "You can have her! I give her to you."

Delshay pointed to the west, in the same direction that the white man and the white woman had been walking. "Go," he said. "I will not kill you."

"Thank you, thank you," Bixby said. He looked at Cynthia for a long moment, his expression a mixture of fear, shame, and guilt. "Cynthia, I—I am sorry," he said.

Bixby started walking west, but the walk quickly turned into a run as he hurried to get away from them before the leader of the Indians changed his mind.

Cynthia watched Bixby leave; then she turned to look into the face of the leader.

Perhaps it was shock, the shock of the attack, of seeing Bixby dissolve in panic, or of realizing that he had just traded her life for his. Whatever it was, it took away all her own fear.

One of the Indians pointed to her.

"I claim this woman as mine," a warrior named Nalyudi, or He Runs About, said, though as he was speaking in his own language, Cynthia had no idea what he was saying.

"No, she will not be anyone's woman," Delshay replied, speaking in English. Then he added in his own language, "She is a woman with powerful medicine. We will honor that medicine."

"She has no medicine," Nalyudi said.

"She has not shown fear," Delshay said.

"She will show fear of me," Nalyudi said. Nalyudi was an anomaly among the Apache. While most

Apache were relatively short, Nalyudi was well over six feet tall and was powerfully built.

"No, I think not. I think Mountain Lion Woman is without fear in her eyes."

"Mountain Lion Woman?" Nalyudi asked. "You have given this white woman a name?"

"Yes,"

"I do not believe her medicine is strong enough for you to give her such a name," Nalyudi said. "I will prove to you that she fears me. Then I will claim her as my woman."

"She will show no fear," Delshay said.

Nalyudi raised his war club, and he let out a menacing, bloodcurdling yell.

Cynthia was resigned to dying now, thinking that it might even be preferable to being a prisoner of the Indians. Because of that, the strange, almost numbing calmness that had come over her before was still present. She showed no fear.

"Nalyudi," Delshay said in English. "Do you agree now that her medicine is strong?"

"Arrrghhh!" Nalyudi shouted in anger and frustration. He turned away from her.

"Come," Delshay said to Cynthia, speaking in English. "You will not be harmed."

"What is your name?" Cynthia asked.

"It is not the way of the Apache to give their name to everyone," Delshay replied. "We give our name only to trusted friends and respected enemies. But I will tell you that my name is Delshay."

"Delshay, I thank you for not killing my husband," Cynthia said.

"You are a strange woman," Delshay said. "You

thank me for not killing your husband, but you do not thank me for not killing you."

"I do not thank you, because my life is still in your hands," Cynthia said.

"Uhn," Delshay replied, nodding. "You are a wise woman. But do not thank me for letting your man live. Though he lives today, your man is a coward, and he will die many times."

"Cowards die many times before their deaths. The valiant never taste of death but once," Cynthia said.

"You know of this, Mountain Lion Woman?"

"Yes. It is something Shakespeare said."

"Your friend Shakespeare is a wise man," Delshay said.

A couple of the Indians took Cynthia gently and led her to a horse, then helped her to mount. Although none of the horses the Indians were riding had a saddle, this was one of six horses that were saddled, and she wondered where they came from and how the Indians happened to have them.

As she mounted, she saw the angry look that the one Delshay had called Nalyudi was giving her. While she had not understood the conversation in which he'd tried to claim her as his woman, she did know that she had made him very angry. What she did not realize was that her action had caused Nalyudi to lose face before the other warriors. And she did not realize what a mortal enemy she had just made.

Chapter Twenty-two

Matt had drawn two queens and an ace. He discarded two cards.

"Two for Mr. Jensen," the dealer said. "Three for the good doctor, one for Mr. Hanlon, and the dealer will stand pat."

"Whoa, Paul, do you actually have something, or are you trying to run a bluff?" Dr. Presnell said.

"My dear fellow," the dealer, Paul Pinkstaff, said. "I never run a bluff."

Matt was playing poker with three new friends he had met in the Dry Gulch Saloon, and they all laughed at Pinkstaff's declaration.

"I know you haven't been here long," Dr. Presnell said to Matt. "But you have just heard what can best be described as a whopper. Paul runs bluffs all the time."

"Those are the ones you need to look out for," Matt said. "You never can tell when they may actually have something."

"Mr. Jensen is a smart man," Pinkstaff said. "I suggest you listen to him. Dealer bets two dollars."

Matt picked up his cards, but his pair of queens wasn't improved. He called, and when Hanlon raised the bet by a dollar, the dealer dropped out, to the whoops and laughter of the others around the table.

Matt called, though he didn't feel good about it. As it turned out, he was right. Hanlon won the hand with three sevens. Matt had been playing for an hour and was down by about ten dollars.

"Mr. Jensen, I will say this for you," Hanlon said as he drew in the pot. "You do lose graciously."

"Whether you are gracious or angry, you are out the same amount of money," Matt said. "So little is gained by being angry."

"You are not only gracious, you are smart," Hanlon said.

"Matt?"

Looking up, Matt saw Sheriff Williams approaching the table.

"Yes, Sheriff?"

"I wonder if you would mind coming down to the office with me. Marshal Gilmore and I have a favor to ask of you."

"Be glad to," Matt said. "If I stay here any longer, I'll wind up losing even more money."

Matt picked up the money that was in front of his chair, then followed the sheriff down to his office. There, he was introduced to Marshal Gilmore and a boy of about twelve, who was identified as Dewey Calhoun.

"Mr. Jensen, are you the same Matt Jensen who rode scout for General Crook several months back?"

"Yes," Matt said.

"Good, I was hoping you were. We've got a little situation here that I'm hoping you can help with."

"I'll be glad to do what I can."

"Son, tell Mr. Jensen what you told us," Marshal Gilmore said to the twelve-year-old boy.

Dewey repeated his story of being out on the Picket Post Road when they encountered Indians. He concluded by telling of hearing the gunfire.

"Did you go back to see whether or not Malcolm was dead or alive?" Matt asked.

"Oh! No, sir," Dewey said with a quick intake of breath. "I should have, shouldn't I? I'm sorry, it's just that I was so scared."

"Don't be sorry," Matt said. "More than likely he wasn't alive, and it wouldn't have done him any good if you had gone back. In fact, it might have just put you in more danger."

"Mr. Jensen, I was wondering if you would let me deputize you while we go out to look for Malcolm," Gilmore said.

Matt shook his head. "No need to deputize me," he said. "I'll just go with you as a private citizen."

"Sheriff! Sheriff!" someone called coming in through the front door at that moment. Seeing Matt, Hendel stopped.

"Hello, Mr. Hendel," Matt said.

"Mr. Jensen, oh, I am so very glad to see you here."

"You know this fella, do you, Jensen?" Sheriff Williams asked.

"Yes, we came out together on the train and then on the coach. He works for Mr. Bixby."

"Oh, yes, the man who is going to own the biggest ranch in Arizona," Sheriff Williams said, his voice disclosing a bit of derision.

"What brings you to the sheriff's office, Mr. Hendel?" Matt asked.

"It's Mrs. Bixby," Hendel said. Then quickly he corrected himself. "Of course, I mean Mr. and Mrs. Bixby," he said.

"What about them?"

"They are missing," Hendel said. "They rode out just after breakfast. I was certain they would be back by now, but they still haven't returned."

"Rode out?" Sheriff Williams asked. "What do you mean by 'rode out'?"

"They rented a rig from the livery and rode out on Picket Post Road to look over land that Mr. Bixby intends to buy," Hendel explained.

"Picket Post Road? That's not good," Sheriff Williams said.

"What do you mean 'That's not good'? Is there something about Picket Post Road that I should know?"

"There's been some Indian trouble along Picket Post," Sheriff Williams said.

"Oh, God in heaven," Hendel gasped, putting his hand over his chest. "Something has happened to her—uh, them," he corrected. "I just know it."

"We're about to go out and take a look," Matt said. "I'll make a special effort to find her."

"I'm going with you."

"Mr. Hendel, that might not be such a good

idea," Matt said. "There's going to be some hard riding ahead of us and—no disrespect intended—the last thing I will need is to have to have someone slow me on the trail."

"Mr. Jensen, I am quite capable of sitting a horse, sir," Hendel replied, his tone petulant.

Matt laughed and held his hand out. "You have convinced me, Mr. Hendel. I'd be glad to have you come along."

"Thank you," Hendel said.

Cynthia mounted the horse they brought for her, and rode with the Indians back to a small encampment. Riding a horse was not a routine thing for a young woman from the city of New York, but she had taken riding lessons and it was something that she had always enjoyed. She was thankful for that, because her skill as an equestrian was serving her well now.

After riding hard for about an hour, they reached an Indian encampment, consisting of about fifteen or so structures. The encampment surprised her, because she thought all the Indians were on large and well-controlled reservations. This small village, if that was what it could properly be called, consisted of no more than a few small, temporary-looking structures. Two of the Indians took her into one of them, where they pushed her down onto the ground, then left her alone.

For some strange reason, she found being left alone to be more frightening than when she was in the midst of them. She sat there, wondering what was gong to happen to her. The shock that had allowed her to take her fate so calmly before was now wearing off and she felt the fear building. But if, as Delshay had suggested, it was her lack of fear that had kept her alive before, she knew that she could not give in to the cold terror that was beginning to overtake her.

After she sat alone for almost an hour, the Indian who had identified himself as Delshay stepped into the little structure. This was the Indian who had spared Jay's life—the one with whom she had discussed Shakespeare. It was odd that he had actually quoted Shakespeare, while knowing nothing about the writer her English teacher had called "the Great Bard."

Despite the relative youth of the Indian, there was about him an aura of dignity and authority.

"What is your white man name?" Delshay asked.

"My name is Cynthia."

"Now you have an Indian name."

"Yes, Mountain Lion Woman," Cynthia said.

"Nalyudi does not approve of your name," Delshay said.

"Nalyudi? Is that the big one?"

"Yes."

"He has become my enemy, hasn't he?"

"Yes."

"Why? I have done nothing to him."

"He wants to take you as his woman," Delshay replied. "But I have forbidden it."

"You have forbidden it?"

"Yes."

"Are you a chief, Delshay?"

"For some, I am a chief," Delshay answered. "I am not a chief of the people who stay on the reservation."

"If you are a chief, then you can tell me why I am a prisoner."

"You are a prisoner because you were not killed. Would you prefer death?"

"I would prefer to be free," she said. "You are a chief. Your people must do what you say. Order them to set me free."

Delshay shook his head. "I think, for now, I must keep you as a prisoner," he said.

"But why would you want to keep me prisoner? I am of no value to anyone."

"You have value to the white man."

"Ha," Cynthia said with a bitter laugh. "You saw how much value I had to my husband."

"Your husband is a coward and a fool," Delshay said.

"Do not be so hard on him," Cynthia said. "He was afraid."

Matt, Ken Hendel, Marshal Gilmore, and Sheriff Williams found Bixby on the road less than four miles from Phoenix. He was bruised and his clothes were torn and dirty, the result of his having fallen several times. He had been running, and he was out of breath, and his face was red.

"Oh, thank God!" he said when saw the four riders coming toward him. "You have come to save me! I knew you would!"

"Where is Cynthia?" Hendel asked. It did not

escape Matt's notice that he called her by her first name.

"Water!" Bixby said. "Please, give me water!"

Sheriff Williams handed Bixby his canteen and Bixby turned it up to his lips, then drank long and deep.

"Mr. Bixby, where is Cynthia?" Hendel asked again, more forcefully this time than before.

"They took her," Bixby said. "The Indians took her."

"How did you get away from them?" Marshal Gilmore asked.

"The axle broke on the buckboard we had rented, leaving us afoot. The Indians came upon us shortly after that. I fought them," Bixby said. "I fought hard, but they captured us. Later, I managed to get away. I tried to save Cynthia as well, but I couldn't, so I figured that the best thing to do would be to come back here for help."

"That was probably the best thing for you to do," Sheriff Williams said. "If you had gone back a second time to try and save her, you would have gotten yourself killed, and maybe her as well."

"Yes, yes," Bixby said, shaking his head. "That's exactly what I was thinking. I see you brought no conveyance. Hendel, I shall require you to return to that accursed corral and secure another buckboard. But, as the first one broke down, I refuse to pay another cent for the replacement."

"Mr. Bixby, you are within easy walking distance of town," Hendel said. "I really feel that I should go with these men to look for Mrs. Bixby."

"Nonsense. You are in my employ, your obligation is to me. Now I am directing you to return to Phoenix, rent a conveyance of some sort, and return for me. If you do not do that, you may consider your employment terminated."

Matt could tell by the expression on Hendel's face that he was about to tell Bixby what he could do with his job. But because he didn't want Hendel to act hastily, he spoke up.

"Ken, if she is still there, we will find her," he said. "I promise you, I'll let you know what is going on. Why don't you do as Bixby says."

Hendel took a deep breath, then nodded. "Very well," he said. "Mr. Bixby, I shall be back within the hour."

"Leave me your canteen," Bixby said.

Hendel took his canteen and handed it down to him.

"Mr. Jensen," Bixby said as he took the canteen from Hendel. "I find it odd that you say you will keep Hendel posted instead of me. She is my wife, after all."

"Of course I will keep you posted, Bixby," Matt said.

Chapter Twenty-three

Phoenix

It was after dark when Matt and the others returned to Phoenix. Matt went to the hotel, intending to give his report to Bixby and Hendel, but when he stepped into the lobby, the clerk called to him.

"Mr. Jensen?"

Matt, who was carrying his .44-40 Winchester in his left hand and his saddlebags across his shoulders, walked over to the front desk.

"Hello, Mr. Peters," Matt said.

"Did you find Mrs. Bixby?" Peters asked.

"No."

"That's too bad."

"I'm just about to give the report to Bixby and Hendel. Do you know if they are in their rooms?"

"No sir, they are not," Peters replied. "Mr. Hendel told me to tell you when you came back that he and Bixby are taking their supper over at the Maison Doree Restaurant."

"Thanks," Matt said. He held up his rifle. "I'll just get rid of a few things, wash up a bit, then join them."

Maison Doree Restaurant

Hendel and Bixby were sitting at a table near the back wall. Hendel was drinking a cup of coffee, which was the only thing in front of him. Bixby had a full plate of food, which he was attacking with some gusto. When Hendel saw Matt approaching the table, he got a quick look of apprehension.

"Did you find her?" Hendel asked.

"No, I didn't."

"Oh," Hendel said, the word coming out like a slow hiss of steam.

"I didn't think you would," Bixby said. He picked up a knife and started spreading butter on a biscuit. "More than likely, she is dead and buried."

"You don't seem terribly troubled by that," Matt said.

Bixby used the knife as a pointer, pointing to Matt as he spoke.

"Who are you to judge me?" he said. "Don't forget, Jensen, I've seen you in operation. I saw how you killed three men in cold blood and now, because I am too civilized and, I might add, controlled to sit here wailing and gnashing my teeth over the prospect of my wife being killed by wild Indians, you think I am a man with no feelings."

"She's not dead," Matt said.

"I mean, when I escaped from them, I knew the chances were—"

"She's not dead," Matt said again, interrupting Bixby in mid-sentence.

"Oh, thank God!" Hendel said.

"How do you know she's not dead?"

"Because we didn't find her."

"If she's dead and buried, you aren't likely to find her."

"The Apache don't bury their dead—at least, not in the sense that you think of being buried. They put their dead in natural tombs—caves—depressions in the sides of mountains—then cover them with rocks. But that is an honor that they only do with their own. If they had killed Mrs. Bixby, we would have found her body—just as we found the bodies of Mr. Malcolm and the six miners that were killed."

"Oh," Hendel said. "Here I was being happy that you did not find Mrs. Bixby's body, while you did find seven others. That was terribly insensitive of me."

"No, it wasn't," Matt said. "It is only natural that you would be concerned more about Mrs. Bixby than the others."

"You are sure that Cynthia is still alive?" Bixby said.

"I'm reasonably sure, yes," Matt said. "If they didn't kill her when they first captured the two of you, then in all probability she will still be alive."

"What will they do with her?"

"They'll make her their prisoner."

"No, you don't understand the question. What will they do with her?" Bixby asked. "Will they— uh—will they—"

"Are you asking if they will rape her?" Matt asked.

"Yes."

Matt shook his head. "I doubt it."

"You doubt it? But you don't really know, right?"

"There is a possibility they could force her into marrying one of the warriors," Matt said. "Maybe even Delshay himself, since his own wife and children were murdered by whites. But that's not the same thing as rape."

"I'd like to know what that is if it isn't rape," Bixby said. "In your own words, you said she would be forced to marry Delshay."

"The Indians have a very strong sense of honor," Matt said. "We may have a difficult time understanding their sense of honor, given that they have done some terrible things, such as raiding ranches and killing entire families. But forcible rape would not be an honorable thing. Marriage, on the other hand, is honorable, even if it is forced upon the woman."

"So you are saying my wife might be forced into a marriage, but it is all right because that would be honorable," Bixby said.

"No, I'm not saying it would be all right," Matt said. "I'm just trying to give you a look at their sense of honor. However, I don't think it is anything you need to worry about right now. As she was just captured, and they know you are still alive, a forced marriage would not be something they would do right away. Here is that word honor again, but the Indians respect an honorable enemy, and that the fact that you were captured, but had the skill and courage to escape, will extend over to the way they will treat Mrs. Bixby."

"What do we do now?" Hendel asked.

"There is nothing more I can do tonight," Matt

said. "But tomorrow, I will gather what supplies I need. Then I'm going after her."

"I will go with you," Hendel said.

Matt held out his hand. "Please, no," he said. "I know you mean well, and I don't mean to denigrate whatever contribution you might make, but the more people there are out there, beating the brush to find her, the less likely I am to succeed. It would be a little like putting a bell on the collar of a cat, if you understand my meaning."

"Yes, I understand. I would very much like to go with you, but if you feel the chances are better for finding her if you are alone, then I will gladly stay behind."

"You are a good man, Mr. Hendel."

"I'm going to have some dessert," Bixby said. "What about you, Jensen, could I treat you to dinner? Dessert perhaps?"

"No, thank you," Matt replied. "I'll need to get some things together tonight, if I'm going out after your wife tomorrow."

Shortly after Delshay left, Cynthia looked around and saw that there was a bed of sorts, made from animal hides. She moved over to lie on it, surprised by how soft and comfortable it was. Before she realized it, she had fallen asleep.

When she awakened sometime later, even before she opened her eyes, she was aware of someone near. When she looked up, she saw an Indian standing over here. She recognized him as one of the ones who had captured her, and also as one of the ones who had helped her to her horse.

"You have rested, Mountain Lion Woman?" the Indian asked. His English was exceptionally good.

"My real name is Cynthia Bixby."

"That is your white man name," the Indian said. "But now your real name is Mountain Lion Woman."

"Mountain Lion Woman," Cynthia repeated.

The Indian squatted down to place a wooden bowl and a wooden plate beside her. There was water in the bowl, and some sort of meat on the plate.

"Eat," he said.

"Thank you," Cynthia said. She reached for the piece of meat, picked it up, and raised it to her mouth, then hesitated just before taking a bite.

The Indian, realizing that Cynthia was afraid to eat, smiled at her hesitation, then reached for the piece of meat and took a bite.

"Eat," the Indian said. "You will like it. It is very good. I cooked it myself."

"What is your name?" Cynthia asked.

"I am called Chandeisi. It means Broken Nose." Even as he explained the name, he ran his fingers across a nose that Cynthia could see was misshapen.

"You speak English very well."

"I attended the white man's school when I was a child," Chandeisi explained.

"Then you have an education? How wonderful," Cynthia said.

"I went to the white man's school," Chandeisi said. "I know the capitals of all the states. I know how to add and subtract, but what good is that for someone who has left the reservation to go on the warpath?"

"Why did you leave the reservation?"

"I left the reservation because the white men killed my wife and children, and killed Delshay's wife and children," Chandeisi said with a sense of bitterness in his voice. "I left the reservation with Delshay and the others."

"Oh, I'm so sorry," Cynthia said.

"It is all right. You did not know."

"What is this thing called?" Cynthia asked, taking in the structure with a broad wave of her arm. "This—house."

"It is called a wickiup," Chandeisi explained.

Cynthia looked toward the opening of the wickiup. "May I look outside?"

"Yes."

When Cynthia looked outside, she saw no one.

"Where did the others go?" Cynthia asked.

"They have gone to make medicine."

"Medicine? What kind of a medicine do they make?"

Chandeisi laughed. "It's not *a* medicine, it is simply medicine," he said. "It is hard for white people to understand, but it is something the warriors do before they go to battle. A powerful medicine gives them strength and courage."

"You are a warrior, but you did not go with them."

"No. I did not go."

"Why not?"

"Delshay asked me to stay here with you."

"To keep me from running away?":

"Yes. And to keep Nalyudi away."

Chapter Twenty-four

Phoenix

With Spirit saddled, Matt led him down the street no more than half a block, then tied him off in front of Donavan's General Store. Going inside, he stepped up to the long counter that separated the customers from the groceries that were on the shelves.

"You're Matt Jensen, aren't you?" Donavan said.

"Yes," Matt said.

"I thought as much. I seen you down at the stage depot when you come in after you shot them stagecoach robbers. What can I do for you, Mr. Jensen?"

"I need a few things for traveling," Matt said. "Some coffee, bacon, dry beans, flour, lard—"

"Ha! You would be goin' after that ten thousand dollars now, wouldn't you? Yes, sir, I figured you would. I told the missus you'd be doin' that."

Matt was surprised by the store owner's comment.

"What ten thousand dollars are you talking about?" Matt asked.

"Why, the ten-thousand-dollar reward Jay Peerless

Bixby is offerin' to anyone that can find his wife and bring her back to him. That is what you're doin', ain't it?"

"No."

"You ain't goin' to look for that woman?"

"Well, yes, I'm going to look for Mrs. Bixby all right. But not because of the reward. I didn't know there was such a reward," Matt said.

"You must be the only one in town who don't know," Donavan said. "I hear tell Bixby woke up Elvis Blanton over at the newspaper at six o'clock this mornin' and had him print up a bunch of flyers. Then he hired a couple of men to post the flyers all over the county. You mean to tell me you ain't seen none of those flyers?"

Matt shook his head. "No," he said, "I haven't."

"Well, walk over there to the table and pick one of them up," Donavan said. "He's got them things posted on ever' fence and tree and in ever' store, saloon, and buildin' in Phoenix. All over the county by now."

Matt walked over to the table Donavan had pointed out, then saw a stack of paper about two inches high. He took the top page off and looked at it.

REWARD!

$10,000 DOLLARS CASH

To be paid to whoever finds
CYNTHIA BIXBY
And returns her safely

Reward offered by Jay Peerless Bixby.
Inquire at Phoenix House Hotel in Phoenix.

Taking one of the flyers with him, Matt started back to the hotel, intending to have a few words with Bixby. He didn't have to go all the way back to the hotel, though, because he saw Bixby standing on the front porch of Sikes' Hardware, talking to a crowd of men who had gathered in the street in front of the store. Bixby was holding up a piece of paper.

"This piece of paper says that I have drawn a draft at the local bank to put ten thousand dollars into an escrow account to be paid to anyone who can locate and return my wife to me."

"Mister, ten thousand dollars don't do you no good if you are dead," one from the crowd shouted.

"What do you mean?"

"If what I'm hearin' is right, then it is more than likely that your wife was took by Delshay," the man said. "Maybe you don't know it but yesterday, the same day he took your wife, he kilt seven men. He's also raided and kilt ever'body at two different ranches. It's a miracle he let you live and—"

"He didn't *let* me live," Bixby said, forcefully interrupting the speaker. "I escaped."

"However it happened, it's a bit of a miracle that you run into him and you're still alive. I don't know whether your wife is still alive or not, but I ain't goin' out there by myself to look for her, and I don't reckon anyone else will either."

"Suppose several of you go together," Bixby said. "There is safety in numbers."

"Hold on here!" Matt called.

"Mr. Jensen," Bixby said. "You have something to add?"

"Bixby, the last thing we need is a lot of people

running around out there, getting in the way, spooking Delshay, and maybe even pushing him into doing something he hadn't planned to do."

"That's just the kind of reaction I would expect from someone like you," Bixby said. "It's no secret that you intend to conduct this search on your own because you don't want to share the reward money with anyone."

"Bixby, I was going out to look for her before I even knew about the reward and you know that. What I cannot understand is why you would do something like this to purposely make it more difficult to find your wife."

"How dare you accuse me of that, sir?" Bixby said. "It is precisely because I do want to find her that I am offering a reward so as to involve the greatest number of people possible."

"Maybe some of you folks would like to come with *me*," someone called.

Matt recognized the man who issued the invitation.

"Pogue Willis," Matt said. "What are you doing here?"

"Same as you, Jensen. Goin' after that reward. That is, unless you think you're the only one entitled to it."

"Pogue Willis?" one of the other men in the crowd said. "Is that who you are, mister?"

"That's right."

"Well, now, that changes things a bit. If I'm goin' to be in a fight, I'd sure like to have someone like you on my side."

"I'll go with you, Willis—but I figure we're goin'

to need four or five others just to be sure," another man said.

"Hell, why don't we all go and form a posse?" Meechum said. "I don't about the rest of you fellas, but if I'm goin' up against Delshay, I want as many guns with me as possible."

"I agree," another shouted. "That is, if it's all right with you, Mr. Willis."

"Yeah, I think it's fine. All right, men, get rifles, bullets, and what food you plan to take. We'll meet here in one hour," Willis said, assuming unopposed command of the posse.

Matt shook his head in disgust, then mounted Spirit and started out of town.

"Mr. Jensen," someone called.

Looking toward the sound of the voice, Matt saw Ken Hendel standing just under the overhanging porch of the apothecary.

"Mr. Hendel," Matt replied, touching the brim of his hat.

"I tried to stop him," Hendel said. "Mr. Bixby, I mean. I tried to stop him from posting that reward."

Matt twisted in his saddle to look back toward the hardware store. He saw the crowd breaking up, hurrying to get weapons and food to join the impromptu posse.

"I swear, Mr. Hendel, if I didn't know better, I'd say that Bixby is purposely making it more difficult for me to find his wife."

"I don't know what happened out there, but the truth is, I think Mr. Bixby is trying to take the edge off a feeling of guilt," Hendel said.

Matt watched Bixby step down from the porch of the hardware store and start back toward the hotel.

"I hadn't thought about that, but you might be right," Matt said.

"Find her, Matt," Hendel said, the words expressing his deepest feelings. "Please find her and bring her back safely."

"I'll do my best, Ken," Matt promised.

Pogue Willis and Billy Meechum waited in the middle of the street for the other members of the posse to return.

"I wonder how many are goin' to go with us," Meechum said.

"Why does it matter?" Willis asked.

"Well, if there's eight more that go with us and we find the woman, that would be only one thousand dollars apiece."

"No, that would be ten thousand dollars for us and none for them," Willis said.

"What? How can that be?"

"You just let me worry about that," Willis said confidently.

It was now three days since Cynthia had been captured and they had changed the location of their camp six times. Every night, just before dark, they would move their encampment, then find a place to spend the night. The next morning, just after sunrise, they would move the encampment again. This, Chandeisi explained, was to prevent the white men from discovering were they were. Chandeisi was constantly by Cynthia's side, for which she was grateful. She had seen Nalyudi looking at her from time to time, and she knew that it was only Chandeisi and Delshay who kept him from claiming her.

After three days, Cynthia felt a need to change clothes, for she was still wearing the same green dress she had on when she was captured. Since she had taken no clothes with her on what she thought would be no more than a couple of hours' drive into the country, she had nothing to change into, and she feared she was stuck with the situation.

To her surprise and delight, Chandeisi came to the rescue by bringing her a couple of dresses made from deerskin.

"These were the dresses of my wife," he said as he handed them to her.

"Oh, Chandeisi, thank you," Cynthia said. She looked at the dresses. "They are beautiful."

The dresses were wonderfully soft, and prettily decorated with porcupine quills and bright, blue beads. There was nothing to wear under the dresses, and at first Cynthia was keenly aware of that fact, but after a couple more days she quit thinking about it.

Each night, Chandeisi helped Cynthia to make a soft bed of stretched skin and fragrant grasses; then he would leave the wickiup to allow her privacy while she slept. Because they spent so much time together, Cynthia was able to engage him in conversation. She did so for two reasons: because she was genuinely curious, and because she thought that it would be good to have a friend in this situation.

"Where did you go to school?" Cynthia asked.

"I attended the mission school at San Carlos," Chandeisi answered.

"Have you ever been off the reservation to live among the whites?"

"No, I have never done that. I have spent my whole life with my people—mostly on the reservation."

"Do you ever wish you could live with white people?" Cynthia asked.

"No, I like living with my own people," Chandeisi replied. "But there are many things I would like to see."

"What would you like to see?"

"I have read that in the tall buildings of the big cities, there are little rooms that you can step into, and those rooms will rise, taking you to the top of the building."

For a moment, Cynthia had to think of what Chandeisi was saying; then she laughed out loud. "You mean elevators," she said. "Yes, the tall buildings in the big cities do have elevators."

"And I have read as well that one does not need a candle or a lantern. You can turn a valve and have light, for the gas is piped in."

"Yes, that is true," Cynthia answered. "And in some buildings, water is piped in as well."

"And is there really a device where one person can speak to another over great distances?"

"Oh, yes, it is called a telephone," Cynthia said.

"Have you seen such marvels?"

"I have them in my home," Cynthia said. "The gaslights, the running water, and the telephone."

"I am puzzled," Chandeisi said.

"What has you puzzled?" Cynthia laughed. "I hope you are not puzzled about how these marvelous things work, because even though I live with them every day, I do not think I can explain the operation to you."

"No, that is not what puzzles me," Chandeisi eplied. "It is just that, with so many wonderful things for the white man to see and enjoy, why must he come to our land?"

"Do you think the white man has done nothing good for the Indian?" Cynthia asked.

Chandeisi shook his head. "I can think of no good."

"What about your education? You have gotten a wonderful education from the white man."

"The white man taught me how to multiply and divide, but not how to skin a rabbit. I have had to skin a rabbit many times. I have never had to multiply and divide."

"You said you went to a mission school?"

"Yes."

"Then you must have learned about Christianity. Do you not feel joy from knowing that your soul has been saved?"

"You are talking about the white man's Jesus God, aren't you?" Chandeisi asked.

"Yes, I am. Do you believe in Him?"

Chandeisi nodded affirmatively.

"Good, good," Cynthia said.

"Why is this good?"

"Because, it is very important that you believe in the one way to the true God."

"There are many paths to the Great Spirit," Chandeisi said.

Cynthia shook her head. "No, there is but one path. Our Father in Heaven will not welcome you into His Kingdom if you do not come to Him through the Son of God."

"You call Him our Father? Does that not mean we are all children of the Great Spirit?" Chandeisi asked. "Are you not His daughter? Is Delshay not His son? Are earth, wind, fire, and water not His creations?"

Cynthia thought hard, trying to remember all of her Sunday School lessons, but no matter how hard she tried, no easy answer came to her.

"I cannot answer all of your questions. I can only tell you how things are," she finally said, hoping that Chandeisi would accept her explanation and press the issue no further.

Chapter Twenty-five

San Carlos Indian Reservation

Although there was a central area to the San Carlos reservation where Indian Agent Baker lived and where the commissary, hospital, and school were built, not all the Apache lived there. In explaining it once, Baker had said that the reservation was like an Indian state and in the state were several small villages scattered about. At the extreme northwest part of the reservation was the most remote of all the villages. Here lived Alope, the daughter of Nopoloto. Nopoloto was the nephew of Cochise and had fought with Cochise until the great chief made peace with the U.S. Army.

The sun had not yet risen, but Alope knew that it was nearly dawn, because she had heard the morning birds begin their singing. Now, as she lay on blankets in her father's wickiup, she contemplated the events that were to happen today.

For a long time, Alope had been in love with a

young man from one of the other villages. Because Cochinay, whose name meant Yellow Thunder, was from another village, he had to have authorization from the council for the privilege of going to Nopoloto to ask his permission to marry Alope. After some consideration and exploration of Cochinay's family, the council of elders gave their consent and Cochinay went to Alope's father to make his petition.

Nopoloto agreed to give his daughter to the young man, on condition that Cochinay give him many ponies. When Nopoloto told Cochinay how many ponies he wanted for his daughter, Cochinay said nothing; he simply rode out of the village.

Hearing how many ponies her father asked for, and seeing Cochinay ride away without so much as a word, Alope feared that there would be no marriage. She wondered why her father had been so demanding. Perhaps love meant nothing to her father. Perhaps Nopoloto wanted to keep Alope with him, for she was a dutiful daughter.

"Do not question me, daughter," Nopoloto said. "I set a very high price to test Cochinay's love for you. If he returns with the ponies, it will prove that his love for you is deep, and it will satisfy a father that his daughter will be well taken care of, and that there will be grandchildren to bless me in my old age."

To Alope's joy, Cochinay returned the very next day and appeared before Nopoloto's wickiup with even more ponies than Nopoloto had asked for.

That was one week ago. In the week since permission had been granted, Cochinay had come to the village to make a home for them. He constructed a wickiup of buffalo hides, putting in it many bear robes, lion hides, and other trophies of the hunt, as well as his spears, bows, and arrows.

Alope had made many little decorations of beads on buckskin, which she placed in the wickiup. She also drew many pictures on the walls of what today would be her new home.

But that would not be until after the council declared them married, so for now, Alope lay on the blankets in her parents' wickiup, waiting for the sun to rise and the marriage to be ratified. Finally, a sliver of sunlight slipped in through the opening of the wickiup, and Alope, anxious to begin the day, got up, picked up a bucket, and started toward the nearby stream to get water.

In the dawn's early light, just outside the little village where Alope lay waiting for the day to begin, Pogue Willis looked around at the men who formed his posse.

"This don't look like no warrior camp. I think this is just a village," one of the men said. "Do you really think the Bixby woman is here?" one of the men asked.

"I don't know if she is or not, but she could be," Willis said. "The way I look at it, there's only one way to find out, and that's to go in and have a look."

"But what if she ain't here?"

"What if she ain't? If you think about it, Lathum, it don't make any difference whether she's here or not. I mean, look at it this way. Every Indian we kill will just be payin' them back for them killing those six miners and Mr. Malcolm," one of the others said.

"But we don't know that these here Injuns is the one that done the killin'," Lathum said.

"It don't matter whether these are the ones or not," Meechum said. "The ones that done the killin' were Apache, weren't they? These here Injuns is Apache. If we kill a bunch of Apaches ever' time they kill some of us, they will pretty soon get the word that the only way they can keep from gettin' killed themselves is to stop their own from killin' us."

"I tell you true, gents, Meechum is makin' sense to me," one of the others said.

"Yeah, I guess if you put it that way," Lathum said. He nodded. "All right, if we are goin' to do this, let's get it done."

There were fourteen armed men in the posse and they lined up abreast. Just before they started, however, a young woman came from one of the wickiups, carrying a water pail. She started toward the stream. Then, seeing a long line of armed white men sitting on their horses just outside the village, she dropped the pail.

"Cochinay!" she screamed at the top of her voice.

"Shoot that bitch!" Willis shouted, and instantly several gunshots rang out. The young woman fell back, the top of her dress red with blood from the many bullet wounds.

The girl's scream and the sound of gunfire alerted the others in the village, and several stuck their heads out to see what was going on.

"Kill them!" Willis shouted. "Kill them all!"

The posse rode through the village, shooting everyone they saw whether it be man, woman, or child.

Many of the villagers were able to get out through the backs of their wickiups by crawling underneath the walls, then running toward the arroyo that traversed the back side of the village. In this way, more than half the village escaped. Finally, when all were either killed or had run, Willis shouted at the others to stop shooting.

"You ain't doin' nothin' now but wastin' your ammunition," he said. "Get down and take a look through all them huts, see if there's a white woman in any of 'em."

For the next few minutes, every wickiup was searched, but there was no white woman to be found.

"What do we do now?" one of the men asked.

"Burn the village," Willis said. "I want these Apache bastards to know that we mean business. For every one of ours they kill, we'll kill ten of them."

"That would mean we would have to kill seventy, and there ain't no seventy dead Injuns here," Lathum said. "There's only about ten or eleven."

"Yes, well, I do think they will get the picture," Willis said as the men began setting fire to the highly flammable structures.

It took but a few minutes before every hut was ablaze. Then, with two dozen columns of smoke climbing into the air, the posse rode away, leaving behind not only the burning wickups, but also the bodies of those they had killed.

* * *

Cochinay was one of those who got away. Catching one of the fleeing ponies, he set out to find Delshay.

"Why did you not join me before?" Delshay asked when Cochinay arrived at his encampment and told him of the raid on Nopoloto's village.

"Before, my blood ran cool, because I wanted only to marry Alope, hunt, fish, and have sons to hunt and fish. But the white man has killed Alope, and now my blood runs hot. I want to join you and kill as many white men as I can."

Delshay nodded, then reached out to put his hand on Cochinay's shoulder. "You are welcome, my brother," he said.

Half an hour later, Chandeisi came into the wickiup where Cynthia was being kept.

"We must leave," he said.

"But we always leave in the morning," Cynthia replied. "Why must we leave now?"

"Because Delshay has said we must," Chandeisi replied.

Cynthia nodded, then began getting together the possessions she had been given. By now she had two dresses, a bowl and a spoon, a comb, a pair of moccasins, and most valuable of all, a tablet and a pencil.

Cynthia had convinced Chandeisi that she needed the tablet and pencil in order to "write her prayers," and because Chandeisi had a genuine respect for the religious practices of everyone, he did not question Cynthia.

When Cynthia left the note, just before they left that night, she felt a slight twinge of guilt, as if she were somehow betraying Chandeisi's trust and friendship. But her desire to be found and rescued transcended any sense of betrayal she might have.

Phoenix

Ken Hendel and Jay Peerless Bixby were sitting at a table in the Dry Gulch Saloon. From the back of the room a woman screamed, but her scream was followed by her high-pitched laughter, then punctuated with the bass guffaws of the men who were with her.

Bixby looked back toward the table with an expression of disgust on his face.

"How can anyone live in a place like this?" he asked.

"Oh, I think it has its attractions," Hendel said.

"Really? And what, pray tell, would be those attractions?" Bixby took in the saloon with a sweep of his arm. "Back in New York, I am a member of the Ambassador Club, where we have a collection of the finest wines and spirits in the world. Would you compare this—this saloon to the Ambassador Club? I tell you, Hendel, it is not by accident that they call this place the Dry Gulch."

Hendel held up his beer. "This beer is brewed here in Phoenix by Andrew Marcus. I think that even you would agree that it is as good a beer as you will find anywhere—and far superior to most."

"The beer is all right, I suppose," Bixby said. "Though I much prefer wine."

"Whoooeee!" somebody shouted as the batwing doors were kicked open. Looking toward the sound, Hendel saw Willis and several of the other men who had ridden out with him this morning when they started their search for Cynthia Bixby.

"Bartender, line up the bottles and start pouring drinks!" Willis yelled. "You've got a thirsty bunch of men comin' in."

A dozen men came filing in behind Willis. All of them were carrying souvenirs of some sort, from bows and arrows to buffalo robes to beaded rugs. A couple were even carrying what appeared to be scalps.

"Let me tell you, boys!" Willis said loudly. "It's goin' to be a cold day in hell before any bunch of Apaches kill any more white men or women."

"What happened, Willis? What are you talking about?" the bartender asked as he began placing empty glasses on the bar, preparatory to filling them with whiskey or beer.

"I'll tell you what happened. We found the camp of that murderin', thievin' bastard Delshay," Willis said. He laughed, then held up his finger to emphasise his statement. "And we rode through that camp like shit through a goose. We must have killed more than half of 'em. The rest skedaddled like scalded-ass rabbits, leavin' the camp behind 'em. So we burned ever' tent, ever' grain storage, we even burned up their dried meat. Yes, sir, even if they do come back, they won't be able to live there 'cause they have got no place to live no more. And what's more, they have got no food to eat."

"Did you kill Delshay?" one of the patrons of the saloon asked.

"No, no, we didn't get him. He's one of them that got away. Which says a lot about him, if you want my opinion. It tells me that the son of a bitch is a coward when it comes to fightin' against real fightin' men."

"I don't know," one of the saloon patrons replied. "I've heard a lot about Delshay, but I've never heard anyone call him a coward."

Willis glared at the patron. "Well, I'm calling him a coward," Willis said. "Are you calling me a liar?"

"What? No, sir, no, sir, not at all, Mr. Willis," the patron said quickly. With trembling hands he picked up his beer, drained the rest of it, then left quickly, chased by the laughter of the members of Willis's posse.

"You ever' see anyone move as fast as that feller just done?" Meechum asked derisively, and the posse laughed again.

"What about Mrs. Bixby?" Hendel asked, surprised by the fact that Bixby hadn't ask about his wife first.

Willis shook his head. "Sorry, we didn't see no white women."

"Did you look?" Hendel asked.

"Did we look? You damn right we looked. In case you forgot, they's a ten-thousand-dollar reward bein' offered up for her. They ain't no way we're goin' out there and do what we done without lookin' for the woman that's missin'. Only, she wasn't there and the nearest I can figure is they must of took her out with them when they left. Either that, or she's dead."

"Do you think that it is more or less likely that she is dead?" Bixby asked.

"Well, I don't rightly know how to answer that,"

Willis said. "But now, let me ask you a question. What if we would happen to find her and it turns out she is already dead? Would you still pay the ten thousand dollars?"

"The bill reads that the reward is to be paid only if she is returned safely," Bixby said. "So the answer to your question is no. Why should I pay the reward if she is dead?"

By now all the drinks had been poured, and Willis picked up a glass of whiskey, then tossed it down. He wiped his mouth with the back of his hand before he replied.

"I'm told by the folks who know them best that Indians don't bury the whites they kill, and like I told you, we did not find a white woman's body," Willis said. "So, if you was to ask me, I would say that they have not killed her."

"But you don't know for sure."

"No, I don't know for sure."

"I didn't think so," Bixby said. "It turns out that you are no different from all the other cretins who live out here. You are incompetent and irresponsible. The truth is, if you lived in New York, there is no doubt in my mind that you would all be incarcerated by now."

Willis took another drink and studied Bixby over the rim of his glass for a long moment.

"Jay Peerless Bixby," he said. "Only you are Jay Peerless Bixby Junior, aren't you now? And it's remembering, I am, that your old man, Jay Peerless Bixby Senior, is the bloke what was sent upriver for dippin' some sticky fingers into Crédit Mobilier. Whether you do your stealin' on the docks or in some fancy office, it's still stealing, now ain't it, laddie?"

Gone was the flat Western twang Willis had acquired, to be replaced by the accent of Hell's Kitchen in New York.

"What?" Bixby asked, his cheeks flaming in color. "How—how do you know about that? Who are you?"

"Let's just say that I am someone you don't want on your bad side, whether it's in Hell's Kitchen or Tombstone, Arizona," Willis replied.

Willis's words had not only surprised Bixby, but everyone else in the saloon as well.

"I never know'd that about you," Meechum said.

"There's a lot you don't know about me," Willis said, still using his New York accent. Then, switching to a Western twang, he added, "But why are we standin' around here jawbonin'? Seems to me like we got us some celebratin' to do. We done what the entire U.S. Army ain't been able to do, and that's find and destroy the camp of that murderin' bastard Delshay."

Chapter Twenty-six

Every time Delshay and his followers broke camp, they took every precaution to erase all signs of having been there. They used tree branches to brush away any tracks, they covered the holes in the ground that were made by the tent stakes, and they even picked up the pony droppings. Such attention to detail was enough to throw off almost anyone who might be searching for them.

Almost anyone.

Matt wasn't just anyone. Having initially learned his craft from his mentor, Smoke Jensen, Matt had a base upon which to build and, over the years, his own experience, intuition, and native intelligence had added to that skill so that he was the equal of or superior to any scout alive.

One thing the Indians could not do was alter where the ponies had grazed. Matt's keen eye caught the uneven cut of vegetation, including some sprigs that had merely been broken, and not consumed. And although the fires had been extinguished and the coals removed, there were a couple of circles of slight discoloration in the sand showing where the fires had been laid.

He was about to move on when he saw a piece of dark green silk stuck in the notch of a tree, and he remembered that Hendel had told him that Cynthia had been wearing a green dress when she left.

This was not something the Indians had merely overlooked, this was something that had obviously been placed there, no doubt at great risk, as the Indians were leaving their camp. As he approached the silk, he saw that it was folded into a small square, and inside the square, he found a note:

To the Finder of this note:

My name is Cynthia Bixby. I can but pray that you are a white man, and one who is aware of my situation. On the 5th of September, my husband, Jay Peerless Bixby, and I departed from Phoenix in a rented conveyance for the purpose of examining some property my husband intended to purchase.

The conveyance broke down and we were put afoot. While walking back to Phoenix, we were set upon by a band of Indians led by one who is called Delshay. Moved to pity by the sight of my husband's great fear, Delshay let him leave unharmed, though he kept me as his captive. It is both my belief and hope that my husband has sounded the alarm as to my condition of captivity, thus putting into motion a search.

I do not know how to tell you where I am, as we move from place to place each day. If you are reading this, that means I have at least been successful in

> *getting word through to the outside world. May I here*
> *hasten to add that the Indians have not mistreated*
> *me in any way. On the contrary, they have provided*
> *me with food, water, and clothing, for which I am*
> *eternally grateful.*

> *With hope for my eventual rescue, I am most sincerely,*
> *Cynthia Bixby*

"Moved to pity by the sight of my husband's great fear, Delshay let him leave unharmed, though he kept me as his captive." Matt read aloud. "I knew there was something fishy about that."

Folding the note back into the little square of green silk, Matt put it in his shirt pocket and started to mount Spirit. That was when he saw him.

Pulling his pistol, he pointed it at a nearby bush.

"If you want to live, mister, you had better come out of there now," he called.

After some hesitancy, the branches of the bush moved and someone came out. It was an Indian, but Matt perceived immediately that he represented no danger. Like with many Indians, it was difficult to ascertain his age, though the man could have been anywhere between fifty and seventy years old. He was holding his hand to his side, and Matt saw that his side was matted with blood.

"Do you speak English?" Matt asked as put his pistol back in his holster.

"I speak English," the Indian said.

"What happened to you?"

"Many white men came to attack my village. They killed many of my people. They killed my wife. They killed my daughters. They killed many others."

"Who were these white men?" Matt asked.

"I do not know."

"Who are you?"

"I am called Nopoloto."

"The village that the white men attacked, was it the village of of Delshay?"

Nopoloto shook his head. "No."

"Do you know Delshay?"

"Yes."

"Do you know where Delshay is?"

"He is not on the reservation," Nopoloto said.

"There is a white woman with Delshay. I am looking for her," Matt said.

"I do not know of any white woman," Nopoloto said. "My village is on the reservation," he said. "Once I was with Cochise, but now I am reservation Indian."

"You say you are a reservation Indian, but you are not on the reservation now," Matt challenged.

"I left the reservation after the attack," Nopoloto said.

"When was this attack?"

"Today. The white men attacked as the sun rose."

"Do you have a horse?" Matt asked.

"Yes."

"You need to have someone look at your wound. Come with me, I will ride with you to the reservation hospital."

It was much later on the same day when Matt rode back into Phoenix, this time accompanied by Indian Agent Baker. They stopped at the office of Sheriff Robert Williams. Williams drank a cup of coffee as he listened to Matt relate to him the story of the attack he had heard from Nopoloto.

"Where is Nopoloto now?" Williams asked.

"He is in the hospital at the reservation, being treated for his wounds," Matt said.

"And Nopoloto says the attack took place on the reservation?"

"Yes."

"I'm pretty sure I know who did it," Sheriff Williams said. "Pogue Willis, Billy Meechum, Karl Lathum, Angus Pugh, and nearly a dozen others are over at the Dry Gulch now, drinking it up. They claim they attacked Delshay's camp."

"I don't think so," Matt said. "I found Delshay's camp. There was no sign of an attack."

"Did you find the woman?" Williams asked.

"No," Matt said. He purposely withheld the information about finding a letter from her.

"I don't think you are going to find her. Not alive anyway."

"As long as I don't find her dead, I maintain the hope of finding her alive," Matt said.

Williams sighed. "Well, if the attack happened off the reservation, it would come under my jurisdiction, seeing as how it was white men who did the attacking. But if it happened on reservation grounds—"

"It did," Matt and Indian Agent Baker replied, speaking at the same time.

"Then you need to see U.S. Marshal Gilmore."

"Do you want to come along with us?" Matt asked.

Sheriff Williams walked over to retrieve his hat, then

put it on. "Yeah," he said. "I'll go down to Gilmore's office with you."

"Did either of you see the attack?" Gilmore asked.

"No," Matt answered.

"I was at the agency headquarters," Baker said.

"Did you hear anything? Shooting, or yelling, or anything?"

Baker shook his head. "The agency headquarters are too far away from Nopoloto's village. I didn't hear anything."

"We did ride out to the village," Matt said.

"What did you find?"

"Nothing."

"No survivors?"

"No."

"No bodies?"

"The bodies had already been moved," Baker said.

"Uh-huh," Gilmore replied. "If they were ever there in the first place."

"Marshal, are you saying the attack didn't happen?" Matt asked. He pointed up the street toward the Dry Gulch. "There is a saloon full of people who are bragging about it."

Gilmore shook his head. "No, they are bragging about attacking Delshay's village. And if that is true, I have no quarrel with them. And without any eyewitnesses or even evidence to tell me otherwise, I have no reason not to believe them."

"You have an eyewitness," Matt said.

"Who?"

"Nopoloto."

"Nopoloto," Marshal Gilmore replied with a derisive snort. "You expect me to arrest more than a dozen white men on the word of one old Indian? And not just any Indian, but one who used to ride with Cochise, making war against us. Like I said, I have no eyewitnesses."

Baker raised his finger at Gilmore. "It is this kind of thing that caused all our problems in the first place," he said. "Geronimo had settled peacefully onto the reservation, until white men murdered his family. Delshay had settled peacefully onto the reservation until white men murdered his entire family. Now, Cochinay has gone to join either Geronimo or Delshay. And all because you aren't doing your job."

"Just a minute, Mr. Baker," Gilmore replied angrily. "The entire U.S. Army has been chasing Indians throughout the West for the last forty years. When Custer and all his soldier boys got themselves killed, it had nothing to do with the marshal's office. I don't know what is going on with Delshay and I don't care. Dealing with Delshay is the responsibility of the U.S. Army. Now, if you gentlemen would excuse me, I have some work to do."

"Mr. Jensen, I'm sorry I suggested this," Sheriff Williams said. "It is obvious to me that the marshal is going to do nothing to help us."

"This is not my jurisdiction, Williams, and you know it," Marshal Gilmore said.

"Right," Williams said, his voice dripping with disgust. "Come along, gentlemen, we are wasting our time here."

"I have to get back to the reservation," Baker said. "And I want to do so before dark."

As Baker started back to the Indian reservation, and Sheriff Williams returned to his office, Matt headed toward the Phoenix House to see Bixby.

"I believe he and Mr. Hendel are at the Dry Gulch," the hotel clerk said.

Matt couldn't help but chuckle. "Bixby at the Dry Gulch?"

The clerk chuckled as well. "Yes, it is hard to imagine, isn't it? Someone like Bixby at a place like the Dry Gulch?"

When Matt stepped into the saloon a few minutes later, the celebration was in full swing. Nearly all the men of Willis's posse were drunk and a few had even passed out. The others were talking loud, telling stories of the great battle that had taken place.

"There was no battle," Matt said as he stepped up to the bar. "I'll have one of Mr. Marcus's beers," he said.

"What do you mean there was no battle?" Meechum demanded. "Are you saying we didn't kill a bunch of Delshay's murderin' Apaches?"

"You killed a bunch of Indians all right," Matt said as he blew the head off the beer that was put before him. "But they weren't murderers, and they weren't with Delshay. You went onto the reservation and attacked a peaceful village."

"How do you know that?"

"Because I spoke to Nopoloto, one of the Indians who lived in the reservation village you attacked.

And I found Delshay's latest encampment. There were no signs of any battle there."

"Did you say Nopoloto?" one of the saloon patrons asked.

"Yes."

"Nopoloto used to ride with Cochise. He's not an Indian you want to get mad at you. We'll be lucky if the entire Apache Nation doesn't go to war because of that."

"Let 'em go to war," Willis said bombastically. "If they do, we'll be ready for them. Right, boys?"

"Right," Meechum replied.

Matt noticed that the rest of the men, at least those who were not passed out drunk, were pointedly silent in response to Willis's challenge.

"It looks like you may wind up fighting this war all alone, Willis," Matt said. "And even you can't draw fast enough, or shoot straight enough, to handle this all by yourself."

"What about you?" Willis asked. "You say you found Delshay's village. Did you see him?"

"No, I did not see him."

"I see," Willis replied. "And did you find the woman?"

"No."

"Well, then, it looks like we are about even, don't it, Mr. Matt Jensen?"

Without answering, Matt walked back to the table where Bixby and Hendel were sitting.

"May I join you?" he asked.

"Yes, please do," Hendel replied graciously.

"I heard you tell them that you didn't find my wife," Bixby said.

"No, I did not." Matt reached for his pocket, intending to show Bixby the note he had found, but before he could, Bixby spoke again.

"There's no need in your going out there again," he said. "Cynthia is dead. I know she is."

Matt shook his head. "I don't believe she is dead."

"I know, I know, you explained all about how Indians don't bury their enemy. But that means nothing to me. I know that she is dead."

"Mr. Bixby, I wish you had a little more confidence," Hendel said. "I am convinced that she is still alive."

"You hold on to that conviction, Mr. Hendel," Bixby said. "In the meantime, I want you to go to the depot and secure two tickets for our return to New York. I have been in this accursed place quite long enough now. I am ready to go home."

"No, Mr. Bixby, I will not purchase a return ticket for you," Hendel said.

"What? What did you just say to me?" Bixby gasped, shocked at the response of the man who had always been subservient to him.

"I said, Mr. Bixby, that I will not purchase a return ticket for you."

"How dare you refuse me!"

"We are not leaving Phoenix until Cynthia has been rescued," Hendel said.

"Cynthia, is it? Since when do you have the right to call my wife by her first name?"

"As it is evident that I am more concerned for her welfare than you, I have assumed that right,"

Hendel said. "Neither you nor I will leave here until she has safely returned."

"You are wasting your noble feelings, Hendel. My wife is dead."

"I don't believe that."

"That's because you don't want to believe it. But I know she is dead."

"How do you know she is dead?"

Bixby bowed his head and pinched the bridge of his nose. "Because, even as I escaped, I saw the savages kill her," he said.

"Then, if you saw that, why did you offer a reward for her safe return?" Hendel asked.

"Maybe it is because I just didn't want to admit it to myself," Bixby said.

Matt applauded quietly, and as he did so, both Bixby and Hendel looked toward him.

"I congratulate you, Bixby," Matt said. "With a performance like that, you should be on the stage."

"What are you talking about, sir?" Bixby asked, the tone of his voice righteously indignant.

Matt took the little square of green cloth from his pocket and put it on the table.

"What is that?" Bixby asked.

"You don't recognize it?" Matt replied.

"No, I don't recognize it. Why should I?"

"But surely you recognize it, Mr. Bixby," Hendel said. "That's a piece of material from the dress Cynthia was wearing the day the two of you left to look at land."

Bixby looked at the little square of cloth, then nodded. "Yes, now that you mention it, it is what she was wearing," he agreed. "I guess I just wasn't expecting to see it here like this." He looked up at Matt. "You found this, did you?"

"I did."

"Then, does this not prove that she is dead?"

"On the contrary," Matt said, unfolding the cloth to expose the note that was inside. "If you read this, it will prove that she is still alive."

Bixby grabbed the note, and as he read it, Matt studied the expression on his face. He recognized the moment Bixby read the crucial words: *Moved to pity by the sight of my husband's great fear, Delshay let him leave unharmed, though he kept me as his captive.*

Finishing the note, Bixby folded it and started to stick it in his pocket.

"May I see the note, Mr. Bixby?" Hendel asked.

Bixby glared at Hendel. "No, you cannot see it. This is a personal letter from my wife to me."

"From the wife you saw killed?" Matt asked.

"Well, I—I—thank God I was mistaken. There was some distance between us. I suppose it is possible that I just thought I saw her killed."

"Show the note to Mr. Hendel."

"I see no reason why I should do that just because you ask me to," Bixby said.

"If you thought I asked you to show Hendel the note, you misunderstood me," Matt said. "I'm not asking you, I'm telling you to show him the note."

"You—you have no right to order me to do such a thing," Bixby said. Then, looking at the determined expression on Matt's face, Bixby broke into a sweat, licked his lips, and with trembling hands, gave the note to Hendel.

Hendel read it, looked up at the moment he

read the line about Delshay letting Bixby go, then returned to the note. After he finished reading it, he returned the note to Bixby without comment.

"Uh, naturally, after receiving this note, my position has changed," Bixby said. "I will not be returning to New York until we have found her. Mr. Jensen, I would appreciate it very much, sir, if you would continue to look for her."

"Call off your reward," Matt said. "Not only were a dozen or more innocent Indians killed because of that foolish reward, it has made my job harder."

"All right."

"Do it now," Matt said.

"Now? Here? Look at them, they are drunk and carrying on—how do you expect me to get their attention?"

"I can get their attention for you, Mr. Bixby," Hendel said.

"You? Ha! How can someone like you get their attention?"

"Watch me," Hendel replied with a confident smile.

Standing, Hendel put his fingers in his mouth, then let out with an ear-piercing whistle. As he promised, it got everyone's attention as the talking halted in mid-conversation while all turned to see what was going on.

"Gentlemen—and ladies," Hendel added, taking in the half-dozen or so women who were in the Dry Gulch, "excuse me for interrupting, but my employer, Mr. Bixby, has an announcement to make."

Hendel sat down and, with some hesitancy, Bixby stood up. He was extremely cognizant of the fact that everyone in the saloon was staring at him, and he cleared his throat before he began to speak.

"I, uh, hereby withdraw the reward offer of ten thousand dollars."

"What?" Willis shouted. "Why?"

"A question has been raised about the efficacy of the attack on the Indian village. It is entirely possible that several innocent Indians were killed and I want no part in it." Bixby sat down.

"You're behind this, ain't you, Jensen?" Willis said. "You're behind this, and you're doing it because you want the reward all to yourself."

Matt stared at Willis for a moment before he answered. "Yeah, you're right," he said quietly. "I'm behind this. And I'm doing it because I want the reward all for myself."

"You!" Willis said, choking on his anger. Turning to face Matt, he moved his hand so that it hovered threateningly just over his pistol. "I've had a bellyful of you."

Chairs tumbled over and tables were scooted across the floor as everyone in the saloon moved quickly to get out of the line of fire. They watched expectantly as Willis and Matt stared at each other. Matt was still seated.

"Stand up, Jensen," Willis said with a snarl. "Stand up. Let's get this done."

"I don't need be standing to beat someone like you," Matt said. "You want to play this out, go ahead and draw. I can kill a little pissant like you as easily sitting as I can standing."

Like the others in the saloon, Meechum had moved to get out of the way. Now, standing to one side of the action, and seeing that Matt Jensen's attention was focused entirely on Pogue Willis, he realized that he had an opportunity he would never get again.

He drew his pistol.

"Draw, Jensen!" he shouted, even as his own pistol was clearing his holster.

Within the blink of an eye, Matt reacted with a draw that was fast and smooth. His practiced thumb came back on the hammer in one fluid motion while his finger put the slightest pressure on the hair trigger of his Colt. There was a blossom of white, followed by a booming thunderclap as the gun jumped in his hand.

Meechum tried to continue his draw, but the .44 slug from Matt's pistol caught him in the heart. When the bullet came out through the back, it brought a chunk of Meechum's shoulder blade with it, leaving an exit wound the size of a quarter.

Meechum's hand came away from his gun and it slipped back down into his holster as he staggered backward, crashing into a table before coming down on it with a crunch that turned the table into firewood. He landed flat on his back, on the floor, his mouth open and a little sliver of blood oozing down his chin. His body was still jerking a bit, but his eyes were open and unseeing. He was already dead. Only the muscles continued to respond, as if waiting for signals that could no longer be sent.

The exchange had caught Willis by surprise, and by the time he looked back toward Matt, he saw that he was looking into the smoking barrel of Matt's pistol.

Willis put his hands up.

"No!" he said. "No, I ain't drawin' on you. I ain't drawin'."

"Get out of here, Willis," Matt said dryly. "I don't like you. If I see you again, I may kill you just for the hell of it."

"You all heard that!" Willis shouted to the others in the saloon. "I want you to remember that you all heard him threaten to kill me."

"If you are still here ten seconds from now, it won't be a threat, it'll be a fact," Matt said.

Willis glared at Matt a second longer, then turning, he hurried from the saloon.

"Ha!" one of the saloon patrons said. "I never thought I would see Pogue Willis turn tail and run."

Several others laughed, though their laughter was nervous and guarded, as if they were afraid someone might tell Willis they had laughed at him.

Matt stood up and looked down at Bixby and Hendel, both of whom were staring at him with shocked expressions on their faces.

"I'm going to find your wife now," Matt said. "I strongly suggest that you be here when I come back with her."

"I'll—I'll be here," Bixby said.

Chapter Twenty-seven

Matt was close.

He was not only close, he was pressing them because they were getting more careless in abandoning their campsites. At this campsite, they'd left the still-glowing embers of a campfire.

As Matt was examining the campsite, he realized that he was being watched. And because whoever was watching him had not killed him, he did not believe he was in immediate danger.

Stirring up the coals, Matt reignited the campfire, then put coffee grounds and water into his coffeepot and set it over the campfire to boil. Within moments, its rich aroma permeated the area. When he knew the coffee was done, he took two cups from his saddlebag.

"Would you join me for coffee, friend?" he called out.

Getting no response from his offer, he put one cup down by the fire and filled the second cup.

Then, sitting on a nearby fallen log, he began to drink.

He heard a movement, then out of the corner of his eye saw the person who had been watching him.

Nopoloto came out from hiding, walked over to the fire, picked up the cup, then poured himself some coffee. Still without talking, he came over and sat on the same log as Matt.

"Agent Baker told me that you tried to seek justice for the raid on my village," Nopoloto said.

"I tried," Matt said. "I wasn't very successful, I'm afraid."

"What happens inside the heart is more important than what happens outside the heart. Because you tried, you are the friend of Nopoloto."

Matt touched his cup to that of Nopoloto as if in toast. It was not a gesture with which Nopoloto was familiar, but he responded quickly.

"I am honored to be the friend of Nopoloto," Matt said.

Nopoloto was quiet until they had finished drinking their coffee. Then he spoke.

"I will take you to Delshay," Nopoloto said.

"I appreciate that."

"But you must do as I say."

"All right," Matt agreed.

Searching around the camp, Nopoloto found a dead tree limb that was about six feet tall, and ended with a Y. He tied the branch to his saddle, then asked for Matt's weapons.

"I don't know," Matt said. "I feel naked out here if I'm not armed."

"You must do as I say," Nopoloto said again.

Matt hesitated for just a moment, then handed his pistol to Nopoloto. Using a small strip of rawhide, Nopoloto tied the pistol to one side of the Y at the top of the branch. Then he did the same thing with Matt's rifle, tying it to the other side. As they rode off, it was obvious to anyone who might see them that Matt was unarmed.

Matt followed Nopoloto, then chuckled as he realized they were circling back to an encampment he had already located, and discarded. Delshay was coming back to previously used encampments, realizing that whoever was following him would continue on.

As they approached the camp, Matt saw three Indians standing on the trail, waiting for them. One of the Indians was the biggest Apache he had ever seen. One was young, perhaps in his early twenties. The one in the middle was Delshay. Matt recognized him from the days when he had scouted for the army. Matt held his hand up, palm out, and was gratified to see that Delshay responded in the same way.

Delshay and Nopoloto spoke a few words in their own language. Then Delshay spoke to Matt in English.

"I have seen you before," he said.

"Yes."

"You were with the soldiers. Are you still with the soldiers?"

"No."

"You have come for Mountain Lion Woman."

"You have given her a fine name," Matt said.

Delshay nodded. "Yes. She has the courage of

a mountain lion. Her man has the courage of
a rabbit."

The other two Indians laughed.

"I have come for her, yes."

"You would take her back to the coward?"

"I will take her where she wants to go," Matt said.

"She will not wish to return to the coward."

"I believe it is for her to decide."

"Yes," Delshay said. "It is for her to decide."

With Matt and Nopoloto leading their horses,
they followed Delshay and the other two Indians
for about a mile until they came to the site of an
encampment. As Matt had surmised, this was one
of the earlier camps he had already discovered.

"You have been here before," Delshay said.

"Yes," Matt answered,

"You track like a wolf," Delshay said. "I knew that
you would find us. That is why I sent Cochinay to
tell Nopoloto to bring you to me."

"I am Cochinay," the youngest of the three Indians who had met him said.

"You are married to the daughter of Nopoloto,"
Matt said.

"You know this?" Cochinay asked in surprise.

Matt had heard about Cochinay and Alope from
Nopoloto when he took him to the reservation hospital.

"Yes, I know this. It is a good marriage for her."

"She is dead. She was killed before we could
marry."

"You are married," Matt said. "In the spirit world,
you are married, and she is very pleased."

Cochinay nodded. "Yes," he said. "Yes, I think that is right."

Matt looked around the campsite for Cynthia. At first, he saw only Indians—then he realized that one of the people he was seeing wasn't an Indian.

"Mrs. Bixby?" he said.

"Mr. Jensen!" Cynthia replied with a happy shout. "You have come for me!" She started toward Matt, but he held up his hand to stop her.

"Delshay, will you let Mountain Lion Woman come with me?"

Before his question could be answered, the big Indian spoke to Delshay. He spoke in Apache, so Matt had no idea what they were talking about.

"Do not let the woman go with him," Nalyudi said.

"Why should I keep her?" Delshay replied *"She is of no value to me."*

"She took my medicine," Nalyudi said. *"You cannot let her go without allowing me to recover my medicine."*

"And how would you do this?"

Nalyudi looked at Matt. *"I will fight the white man for her. If I defeat him, she will become my woman. If he defeats me, she leaves with him."*

"You would do this thing?" Delshay asked Nalyudi, speaking in English now.

"Yes," Nalyudi replied, also in English. "If the white man is not a coward."

Matt realized then that they were talking about him, but the realization didn't surprise him. He had surmised as much during their conversation, even though he not understood one word.

"Mountain Lion Woman called you Jensen," Delshay said. "Is that your name?"

"Yes."

"Jensen, Nalyudi wishes to fight you," Delshay said, indicating the big Indian. "If he wins, Mountain Lion Woman will be his woman. If you win, she will be your woman."

Matt looked at Nalyudi, who was glaring at him. This wasn't going to be a mere sporting exhibition. In all likelihood, this was going to be a fight to the death because Nalyudi was filled with hatred, though Matt had no idea why. However, if this was the only way he would be able to rescue Cynthia Bixby, then so be it.

"All right," he said. "I'll fight him."

Nalyudi explained the rules of the fight. They would each be armed with a war club. They would both have to keep one end of a strip of rawhide, five feet long, in their mouths at all times. This would insure that they maintained close contact during the fight. If one of them let the rawhide strip out of his mouth, he would be required to lay down his club.

Matt nodded his agreement and Delshay presented each of them with a war club, then a long piece of rawhide. The two men put the ends of the rawhide strip in their mouths, then jumped apart to the maximum separation the length of rawhide would allow.

Nalyudi moved in first. He held the club over his head with both hands and as he approached, he brought it down sharply.

Matt barely managed to leap to one side as the war club came down. The miss left Nalyudi exposed, but because Matt had to move so quickly to get out of the way, he was unable to take advantage of the situation. Instantly, both men separated again.

Nalyudi swung again, and this time Matt was ready for him. He blocked Nalyudi's war club with his own. The clash of clubs echoed from the nearby bluffs. Recovering quickly, Matt swung at Nalyudi, but the big Indian was much quicker, and more agile than Matt would have thought. Matt's swing found only thin air. Nalyudi swung in response, and his club connected with Matt's, jerking it out of his hand. Matt suddenly found himself unarmed!

With a victorious smile, Nalyudi began taunting Matt. He made a couple of jabs with his war club, catching Matt in the face with one of his thrusts. That prod opened up a three-corner tear and blood began streaming down Matt's cheek.

Nalyudi could have ended the fight by closing in on him and bringing the war club down to crush Matt's skull. But he was enjoying himself too much, and confidently, tauntingly, he began tossing his own war club from hand to hand.

That was where Nalyudi made his biggest mistake. The hand that could so quickly draw a pistol had no difficulty in reaching out to snatch the war club in mid-toss. It happened so fast that those who were watching, even Nalyudi, were unaware of the sudden change in fortune. Now it was Nalyudi who was unarmed.

Matt jabbed the war club into Nalyudi's solar plexus. That had the effect of knocking the breath out of Nalyudi, and folding both his hands across his stomach, he bent over in an agonized attempt to breathe. At that point, all Matt would have had to do to kill him would be to bring the war club down on Nalyudi's head, for the big Indian was totally defenseless.

Matt started the swing, but stopped it just short of hitting him. Instead, he touched Nalyudi's head as if counting coups. Then he spat out the end of the rawhide strip, tossed the war club aside, and motioned toward Cynthia.

"Come, Mrs. Bixby, I'll take you home," he said.

Gratefully, Cynthia ran to him. Just before she reached him, though, she turned back to Chandeisi.

"Good-bye, Chandeisi, my friend," she called. "Thank you for protecting me."

"Good-bye, Cynthia Bixby," Chandeisi replied.

Suddenly, a gunshot rang out and looking around, Matt saw Delshay holding his hand over a wound in his chest. Nalyudi was holding a smoking rifle, and with an evil smile, he pointed it at Matt.

Three more shots rang out, and Nalyudi went down, felled by bullets from the rifles of Chandeisi, Cochinay, and Nopoloto. Matt realized then that the three Indians had saved his life. Their action was too late, however, to save Delshay, who lay dead where he had fallen.

"Go now," Nopoloto said. "You will not be harmed."

"Come along, Mrs. Bixby. We're going to have to ride double, I'm afraid," Matt said. "But Spirit is a good strong horse, he'll be able to handle it."

"I have a horse," Cynthia said.

"You have a horse?"

"It is one I have been riding," Cynthia said. "It is my horse, is it not?" she asked Chandeisi.

Chandeisi nodded. "It is your horse," he said.

* * *

"I told you the son of a bitch would find her," Willis said when he saw Matt and Cynthia on the road returning to Phoenix. With him were two of the men who had been a part of his posse, Karl Lathum and Angus Pugh. "All we have to do now is kill Jensen and take the girl."

"What good will that do us?" Lathum asked. "Bixby said he wasn't goin' to pay no reward. You heard that same as I did."

"We ain't takin' her for no reward," Willis said. "We're takin' her for ransom. All we got to do is tell Bixby that if he wants to ever see her alive again, he's goin' to have to come up with that ten thousand dollars."

"Where are we going to hit Jensen?" Pugh asked.

"At Weaver's Needle," Willis answered.

Chapter Twenty-eight

Matt knew what it was as soon as he heard it—the whizzing sound of a bullet frying the air but inches away from his head. That sound was followed immediately by the bark of a rifle.

"What was that?" Cynthia said.

Matt didn't answer. Instead, he leaped from Spirit and, in the same motion, grabbed Cynthia, pulling her from her horse. With one hand, he slapped the rumps of the two horses to get them out of danger, and with his other, he pushed the protesting Cynthia behind a rocky ledge. Two more bullets whipped by, one of them hitting a rock, then singing loudly as it ricocheted out into the desert.

By now, Cynthia realized what was going on, and she neither fought nor protested his action.

"Who is shooting at us?" Cynthia asked.

"I don't know, but I'm going to find out," Matt said.

He raised up to take a look and, just as he did, he

saw the white puff of smoke from two rifles. Both bullets came uncomfortably close.

"Stay here and stay down," Matt said. "No matter what you see, or think you see, don't move."

"All right," Cynthia agreed.

Matt got up, then ran across an open area toward a ridgeline that was closer to the spot where the firing was coming from. As he expected them to, the assailants fired again; this time three shots were fired.

"Uhnn!" Matt grunted, grabbing his stomach as he went down. Cynthia screamed.

"Mr. Jensen, no!" she cried.

Willis, Lathum, and Pugh stared at Matt's motionless body.

"We got 'im," Lathum said.

"Maybe," Willis replied.

"What do you mean maybe?" Lathum said. "You seen 'im go down same as I did. Besides, I had a perfect bead on him. I know I hit him. He's deader'n shit, if you ask me."

"I hit him, too," Pugh said.

"Well, I'm glad I'm with two excellent shots," Willis said.

"Hell, Willis, we don't mean nothin' by that," Lathum said. "It's just that we both know the son of a bitch is dead, and we don't know why we're waitin' around up here. Let's go down there and get the woman, then take her in town and get the money."

"Yeah," Pugh said.

"All right, go down there and check him out,"

Willis said. "If he's dead, we'll get the girl and take her back, then get the money."

"Now you're talkin'," Lathum said with a broad grin.

Carefully, the two men climbed down from their perch a short way up the wall behind Weaver's Needle. Then, with pistols at the ready, they started across the rocky valley floor toward Matt's prostrate form.

"Be careful now," Pugh said.

"What's there to be careful about?" Lathum replied. "You seen him go down, same as I did. Hell, he ain't even twitched in the last five minutes. There can't nobody lie that long without at least twitching if he ain't dead."

Matt heard the sound of boots on rock as the two men approached him. He had hoped his ruse would bring out all three, but if it brought only two, that would at least even up the odds between him and whoever else was shooting at him.

"Wait right here," Lathum said.

"Wait for what?"

"Let's put a bullet in his head, just to make sure."

Matt heard the hammers come back on the two pistols, and he waited but an instant before he suddenly threw himself into a roll to his right.

His timing had been perfect—both Lathum and Pugh fired at the same instant he had rolled. The two bullets plowed into the rocky ground where he had been but an instant before. Matt fired twice, the shots coming so close together that it sounded as if there had been only one shot.

Lathum and Pugh went down, both of them dead before they hit the ground.

"Matt!" Cynthia called out, relieved to see that he had not been killed.

"Cynthia, stay where you are!" Matt shouted back. He hoped to get a shot at the third assailant, but the sound of retreating hoofbeats told him that whoever it was was running away.

The sun was setting and the shadows were long when Matt and Cynthia rode down Central Street in Phoenix. They were recognized as soon as they rode into town, and by the time they reached the hotel, nearly one hundred people had turned out to welcome her back.

Bixby and Hendel were standing in front of the hotel, and the expressions on their faces could not have possibly been further apart. Hendel's expression was of absolute joy. Bixby wore an expression of disgust.

"I hope you don't think you are going to get a reward for this," Bixby said. He smiled, a humorless smile. "Remember, you are the one who asked me to withdraw the reward."

"I did not bring her back for the reward," Matt replied.

"Why did you bring her back at all?"

"What? Bixby, what are you saying?" Hendel gasped.

"Look at her, dressed like an Indian and filthy," Bixby said. "She is soiled goods. If she had any sense of self-respect, she would have killed herself before she let those filthy Indians touch her."

Matt was about to tell Bixby that the Indians didn't touch her, but Cynthia held her hand out to stop him. "Is that what you truly think, Jay?" she asked. "Do you think that just because I was with the Indians, I am soiled goods?"

"Indeed I do," Bixby said coldly. "I want nothing more to do with you. When we return to New York, I will have my lawyer draw up a bill of divorcement."

"I wouldn't do that if I were you, Mr. Bixby," Ken Hendel said in a calm and resolute voice.

"Oh? And why not?"

"I would remind you, Mr. Bixby, that the money you have been so freely spending is in fact Cynthia's money."

"Cynthia's money?" Bixby replied. He chuckled. "For an accountant, you have a lot to learn. Once we were married, the money became mine."

Hendel shook his head. "I am afraid you are wrong, sir. By arrangement with her late father, I constructed the estate in such a way as to fully protect Mrs. Bixby. If you divorce her, you will lose everything."

"Well, I didn't really mean to divorce her, I was just expressing my displeasure over—" Bixby started to say, but he was unable to finish the sentence because a dark hole suddenly appeared in his forehead and he fell back, dead from a bullet to his brain.

"Jensen, you son of a bitch!" Pogue Willis shouted from the far end of the street. "That was meant for you!"

"Cynthia, Hendel, get down!" Matt shouted, drawing his pistol.

Hendel pushed Cynthia down, then lay on top of her, protecting her body with his as more bullets flew by.

Cynthia and Hendel weren't the only ones to get out of danger. Those who had gathered on the street to welcome Cynthia back from the Indians suddenly found themselves in the middle of a gun battle, and with curses and screams, they hurried to either side of the street to get out of the way.

Once the street was cleared, only Matt and Willis remained, and they found themselves facing each other about twenty-five yards apart. Both had their pistols in their hands, but Willis held up his left hand.

"Put your gun in your holster, Jensen," Willis said. "If we're goin' to do this, let's do it right. I know damn well I can beat you." Willis holstered his own gun.

"What good would it do you if you do beat me?" Matt asked, putting his pistol in his holster. "The entire town just saw you murder Bixby. I'm either going to kill you, or you're going to hang, one or the other."

"Yeah, that's just it," Willis said. "I ain't goin' to hang." Without a call, Willis dipped his hand toward his pistol. Because he hadn't called it, he had a moment's advantage over Matt, and his gun was in his hand as quickly as was Matt's.

They fired simultaneously.

Willis allowed a satisfied smile to play across his face. "You weren't all that fast," he said.

The smile left his face, to be replaced by an

expression of pain. Then he fell forward, facedown in the dirt.

"No, but I was more accurate," Matt said as he slipped the pistol back into the holster.

Two days later

The westbound train was sitting at the Maricopa depot, venting steam. As Matt walked through a cloud of steam, he saw Cynthia standing alone.

"Mr. Jensen, oh, how wonderful, you did come to tell us good-bye," Cynthia said. "I knew you would."

"Where is Ken?"

"He's with Mr. Prufrock," Cynthia said. "We have had Jay embalmed. We are taking him back to New York."

"Here he comes," Matt said.

Hendel came up to join them then and, unabashedly, he put his arm around Cynthia.

"Is everything taken care of, darling?" Cynthia asked.

"Yes, Mr. Prufrock has been invaluable," Hendel said. "He has made arrangements to ship the body all the way through back to New York."

"I see that there has been a change in your relationship," Matt said, indicating the fact that they were standing together with Hendel's arm around Cynthia.

"A change in the relationship," Hendel said, "but not a change in the way we feel about each other. It turns out that my love for Cynthia was not unrequited."

"I felt trapped in the marriage with Jay," Cynthia said. "I was only able to survive by knowing that

Ken was always there by my side. I feel just awful about poor Jay getting killed, but—"

"Life must go on," Matt said.

Ken nodded. "Yes, life must go on," he said. "We will wait a respectable length of time. Then we will be married."

"Board!" the conductor shouted.

"We must go," Cynthia said. She turned toward the train, then turned back and hugged Matt. "Thank you, Mr. Jensen," she said. "I don't know what would have become of us if it hadn't been for you. If you are ever in New York, please know that you will be welcome."

"Thanks," Matt said. "I'll keep that in mind."

"Board!" the conductor called again, and Ken and Cynthia stepped up onto the train. Ken glanced back one more time and waved at Matt.

Matt waited in the station until the train left. Then he mounted Spirit and headed north. He had no particular destination in mind, but it was late fall, and he wanted to get on the trail before an early winter snow closed the passes.

Cotton Pickens Is Back!

The reluctant hero of
William W. Johnstone's classic
Blood Valley
is back in an all-new adventure!

SIX WAYS FROM SUNDAY

by William W. Johnstone
with J. A. Johnstone
Coming in May 2009

Be sure to look for these other upcoming
Johnstone Westerns:

THE LAST GUNFIGHTER: SLAUGHTER
Coming in March 2009!

BLOOD BOND: DEADLY ROAD TO YUMA
Coming in April 2009!

Critter, he farted. He never did give me much credit for being smart.

I sort of wrestled with myself as I headed that direction. What was some cowboy doing getting into a mining war? But I hadn't been practicing cowmanship for a while now, and thought maybe there might be a job ahead, forty dollars and found, so I proceeded. It was a right peaceful valley, full of sunlight and pine scent on the wind. These here were the Pioneer Mountains, and there were more little gold mines being sunk in the rock hereabouts than I could count. Swamp Creek, the town, sort of mushroomed into a canvas-and-rough plank place overnight, and now all sorts of entertaining types were digging in there, mostly to mine the miners.

The valley was drained by Swamp Creek, which was named for a big old swamp about a mile above town. It was like that creek got constipated for a mile or two there, and spread out every which way. It was said there was no bottom to it, just black muck and more muck in there, and a person would sink in and keep on sinking until the muck closed over his head. It sure was the only swamp around. I steered Critter toward a rocky gray slope that had a lot of pine forest at its base, and more forest high up, where the jagged mountains stretched toward the blue. That poppin' got louder, so I knew I was gettin' close, but so far I couldn't see nothing.

I was taking myself and my sturdy horse into someplace where lead was flying around, and I argued with myself some. My ma, she always told me to stay outta trouble, and my pa, he always told me to stay clear of women, but they's both gone now, so I get into whatever I get into. I wish I'd paid them more heed, because even though I didn't know it then, I was going to get into trouble and women both.

I rounded a bend that opened on a wide gulch feeding into that valley, and now at last I got me a little peek at what the ruckus was all about.

"Critter," I says to the nag, "I do believe they've got a little claim jumping party a-going full tilt."

Up in the middle of that cliff was a mine head. All I could see was the mouth of a shaft driven into the side of that big old mountain, a black hole staring down upon me. And blocking that hole was an overturned one-ton ore car, rusty yeller, and a few chunks of metal I couldn't rightly name 'cause when it comes to hauling rock outta the ground, I'm dumb as a stump.

But I hauled up to study the matter, stayin' well out of range of any hot lead. It was plain enough, even to a dumb-ass cowboy. Up yonder were half a dozen hardcases banging away at someone holed up at the mine. That old boy in the mine, he had him a Sharps, with a big throaty boom, while the rest were using lighter artillery, and no one was gittin' anywhere.

Like that feller at the mine was outnumbered but dug in.

It didn't look like any fair fight either, 'cause I seen some hardcases working around to either side, like they're planning to rush the old boy in the mine, coming at him from the flanks where he won't see much until it's too late.

I got the itchy feeling they were gettin' set to

shoot that old miner plumb dead, probably for reasons I didn't want to think about, such as ownership. It must be quite a mine, I thought, to stir up a kettle full of pain like that.

"Well, Critter, you and me are going to buy into this here fracas," I said. Critter, he rolled an ear back and shook his muzzle in disgust. He was telling me I'm plumb nuts, and I never would argue the case, 'cause he and I both agree to it.

Ahead was a mighty stand of lodgepole pine, sticking straight and true into the air, and I headed that way mostly to keep clear of that Sharps up there, and also to get me a better view of the proceedings.

I steered the horse up a grassy slope and into the forest, which was so thick that afternoon turned to twilight, and I let Critter pick his way over fallen timber, which crosshatched the ground. There was no way to escape making a noise as loud as a steam engine, so I just let the nag poke along, while I kept a sharp eye out for surprises.

Well, I got myself surprised, all right, when a dude in a dove-gray swallowtail coat and black trousers and shiny shoes and black silk stovepipe hat appears from nowhere, pointing a shiny little pepperbox at me, maybe nine barrels in all. A quaint little weapon, outmoded by revolvers, but as lethal as any.

"Hands high," the gent says, so I consider it's my duty to obey, real careful, because pepperboxes are ornery little guns with a habit of shooting off all barrels at once.

I raised my pinkies toward the evergreen limbs

above, and smiled kindly. "Just wandering through," says I. "I'm never one to miss a good show."

The gent looked me over and saw a young cowboy, well armed, skinny as hell, with a few acne patches on my cheeks that were some embarrassing, even if half hid by the scruffy layer of beard I'd not scraped away for a week or two. Me, I saw a smoothly shaven face, black hawk eyes, a trim gray mustache, clean white teeth, fancy dark sideburns, and soft hands that had never done a lick of log-splitting, shoveling, ax-swinging, or plow-wrestling. In short, he was some Fancy Dan. He even had one of them gold watch fobs dangling across his middle.

"Who are you?" the man asked, as if he expected a reply.

"I don't like to spell her out," I said. "I never was too happy with the name, so I keep her to myself."

"Nine barrels. Shall I shoot the first?"

"Cotton," says I, all hasty. "It's not a name I cotton to."

"And?"

"You plumb gonna have to kill me dead before I give out the rest."

He smiled suddenly. "Cotton Pickens," he said. "You've been hanging around Swamp Creek looking for trouble to get into."

I flushed pure red. How anyone got ahold of my rear handle I don't know. I never tell it to anyone.

"This is fortuitous," he said. "I've been looking for you."

Now that was a word I couldn't pronounce, much less figure out. "Put that in words someone like me'd know some of," I said.

"Fortunate," he said. "I heard you are good with a gun, and I thought to hire you."

"Well, I'm not rightly sure I'm for sale," I said. This feller was too clean-shaven for me. My gut feeling is not to trust anyone in a swallowtail coat and a mustache. "But you can give me the what-for."

He shrugged. "This," he said. "We have paper giving us that mine. But that gentleman resists."

"Paper?"

"Deed and mineral rights. We paid the back taxes and bought it at auction."

"But he still figures possession is nine tenths of the law, right?"

"You know some law, Cotton."

"Well, you got to read something in an outhouse, especially when you're as slow to do your business as I am. Outhouses are plumb boring. So I read Blackstone while I'm a sittin'."

"Frankly, it surprises me. But yes, I'm looking for able men, and you'd fit the bill. Forty a month."

That was a heap of money for some half-starved saddle tramp like me. But I wasn't all that sure about this outfit.

"Now, I don't dicker with anyone that's pointing a nine-shot pepperbox at me. It makes me nervous. And I don't think you've given me a name."

"Sorry," the man said, and slid his pepperbox into a slick little underarm holster, where it lay so close it didn't show under that swallowtail.

"Carter Scruples," he said. "I'm a partner in this enterprise."

That sure was an odd handle. I wasn't sure what

scruples meant, but it was something you hid behind most likely.

I quit my twitching now that the mean little lead-thrower was back in its nest.

"I'm not saying yes and I'm not saying no," I said. "I want to see how this here business is transacted."

He shrugged, and nodded toward the edge of the grove. "Have a look, if you want to risk a shot coming your way."

"I think maybe I will," I said. "But I'm going to leave Critter here, safe in these trees."

I slid down from Critter. He objected some, laid his ears back, and I yanked the reins just in time to keep him from taking a bite out of this Mr. Scruples.

"Horse needs subduing," Scruples said. "Either that or it needs its throat cut."

I didn't much care for that observation, and gave Scruples a hard look. But he just smiled pleasantly, like everything was fine here in a pine grove while his hired guns were trying to kill some mine owner.

We eased forward until we reached some brush that bordered the slope, and we could see the action above in relative safety.

"You just gonna kill him, just like that?" I asked.

"Not just like that. We gave him his chance to leave peaceably."

"What'd he say?"

"I wouldn't deem it proper to tell you," Scruples said. "In any case, it'll all be over in a few moments."

It looked like it might be. I studied the scene real careful, and found a few gunmen creeping and dodging up that rocky grade, hiding behind talus. An occasional boom from that big Sharps kept them from rushing, but it was plain a rush was coming, and one man with one long gun wasn't going to hold off a pack of gunslicks. Especially since now the two at the flanks were edging in, taking advantage of cover to stay out of sight.

A few of the gunslicks down below the mine head kept popping away with their carbines, just to keep the mine owner occupied, while them stalkers at the flanks was creeping along the rocky cliff getting ready for the potshot.

Then most everything happened at once. The ones in the middle upped and clambered that steep slope, while the ones at the sides opened fire, and now there were more than six in sight, maybe eight or nine, all a jumping and dodging toward the mine head. The Sharps didn't boom at all, and I wondered if the old boy in the mine had bought the ticket. Lotta lead flying around up there, whanging off that ore car. Then the whole lot of gunslicks whooped up that slope, and the damnedest thing happened. It was sort of shocking actually.

Old miner, he let fly with a couple of sticks of Dupont Hercules with a cap and some spitting fuse wired together, and next thing I know, there was a hell of a eruption as that thing went off, and I seen a couple of bodies fly upward like rag dolls and flop to the earth, no doubt extinct. They sure looked surprised up there. Not a one of them was standing. The concussion had flattened the whole lot. It knocked Scruples and me off our pins, too. Then I heard a maniac laughing up there, behind the overturned ore car, laughing like a bucksaw slicing wood. I have to give those gunslicks credit. They upped and ran toward the mine head and the whole thing happened over again. A couple of sticks of dynamite with a spitting fuse sailed out. I got smart and stuck my fingers in my ears, and tried to hit the ground before the thing went off, but didn't make it. The blast knocked me flat. This time four more of those dudes were writhing on the slope, or tumbling down the talus. Durndest thing I ever did see.

I guess that did it some. The rest of them slicks, they hightailed downslope just as fast as they could scramble, leavin' them dead sprawled around on gray rock. Those two flanking ones just quit and come tumbling down that grade. There was four lyin' mighty still up there, and four more come stumbling into the woods, all deaf as stones and some bleeding red all over.

That's when I saw her. She was just about the most beautiful woman I ever did lay eyes on, a blonde wearing black satin from chin to toe, one of them fancy dresses with more buttons than I can count. She had one of them picture hats topping that soft blond hair, and I just stood there and stared. Where'd she come from anyway?

Scruples, he went over to her and she tucked her arm into his.

"Win some, lose some," he said to her.

She smiled wryly. I ain't seen a smile like that on a lady like that ever before, and I just stood there staring and rocking on my feet. I was dumbstruck. There just ain't any women like that in the whole Territory of Montana. That sort of woman, she's tied up with J. P. Morgan or Vanderbilt, or one of those that live at Newport and have got a lot of gold

Chapter Two

That was it. Scruples and his blond beauty rode away in a shiny black carriage. High up that slope, there were bodies sprawled in the rocks.

That didn't seem fittin' for some country boy like me. Maybe they weren't dead. Maybe they could be helped. But I had me a problem. The minute I stepped out of the pines and onto that rocky slope, that big old Sharps would bark.

"Critter," I says to my nag. "I've got me a job to do, and it scares the britches half off me."

Critter clacked his teeth and yawned. So much for admiration. I thought maybe Critter would salute.

I dug into my kit lookin' for a white flag. If I was going to step out of them trees, I'd need to be waving some white. But I didn't have no white. Just some old cotton underdrawers that started out white, but now was a sort of yeller gray. Well, yeller gray would have to do, so I tied the legs of them drawers to a handy stick, crept up the edge of the grove, and waved the thing around a bit.

I didn't see no action up there, or hear some damned bullet sail by me, so real cautious, I crept out on the rock, takin' my time and waving my yeller-gray drawers around and makin' a lot of noise so's not to surprise that mining bastard up there.

But all I got was a mess of silence.

Well, I thought, it's now or never. Just as a precaution I undid my gunbelt, and hung it over my shoulder as a further peace offerin', though I didn't say nothing about the two-shot derringer in my boot. I did a slow climb over talus toward the lowest of them gunmen, and found him sprawled in the rock, plumb dead. He'd been punctured here and there. So I clambered up that rough gray rock to the next, and found he'd expired, too, and was missing an arm. It wasn't no pretty sight to look at.

The next one was over on the flank, and was one of them two that was creepin' in on the miner. I was gettin' out of sight of the mine head when a voice filtered down to me.

"Stay in sight," the owner of that voice said. I took it for plumb good advice.

"Just checkin'," I said.

"He's dead, and so's t'other, on your left."

"You mind if I come up and palaver a little?"

"You ain't one of them. I saw you ride in."

"That's right, I ain't. But I thought to take care of the wounded and maybe plant the dead, long as the rest of them hightailed out of here."

"No tricks. I got a few more of these little Dupont bombs."

I had yet to see this fellow. Somehow, he was

hidden in the shadows of the ore car, and probably as forted up as a man can get.

I made my way up the talus slope, and finally reached a small flat in front of the shaft, where all the mining stuff lay around and about. The miner, he appeared from somewhere in all that tangle of iron, and that old Sharps was staring at my navel.

"Howdy," I says.

He didn't reply, but grinned toothlessly. He was an old boy, wearing more dirt on him than cloth, and peering at me from bright blueberry eyes.

I got mad. "That's the second time today I've stared into a barrel, and I don't like it. First time, I was looking at an entire pepperbox, and that sight ain't for the fainthearted."

"Sharps is empty anyway," he said, setting it down. "When it comes to fights, I prefer some Dupont." He said it *DOOpont,* and even a dummy like me got the idea he was talkin' dynamite.

He had a row of those bombs there just inside the shaft, and he fetched one to show me his work. "Two sticks of Dupont Hercules, this copper cap in there, with six inches of Bickford fuse crimped in the end, plus a mess of tenpenny nails to do a little damage, all wired nice. Now this here fuse burns thirty seconds to the foot, so these are ten-second fuses. That's so no one picks one up and throws it back at me. Pretty smart, eh?"

Tell you the truth, I was plain itchy standing there next to that thing. I know short guns, and I'm not bad with a long gun, but this thing he was waving around was big enough to kill Paul Bunyon.

"Maybe you oughta set her back in there a piece," I said.

Those blueberry eyes glimmered and glowed, and he whipped a lucifer across some rock, lit the fuse until she sparked orange, and then tossed her off to the right. He dove into the overturned ore car, and so did I, just in time. That sucker lifted the ground from under me, and shot tenpenny nails everywhere. I was right grateful Critter was nowhere near.

"Agnes Cork here. What's your handle?" he said.

I could hardly hear a word, and waited for my eardrums to quit dancing.

"What did you say it was?"

"Agnes Cork, my boy."

"Now wait just a minute here. You ain't no Agnes."

He nodded. "Joseph St. Agnes Cork," he said. "They was trying to line up a few saints when I was born. Now what's your handle?"

"Cotton."

"That's half a handle."

"Agnes, I can't bear to give you the rear half of my handle. Just can't, so you've got to take me as I am."

"Well, invent a name. I just need some pants to go with the shirt."

"Invent a name?" Truth to tell, I'd never thought of inventing a name. But it wasn't a bad idea.

"Sonny, I'll invent one for you. You mind that?"

"Sure I mind. I'll invent my own name, Agnes."

It sure was strange, calling that mining bastard Agnes. I decided to change the subject.

"No one's coming around to plant those four, so it's up to me."

Agnes nodded quietly. "You have a good heart, Cotton."

"Maybe you can help me. It's all rock around here."

Agnes nodded. "Glory hole about fifty yards that way. Miner named Walrus Wank hit a pocket there, but it petered out after a few feet. Still, nice little eight- or ten-foot hole in the wall."

When we reached the first body, Agnes pulled his pockets out and collected a few coins. The man's revolvers were nowhere in sight, and probably got blown into the next county. "They owe me," he said. "I'm charging them for the powder I blew. Must of spent forty dollars defending my mine, and they'll pay. Any more, I'll give it to you to take to Swamp Creek."

"Fair enough," I said.

We carried the dead gunslick over to the glory hole and laid him flat in there, after chasing a rattler out. He sure was perforated. I think about five tenpenny nails had done for him. It was grim work, and I didn't like it none, and besides that it plumb wore me out. But it didn't bother Agnes none, and after a while, we got all four of the gunmen laid out in that little burrow hole, and Agnes had collected thirty-seven dollars and one revolver with a bent barrel.

"That evens it up," he said.

"We gonna pile up some rock here?" I asked.

"Naw," he said. He hiked back to his mine, told me to get well back, and brought one of his Dupont specials, but this one with no tenpenny nails dressing it up and a longer fuse. He lit the thing with a lucifer, tossed it into the mouth, and walked swiftly toward his own mine, arriving exactly when it blew, and after the dust cleared, and my ears quit howling, and I could stand up again, I looked over at that glory hole and there was nothing there except a mess of rock. It was plumb amazing.

Agnes, he just he-he-heed his way back to his own place. He sure had a laugh that made me wonder whether I'd get outa there alive.

I sure didn't know nothing about mining, and I thought I'd better find out.

"How come they were trying to kill you?" I asked.

Agnes, he pulled some tobacco lying loose in his pocket and stuffed it under his tongue. "Just for the fun of it," he said.

"They own this mine? That's what Scruples said."

Joseph St. Agnes Cork, he just cackled. "That wouldn't a got anything if they killed me," he said. "Gold pinched out some whiles ago, and now she's nothing but a hole in the cliff."

"No gold?"

"Pocket mine. Gold along here is in pockets. Clean out a pocket and there's nothing left."

I was getting testy. "So you fought 'em for nothing?"

"Oh, I didn't say that, boy. You got a thing or two to learn about mining. I loved that fight. Now I can sell this here hole for mebbe ten thousand simoleons. Now I got what I needed, and they handed it to me. A man fights off ten, twelve claim-jumpers, why, that hole of his must be worth a lot of moolah."

"You mean you're going to defraud the buyer?"

He grinned, and those blueberry eyes sparked bright. "Oh, I'll salt her a little, and we'll see. A man digs a hole for better part of a year, he ought to get paid for it, right? I'm just angling for some pay, and that Scruples bunch handed it to me on a platter. Until they showed up, I was plumb discouraged."

I didn't like this none. Cork was a crook.

He started cackling again, and I had a mind to get out of there. Critter and I thought to help someone outnumbered ten to one or so, and now four gents lay in their graves and a bunch more were full of nail holes.

"Cotton, you stick around here and I'll teach you some about getting gold out. You want some johnnycakes? I'm of a mind to eat."

I had nothing better to do, so I nodded. "I'm going to fetch Critter, water him, and bring him up here. He likes griddle cakes and he'd be plain unhappy with me if he got a whiff of johnnycakes and he couldn't sink his buck teeth into a couple."

"Does he haul ore cars? I'll put him to work."

"No, Critter ain't never had harness touch him."

Agnes Cork was makin' me huffy again. I wouldn't let no miner lay hands on Critter. Trouble is, Cork was a miner, and they ain't half the man any cowboy is. I worked down the talus slope, plunged into the dark forest, found the nag chewing on bark, and brought him back up there to the mine, where he laid his ears back and snapped a time or two at Agnes, and then tried to kick him, too.

"Horse is just like me," Agnes said, and laughed that mean laugh again.

The miner set to work mixing some cornmeal and water while I scrounged up some firewood. There sure wasn't none anywhere near.

But in time, along about sundown, we got Critter and ourselves fed.

"You got to git now," Agnes said. "I don't allow no one around here disturbing my sleep and slitting my throat. Anyone stirs around here, he gets a knife up to the hilt."

"We'll vamoose," I says, eyeing his little shanty, which was the most disgusting looking dump I ever laid eyes on. If I set foot in there, I'd catch leprosy for sure. "But afore I go, you mind telling me about these claim-jumpers? They offered me forty and found, and I'm just thinking about it. Sure beats starving."

"Oh, Scruples. And his lady friend. They got that palace car in town."

Well, that explained something. Sitting up a slope from Swamp Creek was a regular Pullman Palace Car someone dragged overland, probably using fifty oxen and some braced up wagons. It was right fancy, purple lacquer with gilded letters on the side, and when I got a peek or two at her, I could see wine-colored velvet drapes in there, and heaven knows what, my being too dumb about all that to know a flush toilet from a two-holer.

"What about all that paper? He told me he's got a legal right."

Agnes cackled. "You got a few things to learn, boy. Scruples, he's in cahoots with the mining district recorder, Johnny Brashear, and pays the old souse to find fault in a claim." He eyed me, sizing me up for a ten-year-old. "Mining districts get born pretty casual, long before the government moves in and surveys a place and makes it legal. Miners themselves set up districts, adopt some rules about the size of a claim, stuff like that, and this gets put in a ledger and usually the government gets around to recognizing this stuff years later. But bribe a clerk or two, and you pretty much turn it all cattywumpus."

"Your claim's valid?"

"Bet your ass, sonnyboy."

I didn't cotton to being called sonnyboy, but it was better than being called Cotton, so I just glared at him a bit.

"So them in that palace car, they're not up and up?"

Agnes Cork, he began wheezing so hard I thought he'd choke.

"How come no one's fighting 'em?"

"It's that woman," Agnes said.

I couldn't make sense of that, but it sure did make me curious about her. She was just about the first woman I'd seen in a long time that made my britches go tight. I didn't know they made women like that. She was some better than Sarah Bernhardt. I seen a picture of her once, and thought there sure is some world out there I ain't never seen.

"Boy, you go back to pushing cows around until you're growed up enough to walk into a mining camp. Now, it's getting dark, and I kill anything wandering around my mine in the dark, and I don't ask questions neither."

I think that was a message aimed my way, so I loaded up Critter and climbed aboard, wanting enough light so he could pick his way down that slope without busting a leg. Leastwise, I got out of there without getting shot, and Critter didn't bust nothing.

And I wandered toward Swamp Creek wondering whether to hire on. If all sides was as crooked as it sounded, it wouldn't matter none which one paid me wages.

Chapter Three

I was scrapin' the bottom of my purse in that mining town, and I was wonderin' where my next chow would be coming from. This wasn't no cow town where I could hook up with most any cow outfit, move into a bunkhouse, and fill my belly. No, this here Swamp Creek high in the mountains was different.

It rose up mighty fast, first canvas buildings, then log, and now some sawn wood was showing up here and there and the place was looking like it might stick around a while. There was false-front stores doing a trade. They was a saloon ever' few yards, a few whorehouses with them red lanterns rocking in the breeze, a few shacks where a miner could lie on a bedbug pallet for two bits a night, and a few little whitewashed cottages where folks lived pretty decent.

Now there's plenty of work available in a mining town, and sometimes for two or three dollars a day, too, king's wages, but the stuff you got to do is plain disgusting. If it's hard-rock mines, like in the Swamp Creek district, you've got to go down in some black hole for ten hours, choke on fumes, hope the whole thing doesn't cave in, and spend the whole time hammering and shoveling. The noise is so bad that you're half deaf time you get out of that hole and breathe some real air and see some night sky.

Most of them miners, they're big and tough. Even the little ones are big and tough. They come from all over the world, places I can't even pronounce, and half of them got names I never heard of. Soon as the shift ends, they head for their favorite saloon and toss down boilermakers, or some such. Like most cowboys, I learned the hard way to treat 'em good. Now most cowboys, me included, we think we're pretty tough. Sometimes we work hard, like brandin' time. But truth is, mostly we're just getting carried around on our nags and hardly use our muscles. But miners, they shovel sixteen tons of rock a shift into ore cars, year after year.

So the first time I got into a little punching match with a miner, he just about hammered me down a posthole. It was an education. Once, while sitting in a two-holer, I read about the Seven Wonders of the World, and the Colossus of Rhodes. I ain't got much schooling, and most of it was sittin' in one crapper or another. Most cowboys got educated that way. There was always something to read in there, right next to the corncobs.

This here miner I took a lick at one foolish night in a saloon, he was that Colossus of Rhodes in the flesh, and for certain the Seventh Wonder of the

World, eight feet tall and five feet wide. I was laid up for a week and black and blue for a month. It might not have been so bad if I'd been alone, but there were a dozen cowboys watching me and hooting me on, and they got to see the whole show. We all thought we was tougher than a bunch of rock grubbers, but boy, did we learn fast.

Since then, I've been mighty smiley around them miners, because I don't want to mop up buckets of my own blood. But now I was plumb out of money in a mining burg, and the options weren't good. I could muck rock for two dollars a day, or I could leave town and hope to eat rabbits and squirrels on my way somewhere else. It was depressin' to think about. I've been down in one of them little holes once, and that was enough. I looked at that rock above me, and wondered when a thousand tons of it would land on my head. You sort of get to appreciate daylight down there. Even a cloudy day seems mighty nice when you get out of one of them holes.

Maybe I could find something else for a while. I stared up and down that muddy street, wonderin' how to feed my face and not coming up with much. Well, it was then that a job found me. Some tough gunslick with greased-down black hair, he stops me outside the Eagle Saloon and asks me if my name is Cotton.

I owned to it reluctantly. I can't seem to keep anything quiet, includin' that name.

"Mr. Scruples, he wants to talk with you," this lantern-jawed gent said.

"Oh, I don't think so," says I.

"Unfinished business, Mr. Scruples says. You can

meet him at the Palace Car. But don't delay. If he doesn't hear from you, he'll make other plans."

Unfinished business would be that job offer, and I wasn't of a mind, not after seeing all those bodies scattered around and Agnes Cork tellin' me what Scruples was up to. But I overcame my reluctance, mostly because I wanted another glimpse of that ice blonde. That would be worth the whole trip. Just one little look. Just a few words. Just thinkin' about her made me itch in the britches.

I wasn't too keen about this whole thing, and thought maybe to have a drink first, a little liquid courage, so I headed into the Mint Saloon, and laid my last dime on the plank bar and got a mug of tap beer. The stuff tasted like creosote, and I thought maybe the Saints had brewed it. They didn't drink it, but they wasn't opposed to making money any way they could, so they cranked up their distilleries and pumped out Valley Tan, and beer, too. Their teamsters delivered it regular to mining camps, and without drinking half their load.

I sat real quiet on a stool and listened to the gab around me, and it turned out that the Mint was the place to pick up word about all them little mines. This wasn't a miners' bar at all, but one where prospectors and small-time operators and loners gathered. These gents, they mostly had beards and weathered faces the color of an old saddle and battered slouch hats. Now you take a miner, he's white as a fishbelly, and that's because he hardly sees daylight.

Somehow or other, word had leaked out about Agnes Cork's fight, and those bearded fellows, they were listening hard, and I listened hard, too.

"That Scruples, he sent a regular army after old Agnes, and they got whupped," one said.

"I don't know how long he can hold out. Next time, they'll try something different."

"Cork told me he filed proper on that pocket, but Scruples don't let that slow him down. Scruples tried to buy him out for a few clams, but Cork, he didn't budge. He said he'd sell for ten thousand."

"Must be a pretty good pocket. Agnes Cork, he don't lack for anything. He's paid up at the Mining Supply. I was in there when Cork bought a case of Dupont and some fuse and caps and a new pick, and he just laid down gold coins."

"Coins? Not ore? He must be makin' some bucks."

"You think ten thousand's a bit high for that pocket?"

"Guess we'll find out. Scruples, he's going to try again, I'll wager. You just gotta wonder what's up there in that hole."

Me, I just studied each man, trying to get some handle on him. Mostly, they were loners, I thought. I didn't hear anything bad about Scruples, except he was lookin' for a bargain. We all look for bargains.

"How does Cork get his ore out of there? You'd think Scruples would just jump the mine when no one's around there."

"He must have some secret way of getting it out. Truth is, I've never seen a load leave that mine."

"Whatever it is, he ain't going to tell us how he does it," one of them said. "That's a hell of a hole he's got there. Them tailings keep on growing so he's hauling a lot of rock out of there. He must be in there a quarter of a mile."

It was funny, because I had the answer, straight from Agnes Cork himself. There wasn't no ore. But I kept my mouth shut and sipped that rotten beer which tasted like horse piss. I had no idea why Cork's mine went in so far, if the ore had pinched out and·it was just a pocket.

Well, I finished up my mug and took a leak in the alley. I climbed onto Critter and headed up a steep hill toward this here Palace Car, which glowed purple and gold in the late afternoon light. It sure was out of place, with no railroad anywhere near. But there it was, on the crest of a hill, lording over Swamp Creek, as if whoever lived there owned the whole place. And maybe they did.

Well, there wasn't no hitching post up there, but as soon as I got close, some gunslick with a pair of Colts hanging from his hips butt forward climbs out of the shadows. I watch him close, thinkin' maybe he'll pull one of those short-barrel .45-caliber irons on me, but he simply stared up at me. "The man wants to talk with you. I'll take your horse."

"That's Critter, and he don't like bein' taken any-where."

"I'll take him."

"No, I'll ground-rein him like always."

"I'll take him."

"You tell Scruples I'm not interested," I said, starting to turn Critter away.

But this dude, who's got greased-down hair like the one in town, he grabs my bridle. "I'll take him," he said.

Critter kicked the hell out of him, and the dude dropped to the ground howling, and when he came up, he was waving that revolver in Critter's chest.

"Lugar, stop."

That was Scruples, who was standing on the observation deck at the rear of the Palace Car.

Lugar, he gave me and my nag one of those you're-dead looks, and sulked off toward a barn and pen downslope some. I knew he was itching to spray some lead around, and not just at Critter neither.

"Mr. Cotton, come in."

I didn't really want him to be calling me that, but I wasn't going to admit to being Mr. Pickens either, so I just marched up them iron steps to the platform at the end of the car, and on in.

Holy cats, I ain't ever seen such a place, and I ain't got the words for it. There was a mess of red velvet drapes sort of pinned up with gold tassels, and shimmery stuffed furniture I think my ma called brocade, and damned if there wasn't a big old grandfather clock in a walnut case, and Venetian blinds on the windows, and a mess of them books, all leather and gilt, and vases full of daisies and whatnot, and a mysterious hallway along one side that went to other rooms in the railroad car.

And that blonde, she was nowhere in sight, and I figured it was all for nothing. I'd have given a month's top-gun salary just to see her with her hair down and flowing around her shoulders. But hell, that's Pickens' Luck, and if I planned to live a while, I'd better just get used to it. My supply of women was pretty much limited to the red-lamp variety.

"We like comfort," Scruples said. "And if this district runs out of ore, we'll take our comfort with us."

He motioned me toward a narrow corridor along one side, and we emerged into a compact dining area with a kitchen at the other end of the car. I warn't feeling very pleasured by it. This place was full of stuff, like oil paintings on the wall and tablecloths. I'd heard of them tablecloths, but this was the first I'd ever laid eyes on one. This here one was a mess of white cloth laid over a table, just waitin' to sop up stains. And napkins, too. I'd seen a few of those, but not these white ones sitting in rings of something that looked like silver. Maybe it was pewter. I hardly knew one from another, except it wasn't gold. But there was gold around there. Them picture frames looked to be gold, and them spoons and forks, the handles was gold anyway. And them plates was purple and gold, like the colors outside.

Without asking, he poured me some coffee from a fancy jug, or whatever it was, and handed it to me. He poured one for himself, and motioned me to sit, which I did, sinking into a soft leather cushion. I sure had no notion why people live like that. It seemed a mess of work to me, and no time off to have a beer.

"We have an investment company that's buying up mining properties in the district," Scruples said. "Mostly properties that are delinquent in paying taxes, or have faulty deeds. The problem is, it's hard to remove the previous owners from our property after we acquire it. You saw exactly what can happen. The loss of four of our men sets back our plans, and we'll have to push to return to schedule." He paused.

"We intend to own the entire Swamp Creek Mining District."

That coffee, I'd never tasted the like. It was like them beans got burnt. It was strong enough to stain the rear end of an antelope brown. But I sort of liked the flavor, and thought maybe if I roasted some Arbuckle's beans hard before grinding them up, maybe I could do her.

Scruples, he looked me over amiably, his gaze focusing on me to see how I was responding to all this here stuff, so I just gazed back, wishing that blonde would show up out of one of them closed-off rooms. I didn't half mind this man Scruples, even if he was as real as a three-dollar bill.

He smiled. "We lost about half of our work force," he said. "And that's where you come in. I've made inquiries and found you're handy at a lot of things."

I sort of knew what he was driving at, but long as he was using big words like inquiries, I'd have to sort it out later.

"You could quickly become a top man with the Scruples Company," he said. "Maybe the straw boss. We've ten or fifteen evictions ahead of us, and then we'll own every mining property we think has promise."

"What's evictions?" I asked.

"Oh, persuading people like Mr. Cork it would be wise to pack up and leave."

"That's all? Just talkin' people into leaving?"

Scruples smiled in a way as if he thought I was dumber than a stump, and maybe I am.

"By whatever means," he said.

I knew right then he was working around the truth of it with a mouthful of fancies.

"You mean push 'em out at gunpoint," I said, "and using them guns if I have to."

Scruples smiled. "It's worth a hundred dollars a month to you."

Holy cats, that's more money than I ever seen before, and it made me itch. But I'd have to use my six-guns to kill people just for hanging onto the mines they started up. I thought about that, and I thought about the two slicks I'd met today, the one near the Mint and the one he called Lugar, and I didn't much like the idea.

"I think not, Mr. Scruples," I said.

"I don't ask a second time," he said.

I collected my sweaty old hat and stood up, and holy cats, that blonde walked in, and her hair was down around her shoulders, and I plumb stopped whatever I was doing right then and there.